TARGET PRACTICE

Price counted eight men in the hunting party, seven with long guns. They'd seen him stop to fetch the rifle, and they weren't advancing quite as swiftly now. Surprise had slowed them down, maybe shaken their confidence.

Price was about to shake it harder, while he had the opportunity.

Remounted, reins wrapped tight around his fist, Price raised the Winchester and found his target in a single fluid motion. Far man on the left, surprise turning to fear on one dark face when he saw he'd been marked. The *federale* tried to turn his mount around and ride back out of range.

Too late.

Price fired and saw his target tumble, even as he worked the lever action, swinging right across the line to find the far man on the right. Predictability was dangerous, a trap he always worked hard to avoid.

REBEL GUN

Lyle Brandt

BERKLEY BOOKS, NEW YORK

THE BERKLEY PUBLISHING GROUP
Published by the Penguin Group
Penguin Group (USA) Inc.
375 Hudson Street, New York, New York 10014, USA
Penguin Group (Canada), 10 Alcorn Avenue, Toronto, Ontario M4V 3B2, Canada
(a division of Pearson Penguin Canada Inc.)
Penguin Books Ltd., 80 Strand, London WC2R 0RL, England
Penguin Group Ireland, 25 St. Stephen's Green, Dublin 2, Ireland (a division of Penguin Books Ltd.)
Penguin Group (Australia), 250 Camberwell Road, Camberwell, Victoria 3124, Australia
(a division of Pearson Australia Group Pty. Ltd.)
Penguin Books India Pvt. Ltd., 11 Community Centre, Panchsheel Park, New Delhi—110 017, India
Penguin Group (NZ), Cnr. Airborne and Rosedale Roads, Albany, Auckland 1310, New Zealand
(a division of Pearson New Zealand Ltd.)
Penguin Books (South Africa) (Pty.) Ltd., 24 Sturdee Avenue, Rosebank, Johannesburg 2196,
South Africa

Penguin Books Ltd., Registered Offices: 80 Strand, London WC2R 0RL, England

This is a work of fiction. Names, characters, places, and incidents either are the product of the author's imagination or are used fictitiously, and any resemblance to actual persons, living or dead, business establishments, events, or locales is entirely coincidental.

REBEL GUN

A Berkley Book / published by arrangement with the author

PRINTING HISTORY
Berkley edition / May 2005

Copyright © 2005 by Michael Newton.
Cover design by Steven Ferlauto.
Cover illustration by Bruce Emmett.

ISBN: 0-425-20298-4

BERKLEY®
Berkley Books are published by The Berkley Publishing Group,
a division of Penguin Group (USA) Inc.,
375 Hudson Street, New York, New York 10014.
BERKLEY is a registered trademark of Penguin Group (USA) Inc.
The "B" design is a trademark belonging to Penguin Group (USA) Inc.

PRINTED IN THE UNITED STATES OF AMERICA

10 9 8 7 6 5 4 3 2 1

For Georgia

1

The smart thing would've been to ride on through the village and ignore the posters mounted everywhere he looked along the main road into town. Or he could stop and have a meal in the cantina, wash it down with some tequila, then move on. The point was getting out with no more complications than were absolutely necessary, preferably none at all.

Matthew Price knew that, but still he couldn't go.

The posters hooked him like they were supposed to, drawing in an audience, although for reasons that their artist never would've guessed. He couldn't even credit the crude portraits used in place of photographs, though he supposed the third one, on the left, might've been close enough to catch his eye.

Still, Price supposed he would've missed it even so, without the name. El Lobo Gris.

Gray Wolf.

He'd learned enough Spanish to make out that part and

read most of the rest, though he still had some trouble with long-winded newspaper stories and hadn't the time or the heart to try books. The poster told a simple story, easily deciphered.

Public execution. Saturday, June 23rd.

Price had to stop a moment to recall the day and date. The joke would be on him if he'd arrived too late and still went through the motions for no reason, bringing grief down on himself when no one else would benefit.

He thought about it, concentrating on the mental image of a calendar and blocking out the sun glare from adobe walls on either side of him, as his roan slow-walked toward the village square. Waiting for Price to signal whether they were stopping here or passing on to make another lonely desert camp.

Price marked his days of late by recollecting critical events, instead of counting dawns and sunsets. On the first Sunday of June, he'd killed two men who'd tried to stop him on the road with murderous intent. Wheel off their wagon, one man sweating in the bright sun while he tried to fix it, while his partner sweated worse beneath a tarpaulin in back. Hiding to spring the trap, in case persuasion didn't lure Price off his horse.

It hadn't. Anyway, not quick enough to suit the man who'd soaked his clothing through while lying underneath the tarp for God knows how long, nothing but the sawed-off scattergun for company. His itchy nerves had sprung the trap too soon, and Price had shot them both before they had a chance to take him down.

The shooter in the wagon had been dead before he fell, a clean hole in his forehead over the left eye. Some folk would call it expert shooting, but Price knew that he'd been lucky. Two more inches, maybe less, and he'd have missed the gunman altogether, been blasted from the saddle by a load of buckshot to the chest before he had a second chance to make it right.

Lucky, he called it. And he didn't sneer at luck.

The wheel man had been gut-shot, still alive and crying out for help when Price rode off and left him to the desert. Maybe help would come along, the way it had for Price on one or two occasions, but he reckoned not. He'd left the dying man a pistol, making sure he didn't reach for it while Price was still in range. Whether he used the weapon to relieve himself or saved it for the first pack of coyotes who came sniffing down the blood trail was a choice he'd have to make alone.

We're all alone, Price thought. *In every choice we make.*

Counting from when he'd killed the two half-assed *banditos,* he determined that it must be Friday the twenty-second. Nothing much had happened in the past three weeks, which suited Price just fine. He could've seen to it that nothing kept on happening, at least until the next time. All he had to do was make believe he hadn't seen the posters. Ride on through and spend another night with jerky for his supper, sleeping underneath the stars.

With any luck, he wouldn't dream.

Too late.

He owed Gray Wolf a life, at least in his own mind.

It wasn't strictly true, of course. He'd come to the Apache's aid one day when scalp hunters were bent on making easy money from his hair. It wasn't Price's business then, but he'd stepped in because the odds had rankled him. Because some tiny portion of the weathered flint he called a heart still craved fair play.

Gray Wolf had overcome his innate animosity toward white men long enough to spend a short time on the trail with Price, and he'd stepped in to help when Price was on the verge of being hanged by *federales* for a killing that he hadn't done. Some might've seen poetic justice in it, but Price only saw the rope. The young Apache warrior had arrived in time to stop it, risked his life to get Price off the hook.

So they were even, in the scheme of things.

But not in Price's mind.

The smart thing would've been to ride on through and let it go. Instead, he reined his mount in the direction of the village church.

Cesar Zapata de León was not afraid to die. Some would've said he'd courted death throughout most of his twenty-three years, but that had not been his intention. He fought and put himself at risk for Mexico, for her people, and for the tattered remnants of his family. He didn't fear hanging or the firing squad because he had foreseen this day when he was still a child.

It wasn't so much being executed in the morning that annoyed Zapata, as the company that he was forced to keep.

The *federales* had to kill him. That was understood, one of the rules he had accepted when he chose the path of armed resistance. They were bound to kill him, by their law and by whatever passed for honor in their world. What chafed Zapata's nerves most, in the final hours of his life, was being caged with an Apache and a common thief.

He recognized the insult, but he was in no position to demand a private cell, much less insist that he be shot or hanged without the other two. His enemies had found a way of adding insult to the lethal injury that waited for him in the morning, and they only laughed at his protests, enjoying it.

The bandit and the Indian ignored him. They had staked out separate corners of the filthy cell before Zapata joined them, and he left them to it. Huddled closest to the door, the thief had proved to be a sniveler, pleading with jailers when they brought the plates of beans with stale bread on the side. It was a hideous mistake, he told them, almost weeping. He had stolen nothing, harmed no one. The witnesses against him were malicious liars, doomed to burn in Hell. The guards ignored him, and the third time he had launched into his spiel, Zapata threatened to baptize him with the cell's slop bucket if he didn't shut his mouth.

The threat had worked, at least so far.

There'd been no word from the Apache. His dark eyes had scanned Zapata on arrival, seemingly found nothing to concern them, and resumed their study of the single window mounted high up on the eastern wall. A giant might've glimpsed the village street outside, standing on tiptoe. Otherwise, the barred window served only to admit daylight and flies. What the Apache found to fascinate him there, Zapata couldn't say and didn't care.

He'd been surprised to find an Indian in jail, awaiting execution. Normally, the *federales* shot Apaches on sight, without regard to age or gender. Zapata had no sympathy for the savage raiders who had killed half a dozen members of his family in bygone years. He understood their struggle, in an abstract sense, but he couldn't compare it to his own. Their worlds were separate and always would be, with Apaches living in the past while Mexico struggled to build a bright new future.

It would have to carry on without Cesar Zapata, though. That much was clear. His people couldn't help him now. It would be madness to attempt a rescue, probably the very thing his captors most desired. Why settle for one rebel's blood, when they could kill a dozen, twenty, fifty?

They would advertise the execution, build it up into a spectacle, hoping Zapata's comrades could be lured to take the bait. Why else postpone his death, when both sides knew there'd be no pretense of a trial? Zapata trusted that his comrades would be wise enough to stay away.

If they were not . . .

He heard the jailers coming. It was time to eat again, more bread and beans, the menu calculated to ensure foul air inside the cell. Zapata saw the bandit in his corner, screwing up his courage for one more appeal, but when Zapata cut his eyes in the direction of the slop bucket, the other man sank back into himself, face twitching spastically.

No word from the Apache. Just as well.

The jailers were an odd pair, fat and thin, but neither of them smiled. The thin one juggled three plates while the other held a shotgun ready, standing well apart for a clean field of fire. There was no personal service. They set the plates down near the middle of the cell, backed out, and locked the door behind them. Footsteps faded down the hall.

Zapata and the young Apache moved as one, watching each other, going for their plates. Up close, Zapata smelled the Indian and wondered what *he* smelled like to his age-old enemy.

No matter, he decided. Soon, they'd both be food for worms.

But in the meantime, he would eat the gruel his jailers brought to him and keep his strength. Tomorrow morning, when they killed him for the pleasure of an audience, at least Zapata knew that he could face death as a man.

The church was dark inside, air heavy with the waxy smell of candles burning on an altar where the Virgin Mary stood and watched with tiny flames reflected in her painted cycs. Price estimated sixty candles, maybe seventy, with some of them burned down to nubs and others looking fairly new. He marveled that so many people came to church on any given day, deciding that there must be more to pray for in the villages where life creeps by the people at a snail's pace and they still feel left behind.

It was a moot point, since he hadn't come to pray.

The place seemed empty at a glance, not huge like some he'd seen, but larger than the other buildings on the dusty village street. Peasants would starve in tattered rags before they let their church go wanting. It was one more part of "civilized" society Price didn't understand, but he still recognized it—and the fact that he could take advantage of it on occasion.

Like today.

"Hello?" His voice was small and hollow in the church, with its peaked ceiling fifteen feet above his head, thick walls, and hopeful pews that Price suspected wouldn't fill completely if the villagers turned out en masse to hear the padre lecture them on sin.

Where *was* the padre?

Price moved down the center aisle, his boot heels clicking softly. Halfway down, he paused to verify that floor-length curtains on both sides of the confessional were tied back, that no one crouched inside, recounting a parade of sinful deeds or dreams.

I've got one for you, Price thought to himself, and almost smiled.

"Hello!" he tried again, louder this time.

The padre answered from a cubbyhole somewhere in back. Price moved in that direction, bent on meeting him halfway. It seemed the least that he could do, under the circumstances. He was not surprised to see the sixty-something priest emerge, tired face and thinning hair, the drab brown cassock hanging on his body like an old hound's skin.

This kind of village wasn't where the popular and well-connected priests were found. It was the sort of place where novices were sent to cut their teeth, and old men were put out to pasture in their final days. It wouldn't take much skill or effort, marrying a couple now and then, baptizing the occasional baby, and saying funeral masses for the poor. Price could've sketched the aging padre's story without asking, but he didn't care.

The most important thing was already confirmed.

The priest, though stooped with age, was nearly Price's height.

"Buenas tardes," Price said, smiling now.

"Good evening, my son. May I help you?"

"I'll bet you can." As he spoke, Price eyed the ropes securing the confessional curtains. They looked like some kind of velvet, maybe half an inch thick. Soft enough that they wouldn't hurt an old man's wrists or ankles much, yet strong enough to keep him down a while.

"Well, then?"

The prodding question made Price realize he'd lost a moment somewhere. He'd been doing that from time to time, since all the bloody business in Redemption and the vengeance ride that followed, and he knew he'd have to watch it. Blanking out that way with anyone but a decrepit preacher might just get him killed.

On second thought, Price wasn't sure how many preachers he could trust either.

"Sorry, Padre," he said, turning to face the priest again, "but I'm afraid I need your duds."

"Excuse me?"

"Just the robe, that is." Price thought the dangling hood would serve him well. It could conceal a multitude of sins.

From his expression, Price supposed the priest hadn't decided whether he should laugh at this strange gringo or be frightened. At the moment, he was stuck somewhere between the two extremes. "I still don't understa—"

The sudden pressure of the Colt Peacemaker's muzzle on his forehead cleared it up.

"The robe, that's all," Price reassured him. "And a few more minutes of your time. I'll make you comfortable and trust you to be quiet. How's that sound?"

Price knew that lying was a sin, but he forgot its number on the Big Man's list. No problem, since he had all kinds of other sins lined up to go within the hour.

Price led the priest to his confessional, received his robe, then sat him down inside the booth reserved for listeners. He tied the old man's hands behind him, then secured his legs. Lastly, he cut a strip of curtain where it wouldn't show much when the rest was shut and gagged the padre with it, nice and tight.

"My turn to help the fallen," Price informed him as he slid the curtain shut.

Antonio Lopez y Vega didn't own a pocket watch, but months and years of mind-numbing routine enabled him to judge the time within two minutes while he was on duty. It was coming up on half an hour since he took their last meal to the three on tomorrow's death list. He would go back with Ismael to fetch the plates in five or ten more minutes, and the prisoners would get no breakfast.

He was nearly done with them forever, and it didn't bother Lopez in the least. He got his pay on time, most months, and there was seldom anything about his job that qualified as dangerous. This time was somewhat different, with rumors that a band of rebels might come after one of the condemned, but the commanding *federale* had assured Lopez that he was safe.

More to the point, he had been right.

Lopez had learned to take whatever *federales* told him with a hefty dose of salt, but Lieutenant Cruz had been right on that score. No one had come to help the rebel, and to-morrow he would die beside the sniveling thief and the stoic Apache. Soon enough, they would all be gone and Lopez could return to watching drunks, swabbing the cell when they were careless with the slop bucket. It was demeaning work, but Lopez had no real ambition and it still beat starving, as so many of his countrymen would do before year's end.

Call it security. He had no craving for adventure, much less danger. Even as a child, Lopez had left most of the rough-and-tumble games to other boys. Some had despised him for it, called him names that stung like cactus needles, but he'd only fought the ones who put their hands on him, and then he'd mostly won.

There was no fighting now, to speak of. Now and then they had a rowdy prisoner, emboldened by tequila, but it only happened once in a great while. His charges, for the most part, offered no resistance and required no special handling.

"You want the gun this time?" Ismael Ornelas asked him. "When we go?"

"What for?"

"A change. You always get the plates."

"It's no great privilege."

"All I thought, it's something different for once."

Lopez distrusted change. "I'll get the plates," he said.

Ornelas shrugged and sent a tremor through his double chin. "As you like it," he said.

Lopez was working out an answer in his head when he heard footsteps moving toward them, down the flagstone corridor. He blinked and frowned. Ornelas squared his heavy shoulders, putting more strain on his tunic's buttons.

"Padre?" Lopez hadn't been told the priest was coming, hadn't known one of the dead men waiting had requested a send-off. Lopez disliked surprises, all the more so when he had three prisoners to watch.

The priest was closer, but still hadn't answered him. Lopez half-recognized the shoulders stooped with age and care, but he had never seen the padre raise his cassock's hood.

"Father Ybarra?"

"Not today."

A gringo stared at Lopez from the hood's deep shadow, and the hand extending from the robe's right sleeve was wrapped around a six-gun. Lopez stared into its muzzle and saw death. Same thing when he glanced up to meet the gringo's eyes.

"I know two ways to do this," said the gringo in passable Spanish. "One way, you both live to tell the tale."

"What do you want?" asked Ismael. No great thinker, that one.

"I'll give you three guesses," the gunman replied, "and the first two don't count."

Zapata heard his keepers coming back to take away the plates. His last meal had been nothing to write home about, but then again, he had no pencil and no writing paper. Truth be told, he had no home.

The government he fought against had seen to that.

He considered some act of rebellion—cursing the jailers perhaps, or heaving the slop bucket at them—but he guessed the one who brought the shotgun wouldn't hesitate to use it.

And as strange as it might sound, Cesar Zapata didn't want to die *tonight*.

He wasn't sure what waited for him in the morning, whether it would be a rope or firing squad, but Zapata was suddenly jealous of life. Every moment remaining seemed precious, and he couldn't bring himself to throw away that scrap of time.

Tomorrow, when they took him out, there would be time enough for gestures and denunciation. While the ghouls heaped scorn upon him, he would spit in their faces, remind them with his dying breath that he had fought and died to save *their* country and *their* children from a tyranny they didn't even recognize.

And even now, he didn't feel the effort had been wasted. From the beginning of his struggle, he had known that it might end this way, or with his body broken on some dusty battlefield. Death came to every man in time, but some scarcely noticed because they had lived in the shadows and groveled for crumbs from their rich master's table. For men such as those, death wasn't tragic; it was a relief.

For men like Cesar Zapata de Léon, it was a rite of passage into history.

But he would rather live to fight again, if he could find a way. Unfortunately, there was no one left to help him, none nearby who sympathized with his crusade. Zapata might have bribed the guards to let him go, if he was rich enough, but peasant revolutionaries in the great state of Durango weren't exactly worth their weight in gold.

Zapata was surprised to see a padre with the jailers, but this was his first time in a death cell and he reckoned it was part of the procedure. The same murderers who planned his execution might well plead concern for his immortal soul. The Church, in turn, had never stopped a wealthy man from stealing someone else's property or trampling on their lives, as long as he donated part of the proceeds to keep the padres fat and happy.

Zapata would not bow before them. That was already decided. He had nothing to confess, and any statement he desired to make could wait for morning, when he had a captive audience.

Keys jangled at the door, and in the heartbeat that remained before it opened wide, Zapata realized what had been nagging at him since the guards came into view.

Both men were empty-handed. There was no shotgun.

Zapata glanced at the Apache, wondering if he had noticed that their keepers were unarmed. The long-haired warrior had a curious expression on his face, inscrutable.

Useless.

Zapata thought perhaps he could take both of them alone, if he was swift enough. Scoop up the bucket, fling its stinking contents at the nearest of the two, and then charge through the stench to knock them down. He was already leaning forward, muscles bunching in his thighs and shoulders, when he realized his critical mistake.

There *was* a gun, but it was in the padre's hand.

And it was pointed at the guards.

Both jailers stepped into the cell. The priest followed, keeping a safe distance and pointing with his weapon toward the corner where he wanted them to stand. The pair obeyed him silently. Beneath the cassock's hood, Zapata saw a gringo's face. Nobody he had seen before. The gunman's eyes met his, moved on to rest for half a second on the thief, then found the Apache.

"You ready to get out of here, or what?" the padre said in English.

The Indian was standing. "This creates another debt," he said.

"You want to talk about it now?"

"Later maybe."

The padre smiled, waggled his pistol toward the other prisoners. "These friends of yours?"

"They die tomorrow," the Apache said, already near the open doorway. "This one steals from houses, and this one"—he nodded toward Zapata—"makes war on the government."

"I've felt that way myself a time or two," the gringo said. And then, to those confined: "Whoever wants a running start, this is your chance. Call it a one-time offer, closing when I shut the door."

The thief was up and past him in a stumbling rush. Zapata followed, knowing only that he had a second chance, not where the path would lead. When he was clear, the gringo closed the cell door, locked it with the fat guard's keys, and put the key ring in a pocket of his baggy robe.

"Freedom!" The thief was grinning, while fat tears ran down his face. Without another word, he turned and bolted toward the street exit.

"My horse is tied out back," the gringo said. "A couple more were waiting when I got here. At a guess, I'd say we haven't got much time."

The gringo and the Indian moved toward the jail's back door. Zapata hesitated for a single beat, then followed after them.

Price half expected to find *federales* waiting when they stepped into the meager shade behind the jail. There wasn't much in terms of cover—wasn't much in terms of *town* when he got right down to it—but they could've thrown a skirmish line around the backside of the small adobe lockup and cut loose with everything they had as Price and his companions were exposed.

Nothing.

His roan stood where he'd tied it, with two other horses, prior to circling around and coming in the front way like the jailers would expect a priest to do. Price knew that he'd been lucky there were only two of them, and slow-witted to boot, but he and the men he'd released were still a long way short of free and clear.

He had the only guns among them, so he took the rifle from his saddle boot and handed it to Gray Wolf. "Just in case," he said.

"More debt," said the Apache with a frown.

"Yeah, yeah. Let's ride."

The Mexican—Zapata, as the posters called him—was already mounted by the time Price shed his stolen robe and climbed aboard the roan. He waited for them, though, instead of bolting as the thief had done. Price didn't know if that was good or bad, in the long run, but they were in this thing together for the moment, come what may.

Just then, as if in answer to his thought, a shot rang out from the direction of the village square. A second later there were three, four, five more shots in rapid fire.

"There goes the runner," Price told his companions. "We're up next."

He spurred the roan, Gray Wolf racing beside him on a gray, Zapata on his borrowed piebald pony gaining on the other side. Price guessed they'd have a few short minutes while the *federales* ran to check the jail, see how the thief had slipped away. Unless they had spare keys, they'd need some time to liberate the guards, but questions could be answered through the bars. And once they were, he guessed a posse would be coming on in hot pursuit.

How long?

Not long enough.

The sun was dipping lower in the west, but it wasn't hidden yet and dusk would linger for another hour once it set, before full darkness hid their tracks. Hard-riding hunters would be after them by then, might even overtake them on the desert flats.

Which meant they'd have to fight.

Price had a spare revolver in his saddlebag, but there was no time to retrieve it now. He focused on the empty land outside of town and realized he didn't even know the place's name. That worked out well enough, Price thought, since no one in the village knew his either. They were strangers all around, and if the *federales* killed him, no one here would give a damn.

Five minutes after stepping from the jail, they were already out of town. Price didn't know if anyone had seen them go, taking the back way, but it wouldn't take much of a tracker to discover horses missing at the jail and follow them from there. Any delay would come from rallying the troops, collecting weapons, maybe saddling their animals.

Was it enough?

Maybe—and maybe not.

It hadn't taken long to spot the thief and bring him down, but that might work in Price's favor if it spread confusion in the village, maybe sent the *federales* off to look for other fugitives on foot. The way it stood, he'd take what he could get and let his Colt speak for him, if and when the hunters ran them down.

He was an outlaw now, and it surprised him that he felt no different than before. In fact, aside from the excitement of the chase, Price felt nothing.

Nothing at all.

2

Lieutenant Jose Cruz Escalante trembled on the edge of an explosive rage that might consume him if he let it slip beyond control. He felt the hot blood in his face, the headache pulsing at his temples, keeping time with his accelerated heartbeat. Fists clenched, nails digging half-moon scars into his palms, he stood before the worthless peasants who had threatened his career and he used his last ounce of restraint to keep himself from striking them.

"And are you *sure*," he asked the two doomed men, "that no one mentioned any destination? *Nothing?*"

"No, sir," the scrawny one replied, bracing himself for yet another verbal hurricane. The fat jailkeeper had begun to weep and couldn't find his voice, but shook his head. Another negative.

They stood outside the jail's front door, late afternoon creeping toward dusk but still as hot as Hell, with little shade to speak of. Twenty feet or so from where Cruz stood, a body lay facedown on dirt stained to the shade of rusty iron. One out of three had paid the price for spitting in his face, but Cruz was far from satisfied.

"And, once again, you've never seen this gringo? Neither of you?"

"No, sir," answered the thin man. A snuffling head shake came from his overweight companion in disgrace.

"Lieutenant Cruz!"

He turned to find a corporal coming from the church, dragging behind him an old man Cruz vaguely recognized. The padre?

Yes.

"I found him, sir," the corporal said. "Tied up in the confessional. He says—"

Cruz raised a hand to silence him. "Father . . . what is your name?"

"Ybarra. Have you found the man who violated holy ground?"

"I need your help for that."

"You have my prayers."

"I need your information, Padre. Did you recognize the man who robbed you?"

"No. He was a gringo, not the kind you see in church."

"You'd recognize his face again?"

The aging priest considered it, then nodded.

"That's all for now." Cruz turned his back to signal that the interview was finished. As he did, Sergeant Aguirre came around the north side of the jail on horseback, trotting forward.

"Sir!" The sergeant snapped a crisp salute.

"Report."

"The men are ready, sir. We have the trail."

"Well, then, what are you waiting for?"

"Your order, sir."

"Go after them, for God's sake! Go, and bring them back by any means required. I'm owed two horses and three lives."

"Yes, sir!" The sergeant wheeled away and galloped out of sight. A moment later, Cruz heard horses racing southward out of town.

The fugitives had half an hour's lead at least. Some of that time had slipped away while Cruz's men were checking out the jail, releasing the two guards, and fetching him to see the mess they'd made. More time had passed after he'd started barking orders, while Aguirre had picked seven men and led them off to saddle horses for the chase. How far could three men ride in the allotted time?

The worst that could happen would be a split, if they divided forces and rode off in two or three different directions. More time would be wasted then while Aguirre puzzled over which one to pursue, deciding whether he should split his own force and attempt to bag them all, or simply go for one.

Cruz needed all of them, to salvage something from the mess in which he found himself. Ideally, he would have the three trussed up like hogs for slaughter, babbling answers to his questions as he squeezed them to find out who'd planned and organized the break. That would be the best solution, but he'd take the three head-down across their saddles as his second choice.

He turned back toward the jailers, scowling. "Dispose of that," he ordered, nodding toward the corpse. "When that's done, you're confined to quarters. I will hear your full report and judge your case tomorrow, eight o'clock. You have the night to make yourselves presentable. Dismissed!"

They stiffened to a semblance of attention, offering awkward salutes. Cruz turned his back on them and stalked

back toward his quarters at the far end of the street. He
craved tequila, but he also knew that it would cloud his
mind, and what he needed now was crystal clarity of
thought.

So many questions still unanswered in his mind.

Who was the gringo? Which of the condemned had he
come calling for, and why? Was he a mercenary hired for
the occasion, or a friend of one he'd liberated? Once they'd
gotten out of town, where would the vermin go to hide?

Cruz knew the thief, a pig named Calderon, was not the
target of the jailbreak. He had bolted by himself to meet his
death. The others had let him go without a protest. Simple.

That left the Apache and Zapata. Nothing linked them in
the world outside their prison cell, and neither was the sort
to have a gringo friend. Were they?

And yet, the gunman had appeared and liberated both of
them, presumably one of his choice, the other incidentally.
Or was it *both*?

The throbbing of his headache had increased. Lieutenant
Cruz decided that a small shot of tequila wouldn't hurt him
after all. In fact, with any luck, it just might help him find
an answer to the riddle that confounded and humiliated
him.

Before he had to file his own report and face the wrath
of his superiors.

The roan was holding up all right so far, and neither of the
other animals was falling back. Gray Wolf rode silently beside Price, on his left, holding the reins in one hand while
his other clutched the Winchester. Price caught Zapata
shooting sidelong glances at him while they covered
ground, but riding flat-out through the sunbaked desert with

a posse coming on somewhere behind them wasn't a conducive atmosphere for questions.

They'd need to rest the horses in another thirty minutes, give or take. Riding the animals to death would seal their own fate in the bargain. Gray Wolf knew it, and Price hoped Zapata knew it too.

He'd half-expected that the Mexican would ditch them when they were a mile or two from town, peel off to who knows where, but he was sticking. It might've helped him if Zapata had gone off alone, forcing the trackers to decide which trail was worth their time and sweat. Price thought about it, figured he could stop and *make* the unarmed stranger choose another course, ride off toward any compass point except the south-by-southwest direction Price and Gray Wolf were pursuing, but he let it go.

Where were they headed anyway?

Price didn't have a clue. He'd come into the village riding north to south, and so continued on that way, instead of doubling back. When they were clear of town, he'd followed Gray Wolf's lead, hoping that the Apache knew the territory, maybe had some hideout they could make for in a pinch.

And it was pinching now, no doubt about it.

They couldn't count on *federales* being slow or stupid. It hadn't taken long at all for somebody to drop the first runner, and Price knew they'd be looking for a clean sweep, bent on taking down the other fugitives—and him, for helping them escape. It was the kind of insult soldier types could never forget or forgive.

If he was caught, Price knew he'd join the others in a hanging cell. But something told him their pursuers wouldn't be concerned with taking prisoners this time.

Another two or three miles, Price decided, and he'd stop

to give the roan some water. Let it walk a while, before the next hard run. He watched the cruel sun inching lower toward a line of distant mountains, lost in haze. Call it another hour anyway before dusk brought a measure of relief from the oppressive heat. Another thirty, forty minutes after that before full darkness hid their tracks.

Too long.

The hunters were already after them. Price felt it, even if he couldn't offer proof. They needed someplace to lay up and meet the enemy, maybe surprise the *federales* with a volley that would help the odds.

More trouble, and he had nobody else to blame for it.

Gray Wolf was glancing backward every hundred yards or so, checking their trail. They'd gone another quarter mile before he called to Price above the sound of running horses.

"Riders!"

Price looked back and saw their dust. He couldn't judge the hunting party's size, but he supposed there'd be enough to do the job if they were fast enough, and lucky. He could almost guarantee that some of them wouldn't be going home alive. As for the rest . . .

He pushed the roan, to see what it had left. The animal huffed at him, but it found a bit more speed. Not quitting yet. He missed the Appaloosa, shot from under him five weeks ago, but Price had no complaints about the roan.

A little farther. Just a little.

Someplace we can make a stand.

Images of blood and thunder filled his mind, but they were nothing new. Without stopping to sort them out, he couldn't say if they were memories of showdowns past or promises of things to come.

Whatever, he was riding for a fight. The only thing he didn't know right now was where and when it would occur.

•   •   •

Cesar Zapata craved a weapon, but he couldn't ask either of his companions for a gun. The gringo and the Indian were friends somehow, as alien as that concept might seem. Zapata wished now, with the *federales* gaining steadily, that he had left the other two and struck off on his own once they had passed beyond sight of the village.

Too late now.

Zapata didn't curse his luck regardless, for the chase was better than a cage. Given a choice, he'd rather be shot from the saddle like a man than spill his blood before a jeering audience of peasants who couldn't understand that he was dying for their sake.

If they were overtaken by the posse and he saw no hope of breaking free, Zapata made up his mind to reverse direction, charge his enemies, and make them kill him here. He wouldn't let them bind his hands again and hold him for the firing squad, the hanging rope.

He hoped Dolores wouldn't grieve too much, too long. This was the path that they had chosen, coming to its lonely end. They'd never quite discussed it—never really had to, after all their family had suffered—and Zapata knew she understood the risks. He simply hoped she wouldn't take his death too much to heart and let it color everything that happened in her life beyond this day.

The first gunshot was far away, more echo of a sound than sound itself. Zapata ducked his head regardless, instinct taking over now that battle of a sort was joined. He didn't know if their pursuers were within effective rifle range, much less if they could hit a moving target from a running horse, but as a soldier he was bound to take the few precautions still available to him.

Zapata rode at breakneck speed, hunched forward on the

unfamiliar saddle, trusting his freedom and survival to a stolen horse. It hadn't failed him yet, but he had no idea how strong it was, how much endurance it possessed. If it gave up the race, he was as good as dead. If it collapsed, the fall might kill him quicker than a *federale*'s strangling rope.

Zapata rode, and still the others seemed to pull away from him. It wasn't planned, simply a question of their animals and native skill. The Indian named Gray Wolf was like a centaur, speeding over open ground as if the horse was part of him. The gringo wasn't quite as skilled, but nearly so, and he alone among them rode a mount accustomed to his touch.

Zapata had never been a horseman in the normal sense. He was a peasant farmer's son, whose family had once kept two old burros, then been forced to sell them when the state raised taxes one more time. In later life, as a *bandito* and a soldier, he had learned to ride, but still Zapata felt more comfortable on his own two feet. Moreover, he believed a horse could sense that reticence and thus sometimes refuse to serve him as it might a better rider.

More gunfire.

Zapata ducked lower, feeling the saddle horn against his breastbone, and the horse's mane against his cheek. The shots were scattered but more numerous, increasing the odds of a hit by dumb luck. Zapata heard no bullets whistling past his head, a sound with which he was familiar, but that didn't mean the *federale* marksmen were deficient.

If they drew a little closer, if the officer in charge of the detachment let them stop and aim next time, there could be hell to pay. His horse, a larger target, could go down at any time and pitch him headlong to the arid ground. If the fall didn't cripple or kill him, his enemies would.

Keep riding!

Dusk was approaching, and riflemen could only hit visible targets. Zapata had no faith that he would see the sunset, but he had to try. A part of him had never learned his father's failing.

He had never learned to quit.

A few yards out in front of him, Gray Wolf glanced backward, then the gringo took his turn. Neither checked on Zapata. They were gauging distance from the *federales,* and he might as well have been invisible. It could've rankled him but didn't, since he thought all three of them would soon be dead.

Maybe, at least, the other two would sell their lives, take some of the pursuers with them when they fell. That way, it wouldn't be a total waste. Less soldiers to harass his people later, when they mounted new campaigns.

The next rattle of shots was closer yet. This time Zapata heard a slug whip past him on his left, the gringo's side. It wasn't close enough for him to *feel* it, but that time was coming. Soon.

Zapata tried to make himself a smaller target, craning forward in the saddle, crying to his horse for greater speed.

Sergeant Luis Aguirre rode through gun smoke, praying that that the bullets racing on ahead of him would find their marks. They didn't, and he spit a curse in place of the traditional *Amen.*

It had been wishful thinking, anyway. These days, the Lord always used others to perform his dirty work.

Aguirre knew Lieutenant Cruz wanted the prisoners alive, if possible, but it would mean Aguirre's stripes—

maybe his life—if they escaped a second time. He had to take them back, dead or alive, and dead was always easier.

Hard logic notwithstanding, even as he gained upon his prey, Aguirre worried that he wouldn't overtake them. They would slip away somehow, he feared, if darkness fell while they still had a lead. Even this close, Aguirre knew that he could lose the race.

And so much more.

Lieutenant Cruz had no authority to kill him, if Aguirre went back empty-handed, but he could murder the sergeant's career. Stripped of his rank, assigned to every filthy job that came along, Aguirre could be driven to resign or set up for a court-martial on petty charges. If the evidence was stacked against him, it might even seem he was responsible for the escape. Aguirre knew he would be nothing in civilian life, and he couldn't survive in jail.

The answer to his plight was simple: Kill the fugitives and help Lieutenant Cruz save face, thereby helping himself.

If only his men could shoot straight.

Another volley sounded, belching aromatic gun smoke, and he saw the targets duck, trying to hide in plain sight. None of them fell, though, and their horses didn't stumble.

Damn it!

How much longer could they ride this way, pushing their horses to top speed? Could they outrun the sunset and find sanctuary in the dark? Aguirre's men were not equipped for searching after nightfall. They carried no torches, no provisions for a long chase through the desert. If Zapata regrouped with his rebels, if the Apache found his tribesmen, then Aguirre and his seven hunters were as good as dead.

"Faster!" he bawled to no one in particular. His column had already broken formation, racing across open ground in a ragged skirmish line while each man tried to drop one of the fugitives.

Each one of them except Aguirre.

In deference to his rank, the sergeant carried no carbine, and his pistol couldn't touch the targets at their present range. Aguirre knew when he should fire, and they had yet to reach that point. Meanwhile, the others did their best, perhaps hoping for some reward if they brought down the distant riders.

Not so distant now, Aguirre realized. He checked the western skyline, saw the sun kiss far-off mountain peaks and sink behind them. They were running out of daylight.

Running out of time.

Aguirre's horse was laboring. It was accustomed to long marches, but pursuit was different, running for miles through brutal desert heat. No man could do it and survive. The animal was weakening.

Aguirre cursed it, lashed it with his plaited leather quirt. The animal snorted, kept running, but it gained no further speed. It had no more to give.

The bitter taste of failure mixed with trail dust in Aguirre's mouth and sickened him. A hand was moving toward the holster on his right hip when he caught it and returned it to the horse's reins. His bullets would be wasted at this distance, and Aguirre knew he couldn't reload at full gallop. If he tried, he'd either drop his cartridges or take a deadly spill, leaving his men without a leader.

Wait then.

All he needed was another hundred yards. One-fifty would be better, but Aguirre had no faith in miracles. If he could hold his present pace that long, without killing his horse . . .

Shots echoed from the carbines ranged to either side of

him, stinging Aguirre's ears. He gripped the reins, white-knuckled, ready for another dose of failure. No one on the line was more surprised when one of the three human targets toppled from his saddle, twisting gracefully in midair on his way to meet the ground.

At last!

Aguirre took a last cut with his quirt, then let it dangle from a rawhide loop around his wrist. He drew his long-barreled revolver, thumbing back the hammer as his index finger found the trigger's curve.

Price saw the bullet strike Gray Wolf. It was a fluke, glancing in that direction as a crimson spout erupted from below one shoulder blade; then Gray Wolf cartwheeled from his saddle and the horse ran on without him. Looking back, Price saw the young Apache crumpled in a boneless heap, one leg twisted beneath him in a posture no man living could assume. The lever-action Winchester lay near his outstretched hand.

The roan carried Price onward for another thirty yards before he hauled back on the reins and brought it to a halt. Zapata, on the piebald pony, passed him by at speed, head turned and mouthing some remark Price didn't catch.

Price raised a hand and wished him *adios,* then wheeled his animal around and spurred it back toward where the young Apache's body lay. The *federales* were advancing at a gallop, still perhaps a hundred yards distant, reloading single-shot carbines as they rode.

Price reached his friend and stepped down from the saddle. There was no point checking for a pulse. He took the Winchester and brushed it free of grit, examined it to reassure himself dirt hadn't plugged the muzzle when it fell.

All clear.

He counted eight men in the hunting party, seven with long guns. They'd seen him stop to fetch the rifle, and they weren't advancing quite as swiftly now. Surprise had slowed them down, maybe shaken their confidence.

Price was about to shake it harder, while he had the opportunity.

Remounted, reins wrapped tight around his fist, Price raised the Winchester and found his target in a single fluid motion. Far man on the left, surprise turning to fear on one dark face when he saw he'd been marked. The *federale* tried to turn his mount around and ride back out of range.

Too late.

Price fired and saw his target tumble, even as he worked the lever action, swinging right across the line to find the far man on the right. Predictability was dangerous, a trap he always worked hard to avoid.

This time, the *federale* had his own piece shouldered, lining up a shot toward Price. He took it as the Winchester recoiled, and Price could hear the heavy bullet zing past to his left, maybe a foot off target. *His* shot wasn't perfect either, but it tore a blowhole in the left side of the *federale*'s rib cage and the wounded man rolled backward off his horse's rump.

Click-clack. Ejecting empty brass and chambering a live round as he swung back to his left. The mounted skirmish line had halted now, a straggling non-formation, while two horses without riders galloped back the way they'd come. Price marked their leader as a sergeant, armed now with a pistol in his hand but still well out of range for placing shots dependably. The other five had carbines capable of reaching him, but they were frozen by the shock of seeing two

comrades cut down. Frozen for maybe two, three seconds
at the most, before they snapped back into action.

Price lined up another target, shot the *federale* nearest to
the sergeant, on his left, then spurred the roan into a charge
before that body hit the dust. He held the reins and Winchester together in his left hand, rifle braced sideways
against the saddle horn, and drew his Colt Peacemaker as
he closed the gap to close-up killing range.

The *federales* panicked, shouting at their animals and at
each other while they hauled on reins, two of them shud-
dering from a collision as they turned to flee. The two entangled horses reared and whinnied, flailing air with their
front hooves. Price veered in that direction, heard a rifle
shot from somewhere to his right, and ducked instinctively,
but it was nowhere close.

Three *federales* were in full retreat, the sergeant leading
by example, when the last two broke apart, cursing each
other, and prepared to follow suit. The nearer of them
risked a glance at Price, to see how close he was, and took
a .45 slug through his gaping mouth. Its impact punched
him from the saddle, somersaulting backward to the
ground.

The other clumsy one was grappling with his horse and
firing off a stream of Spanish curses when he should've
concentrated on his target. Carbines were invented for the
cavalry, but mounted shooters had to aim like everybody
else. This one was in a hurry and he squeezed off from the
hip, one-handed, as if hoping luck would guide the bullet
home.

It didn't work.

Price shot him in the chest from twenty feet, a killing
wound that dropped him twitching to the sand. One boot
was hung up in its stirrup, though, and when the *federale*'s

horse bolted, it took him on one final jolting ride across the desert.

Price faced toward the north and saw his last three adversaries riding hell-for-leather back toward town. He spared Gray Wolf a parting glance, then set off in pursuit.

Zapata knew he should've ridden on, but when he saw the gringo stop and turn around he couldn't help himself. He had to see what happened next.

And what he saw astounded him.

Zapata watched the gringo fetch his rifle, then proceed to drop two *federales* on the run. He'd shot a third after the idiots reined in to gawk at him, but even that was not the limit of his sheer audacity.

Zapata nearly cheered the gringo when he charged the *federale* skirmish line, but he'd expected to hear the carbines speak and see the brave fool blasted from his saddle. The gringo was outnumbered five to one, long guns against the pistol he had drawn for close-range work.

Zapata cursed himself for stopping, when he should have used the precious time to put more ground between himself and his pursuers. When the gringo fell, Zapata would be alone, unarmed, and well within the range of their carbines. He clutched the reins, prepared to flee while yet a shred of hope remained.

And then, the *federales* broke.

There was no bottling up the whoop of glee that burst free from Zapata's throat that time, watching the hunters turn and run. Two of them collided in their haste, and by the time they drew apart the gringo was upon them, his *pistola* spitting death. Zapata watched them drop, one-two, and marveled as his liberator set off riding hard behind the three survivors.

No! his mind cried out. *Come back!*

No matter how the fleeing *federales* whipped their horses, it would take more than an hour to reach the village once again. There, they'd have to get fresh horses, gather reinforcements, and return in full darkness—if they returned at all. Zapata guessed the cowards might wait until sunrise, then come back with Indian trackers to guide them if some could be found. Either way, he could ride through the night and be free for a while, maybe give them the slip altogether.

But not the gringo.

Even in the dusk, Zapata saw him gaining on his targets, getting more speed from the roan than any horseman could expect after their long flight through the wasteland. Muzzle-flashes winked afar, and echoes of the gunshots reached Zapata's ears a second later. He remembered watching lightning as a child, counting the seconds afterward until he heard a peel of thunder, calculating how far off the storm was. Zapata hadn't played that game in years, but he remembered how.

Watching the battle, he was drawn to close the gap. Zapata's common sense warned him again to turn and ride away as quickly as he could, but he moved slowly toward the fight instead. If he'd been armed, perhaps he would've rushed to join it, but he was a spectator this time and so kept a respectful distance.

Even so, he saw the gringo overtake his quarry, firing as he rode and dropping one *federale* with a shot from the flank. As if it was rehearsed, Zapata saw the target plunge headfirst into a cactus patch.

Two left, and one of them—the leader?—rallied nerve enough to turn and face his enemy at last. Both fired revolvers, with the gringo still advancing, and the *federale* crumpled from his horse to find a sandy resting place.

The lone survivor galloped on, bent low across his saddle horn. The gringo gave up chasing him and aimed with an extended arm, a duelist on horseback. Zapata hissed at him to take the shot before his target dwindled out of range, but still the gringo waited . . . waited. . . .

When it came, the shot seemed louder than the others all together. And it seemed that he had missed, the *federale* riding on another fifty yards, almost beyond the range of naked eyes as dusk lowered, but then the *federale* rolled off to the left and landed on his back, with arms outflung.

Zapata sat and waited, watching as the gringo turned southward again. He took his time returning to the point where it had started, probably reloading his six-gun. He passed Zapata, sitting in near-darkness now, and stopped beside the crumpled figure of the Indian.

"He was your friend," Zapata said.

"I wouldn't go that far."

Zapata was confused. "You risked your life to free him, and to pay back his killers."

"We had a history," the gringo said.

"A man of such loyalty can do great things."

"I doubt it."

"Let me prove you wrong," Zapata said. "Come with me. There are people you should meet."

The gringo paused, then shrugged, as if to say *Why not?* "My name's Matt Price," he said, nudging the roan forward and offering his hand.

His grip was firm and dry.

"Cesar Zapata."

"I got that much from your poster. Where are we going?"

3

They traveled slowly westward for the next three hours, taking it easy since none of the hunters would be fetching reinforcements from the village, pointing out their trail. Price almost felt relaxed, riding beneath the stars, fairly secure that no one else would be trying to kill him before the sun rose.

"What did you mean," Zapata asked him in due time, "that you and the Apache were not friends?"

"We didn't know each other well enough to qualify," Price said. "It takes time, making friends. We helped each other out of trouble sometime back. He called it even, but I had my doubts. Turns out it was a wasted effort anyway."

"You think so?" asked Zapata.

"Well, he's dead. That wasn't what I had in mind."

"But he was free. They didn't have a chance to strangle him or stand him up against a wall."

"You think it matters?"

"How we die?" Zapata nodded. "Certainly. A man's life ought to count for something. Likewise with his death."

Price wasn't sure he bought it, but there was no point in arguing philosophy. "It's funny," he remarked. "I didn't even know what he was in for."

"Murder, so they said. There have been raids on certain farms. Some travelers were killed last month, outside Gómez Palacio."

"The *federales* thought Gray Wolf was part of it?"

"He was Apache," Zapata said. "What more proof do they need?"

Price understood the mind-set, might even have shared it at one time. Some things weren't crystal-clear these days, as they had once appeared. "I guess you feel about the same," he said.

"My people have made war against the red men for three hundred years, it's true. The land was theirs, and my ancestors stole it. Who can say they're wrong? Still, we fight," said Zapata, "but we also marry. It's the same where you're from, I suppose."

"More bitterness than anything," Price said. The talk had drawn his mind back to a small town called Redemption and the people there who practiced tolerance, doing their best to make life color-blind. Price thought about his time there, what he'd lost, and then the aching rage was back, nowhere to go with it since he'd eliminated all of those responsible.

"I see a sadness in you, Matt Price."

"That's just the same as saying I'm alive." He changed the subject. "Posters back in town claim you're some kind of revolutionary. What's the deal on that?"

"It's true," Zapata said, "that I rebel against the present government of Mexico. You know Porfirio Diaz?"

"I know of him. He runs the country."

"With a fist of iron, and for his own enrichment. He was once deposed, ten years ago, but he returned from exile and he rules the roost again. We have to do it right this time, and make him answer for his crimes."

"That's what you aim to do?"

"I'm not alone," Zapata said. "Far from it."

Price stayed clear of politics whenever possible. Experience had taught him that today's reformers often lost sight of their goals, becoming next year's petty tyrants. Sometimes not so petty.

"Well, I wish you luck," Price said. "At least you've got another chance now."

"Thanks to you."

"Don't make more of it than it is," he cautioned. "I was looking for Gray Wolf, nobody else."

"Ah, but you could've left me in the cell, yet you did not. Things happen for a reason."

I wonder, Price thought, but he kept it to himself.

They found a place to camp around midnight, atop a ridge where Joshua trees had put down roots and shielded them on two sides from the chill night breeze. The high ground would be their advantage if intruders came along, and in the absence of a fire they weren't exposed to hostile eyes. A trickling stream that fed the thorny trees also provided water for the men and weary horses. Dry grass served the animals as forage and supplied a bed of sorts.

Supper was jerky and hardtack washed down with springwater, the same thing they would have for breakfast when the sun rose. Almost as an afterthought, Zapata checked his stolen saddlebags and found a small flask of tequila tucked beneath a parcel wrapped in tissue paper. After they had shared a sip of liquid fire, he tore the package open and revealed a set of flame-red women's pantaloons.

"Looks like we spoiled somebody's plans," Price said.

"Oh, yes, I think so," said Zapata. "This one will have more to think about than love tonight. And those you've cheated by releasing me will not forget it, I'm afraid."

"No problem," Price replied. "I didn't sign my name back there."

"Diaz has ways. His eyes and ears are everywhere."

Price thought about his only living relatives, a sister in New England, and the years since they'd last been in touch. The son he couldn't claim. "He'll need a long arm to reach anyone I care about."

"You are alone then?" asked Zapata.

"Last I checked."

Zapata seemed about to say something, but stopped and shook his head, as if responding to some silent argument inside himself. "Until tomorrow then," he said, and settled back to use his saddle as a pillow. "Thank you for my life."

"De nada," Price replied, and closed his eyes against the night.

No rooster crowed at sunrise in the desert, but a sage hen's clucking in the chaparral nearby roused Price before the pale light pierced his eyelids. Stiff and chilled, he rose and dusted off his clothes, shaking the horse blanket he'd slept beneath to make sure it was free of crawling things.

Zapata woke up to the blanket's flapping sound and blinked at his surroundings, then produced a smile to greet the day. "No walls," he said. "No bars."

"No coffee," answered Price.

They shared more stringy beef and stale biscuits, sharing

the one canteen before Price topped it at the spring. A crimson dawn flamed in the east as Price finished saddling the roan.

"Sailors take warning," he said to the horse.

"Sailors?" Zapata queried.

"It's an old saying up north. 'Red sky at morning.' Never mind."

"We should be safe," Zapata said, still smiling. "We are far off from the sea."

"Speaking of trips, I'm still not clear on where we're going."

"In the mountains there," Zapata answered, pointing, "are my people. We should reach the camp this afternoon, if nothing slows us down. They will reward you for your service to the cause."

"I've got no use for a reward right now," Price said.

"Perhaps a cup of coffee then."

Price mounted, settled comfortably on the roan. "I've been thinking that your people may not be too thrilled to have a gringo dropping by. They don't know me from Adam, and your business isn't what I'd call secure."

"They will accept you if I say so," said Zapata.

His tone led Price to reconsider how things stood. "So, you're not just another soldier then, I take it."

"Some call me a leader. I think we all serve Mexico, but there are times when hard decisions must be made."

"And you make them?"

"Sometimes. Diaz and Neron force my hand."

"Who's Neron?" Price inquired as they rode toward the mountains still swaddled in haze.

"Lazaro Neron Constanzo," Zapata replied. "He is Durango's governor, appointed by Diaz. A creature of his master. He corrupts whatever falls within his reach."

"I guess he doesn't wish you well."

"He wants me dead, Matt. Of that, you can be sure."

Throughout that morning, Price had the illusion that the mountains were retreating from them, edging backward in a kind of dream world where he couldn't close the gap no matter how he tried. At last he gave up watching them and concentrated on the high desert around him, watching hawks and vultures circle overhead, keeping an eye out on the trail for rattlers that could spook the roan and send him bucking off across the countryside.

At noon, Price glanced up once again and found the peaks had rushed to meet him. They were riding into foothills now, the air already cooling slightly, while the greenery became more plentiful. It started with low ground cover, locoweed and sourgrass, pigweed and prickly poppy, fading into righteous trees at higher altitude. Price could already smell the white pine, cedar, and the alligator juniper before they reached the tree line, climbing steadily.

Price knew these mountains more by reputation than first-hand experience. They were the great Sierra Madre Occidental, smaller than the Rockies but impressive on their own account. Beyond them, on the western side, Durango would turn into Sinaloa, sloping downward to the sea. Price hadn't seen a beach in ages, and he didn't think his short-term future offered any sand and surf.

"We're getting close, I take it?" he inquired.

Zapata glanced up at the sun. "Another hour, maybe less."

"I'm not much of a mountain climber."

"Fear not, Matt. You'll find comfort with my people."

Price had his doubts, but didn't voice them. He could spare an hour from a life devoid of destinations, after all.

When he was going nowhere, anyplace could feel like home.

Rufio Duarte was sipping bad coffee and making it last when the runner found him. He was little more than a child, barely half of Duarte's twenty-six years, and he had trouble keeping the excitement from his face.

"Riders are coming, *Capitán*!"

"I'm not your captain," Duarte reminded him. Rising, he poured the dregs of his coffee into the morning fire's ashes. "How many are coming? From where?"

The youth blinked and turned shame-faced. "They told me to tell you. Say 'riders,' they told me. That's all, *Capi*—"

"It's not your fault," Duarte said, cutting him off. "Next time, you tell them I want details. That's an order."

"*Sí!* I will!"

Duarte brushed past him, felt the runner on his heels as he moved toward the lookout point. Stopping, he turned and told the boy, "That's all for now."

The boy looked disappointed, but he nodded, slowly turned away. Duarte almost smiled at the exuberance of youth, but he was not in any mood to smile this morning. Cesar was most likely dead by now, which meant he was in fact the *capitán*, unless some other chose to challenge him.

Duarte didn't need to ask the boy which lookout point, because they only had one. Their retreat was fairly spacious, but the only access short of scaling or descending cliffs bare-handed was a narrow, winding trail that wriggled through a rocky cleft where new arrivals had to move in single file. He kept two riflemen always on duty there, one for his eyes, the other to make sure both stayed awake regardless of the hour.

Duarte didn't hurry as he climbed the mountain trail that terminated at the lookout point. He didn't like to run unless there was a bona fide emergency, because it spooked the others and it also made him look undignified. Duarte had a kind of waddling stride when running, even though he wasn't fat. He'd tried to change it, but it had outlasted puberty and still made Cesar laugh from time to time.

He won't be laughing anymore, Duarte thought, and felt a lump form in his throat. They were like brothers, growing up, and now . . .

He hoped Dolores wouldn't fall apart today. Duarte hadn't seen her yet this morning, knew he ought to check on her and see how she was doing. Maybe he could offer comfort in her time of sorrow, help her to forget. If she was grateful for his efforts, what would be the harm in that?

A sudden stiffness made the uphill hike more difficult. Duarte concentrated on his mission of the moment, answering a summons from the guards. If this had been the army, a report of danger would've passed through half a dozen underlings before it reached Duarte's ears, by which time it might be too late. He'd rather make the climb first thing and find out what was wrong than wait and watch the enemy march into camp while he sat idly on the sidelines.

The final thirty yards were steep enough to leave Duarte winded, but he never slowed his pace. The lookouts wouldn't call him if they weren't concerned. They knew which visitors were authorized and when to use their rifles on trespassers. If it had been the *federales,* Duarte's warning would've been the sound of gunfire, calling him to rally every able-bodied person in the camp and man the barricades.

Besides, he knew that Cesar wouldn't tell his captors

where the camp was hidden. He would take that secret to his grave, no matter what the bastards did to him.

Duarte huffed across the final fifteen yards, and found the lookouts peering down into a wooded valley far below. The trail was plainly visible from that angle, a well-worn track amongst the trees. Two mounted figures were a half mile out and moving toward the bottleneck.

"*Jéfé,*" one of the lookouts said before Duarte had a chance to speak. "We wanted you to see these two."

"We don't know what to do," the other added.

Duarte waited with a hand outstretched. "The glass."

The guard who'd spoken first handed a pocket telescope to Duarte. Duarte drew it out to full extension, raised it to his eye, and spent another moment trying to regain his fix on the advancing horsemen.

"Lower, *Jéfé,*" said the second guard.

"Ah, yes." He had them now, picked out the leader, and Duarte's heart kicked hard against his ribs. "It can't be!"

The first guard nodded. "That's what *I* said, eh, Chico?"

"Tha's right. You said it."

"*Cállate!*" Duarte snapped at both of them. He had to think, and quickly. Had to sort through all the questions swirling in his head.

How could Cesar be there, on the trail below, when he'd been locked up yesterday and scheduled for a rope this morning? Who was his gringo companion, riding several yards behind Cesar and studying the trail ahead as if he feared a trap? Was he an ally or an enemy? How could a gringo be a friend?

Duarte scanned backward along the trail until it disappeared in shadow and his glass lost focus. It was just the two of them, as far as he could see. There were no *federales* coming up behind them, no one else visible at all.

Duarte didn't like it, but he had a choice to make and he could not delay it. "Let them pass," he said, "and keep a sharp eye out for anybody else."

"Sí, Jéfé."

He returned the glass and left the lookouts. When the trees concealed him from them, Duarte started jogging, but he took care in his haste. It wouldn't do to slip and break an ankle now, of all times. He must tell Dolores that Cesar was coming home. Duarte fancied she might bless the lips that brought such news.

And if she had cause to regret it later, well, the fault would not be his.

Price waited for the bullet, but it didn't come. He had been restless since they left the flat land and began to climb through trees, along a trail Zapata knew by heart. Price might've found it, if he'd search the tree line long and hard enough, but his companion had gone right to it and they'd passed into a world of shade and dappled sunlight, where the ground went up and up without respite.

If it's a trap, Price thought, *he's gone the long way round to get me here.*

It made no sense, of course. He'd saved Zapata's life, albeit through a kind of accident. Price couldn't think of any reason why the Mexican would want to kill him, but he knew the racial thing was never far away when white and brown rubbed shoulders in the West. Zapata didn't seem to think that way, but Price was no mind reader.

What he *did* know was that since they'd found the forest trail, he couldn't shake a sense of being watched. He couldn't point a finger at the watchers, couldn't even swear that they existed, but he'd learned to trust his instincts when it came to matters of survival. Following Zapata on the narrow track, Price kept his right hand near the holstered Peacemaker.

The last bit of the trail was worse than he'd expected, where opposing cliffs closed in to form a chute some fifty feet in length. Worn gravel under hoof, and just a slice of blue sky thirty feet above his head. His stirrups nearly brushed the stony face on either side. It would be wasting lead to use a weapon there, Price thought, when anyone could drop a fat rock on his head and get the same result.

"I guess you don't use wagons much," he said, his voice echoing.

Zapata answered without turning. "Some cannot pass through the tunnel. It defeats them. Are you feeling well?"

"I'll make it," Price replied.

Unless somebody drops that rock.

But he couldn't deny a feeling of relief when they broke through and into daylight. The trail ran on another hundred yards through looming trees before they reached a spacious clearing and Zapata's camp.

The word had gone before them, verifying Price's hunch that they were under scrutiny. Without Zapata, he supposed that hidden shooters would've stopped him well before he reached the skinny canyon. Zapata's people had a good thing going so far, but Price knew a fortress could become a death trap if it was besieged.

A cheer went up from the assembled folk, some of them crowding forward, anxious for a chance to touch Zapata and make sure he wasn't a mirage. Laughing, Zapata swung down from his horse and let someone lead it away. Price followed his example to a point, but held the roan's lead in his left hand. Kept the right hand free.

First in the ranks to meet Zapata were another man about

his age, somber despite his smile, and a woman Price thought must be several years younger. The man clutched Zapata's hand and clapped him on the shoulder, stopped just short of an embrace. The woman threw herself into his arms, beaming and weeping at the same time, as she kissed Zapata on the cheek. Others were satisfied to speak his name or brush his clothing with their fingertips.

The happy folk didn't crowd Price, staying well back from the gringo in their midst until Zapata introduced him in a burst of rapid Spanish. Price caught most of it, the critical "amigo" naming him a friend, and felt the mob in waiting warm to him a little.

Not much maybe, but at least he didn't think they'd try to lynch him on the spot.

"Matt," Zapata called to him, "come meet my heart and my right arm." He introduced the woman first. "Dolores is my baby sister."

"Baby! I am not—"

"And Rufio Duarte is my best friend in the world. My second in command."

Duarte's grip was there and gone before Price had a chance to gauge his strength. His eyes told Price that there was only room for one bosom amigo in Zapata's world.

"I deal with any problems that arise," Duarte said.

Price met his level gaze. "I'll bet you do."

Dolores Zapata stopped listening to her brother's short homecoming speech and studied the stranger's face. His skin was darker than her own, bronzed by the sun, with lighter scars just visible above his left eye and beside his chin.

Handsome?

She barely had a gauge by which to judge such things, but Dolores knew what pleased her eyes. He wasn't pretty, like the rich boys she'd seen once in Gómez Palacio, who oiled their hair and their frail goatees to make them look like pouting devils. She might've called him rugged, certainly the product of a hard life, but when his eyes locked with hers—

She turned away, blushing, and found Duarte frowning at her. Dolores knew that look, had been on the receiving end often enough to recognize the way his eyebrows bunched together in a nearly solid line above his nose. She had displeased him somehow, but she didn't know what it could be, unless . . .

He's jealous, she decided, almost laughing at the notion. *Jealous of a gringo I just met!*

It would've been a good joke, but Dolores had no one with whom to share it. The handful of girls her own age still unmarried in camp adored either Cesar or Rufio. Some lusted after both, if truth be told. They sat around imagining that one or both men noticed and returned their feelings. If Dolores claimed that Rufio was interested in her, they might be angry and they'd certainly turn catty, mocking her, if nothing worse.

She heard the stranger's name spoken and focused for the first time on the story Cesar was recounting. He described the flight from prison, the pursuit by *federales,* and the death of an Apache called Gray Wolf. Then he related how the stranger turned and charged the enemy, guns blazing for his slain amigo, and left none of them alive.

Dolores shot another glance at Matt Price. She had already guessed he was a hard man, for none other could've rescued Cesar. Now she knew he was a killer who befriended savages. Why did she still feel drawn to him in such a way that she had not experienced before?

It was ridiculous. A gringo gunman, probably an outlaw, certainly a stranger who would likely ride away as soon as he'd collected a reward for Cesar's life. And yet, she'd known bad men, despite her tender years. There'd been a few in camp, before Cesar and Rufio got rid of them by one means or another, animals who sought either to profit from the revolution or avenge themselves for some old injury. She still recalled the gasping face of one Cesar and Rufio had hanged for rape.

But Price seemed different somehow. If pressed, she might've said he was a hard man but not evil, capable of cruelty but deriving no amusement from it. A killer who did not enjoy his work.

A man like her brother, in fact.

When Cesar finished speaking, there was general applause, and several people tendered private thanks to Price for their leader's safe return. He nodded, clasped whatever hands were offered, but Dolores saw he was uneasy with the praise, a man who didn't like to be the focus of attention, unlike Rufio.

Dolores suddenly wished she could draw him away from the crowd, whisk him off to some quiet corner of the camp or a place in the woods she'd discovered and kept to herself.

What would you do there? asked a small voice in her head.

They'd talk, of course. What else would she consider doing with a man she'd only met, who'd never spoken to her once?

Blushing again, Dolores turned and went to join her brother's entourage as he moved toward the center of the camp. She knew that Rufio was glaring, so she made a point of quietly ignoring him. And when Price followed, finally relinquishing his weary horse, Dolores couldn't altogether mask her smile.

"You know nothing about this gringo, Cesar. He could be a spy."

"Spies don't kill *federales,* Rufio. They don't break rebels out of prison."

Duarte sipped his coffee through a frown. Their beefsteak supper was a fading memory, sitting like cold stones in his stomach. It had been a celebration of Zapata's safe return, but Duarte's joy was hedged with reservations. He felt duty-bound to show Zapata it was wrong, bringing the stranger into camp. Bad for the cause and for their people.

"He's an outlaw, used to killing."

"So are we," Zapata said. "And please make up your mind. Is he an outlaw or a spy?"

Angry, Duarte shrugged. "Maybe he's both. Why not?"

"You think the *federales* had him break me out of prison, then he shot them down for fun? You didn't see him, Rufio, with the Apache."

"All the more reason we should be rid of him. Apaches are the enemy, as surely as Diaz and Neron."

"We've fought them, Rufio, it's true. But this obsessive hatred of their race demeans you."

Duarte felt his cheeks flush, hoping that the firelight and his dark complexion covered it. He took time prior to answering, weighing his words. "I'm thinking only of your welfare and our cause," he said. "Bringing a stranger here was rash, Cesar. He knows the way now. If he means to hurt us—"

"Rufio," Zapata said, interrupting him, "he saved my life when all he had to do was take the Indian and leave me in the cell. I've seen his loyalty and what he'll do to those who harm his friends. A man like that won't hurt us. He can only help the cause, if he decides to stay."

Duarte winced. "You've given him that choice, Cesar?"

"I have."

"Without consulting me?"

Zapata's gaze acquired a flinty edge. "I didn't know it was required, amigo."

"No, of course not. What I meant to say—"

"You've made your point. We disagree."

"And what has he decided?"

"Nothing yet. I've welcomed him to stay while he makes up his mind."

"With free run of the camp."

"He freed me from a cage," Zapata said. "I won't repay that act by putting him in one."

"I only meant that there are things he shouldn't see."

"Like what?" Zapata challenged. "He's already seen the camp, as you point out. What else have we to hide? Is there a cache of gold that I don't know about?"

Duarte scowled. "Joke if you please. He's dangerous. A murderer."

"And what are we?" Zapata raised his open hands. "Do these seem clean to you? They're bloody. Have you checked your own?"

"We're soldiers!" Duarte said. "This is a war. We have good cause."

"And if he joins us, so will Price."

"Your mind's made up then?"

"*Sí*. It is."

"I hope he doesn't disappoint you."

"If he does," Zapata said, "I'm sure you'll be the first to let me know."

"Good night, Cesar. And welcome back."

"Sleep well, old friend."

Duarte didn't think he'd get much sleep, but he was smiling as he left Zapata. There was nothing to be gained from showing those around him how he seethed inside. Zapata thought him foolish for not trusting Price on an hour's acquaintance, but Duarte knew he wasn't the fool in this play. It was madness trusting a stranger with the location of their camp, their strength, the number of their weapons.

A stranger and a gringo too. What had the pale men from El Norte ever done for Duarte and his people? In his father's day, they'd stolen half of Mexico and made it part of the United States. When they came south across the Rio Grande, it was always for some profit to themselves: cheap labor, minerals and oil, Mexican cattle stolen off the range or purchased at a fraction of their value. In towns along the border, they behaved like savages and turned Mexican women into whores.

Duarte had no love for Anglos or Apaches, and he didn't care who knew it, but he saw that he'd be forced to mask his feelings in the future, if and when Zapata asked for his advice. It stung him that their years together counted less in Cesar's eyes than one night on the trail with some gringo who'd saved his life by accident.

What if Dolores felt the same?

What if she felt much more?

Duarte had seen the way she looked at Price, and it was gnawing at his gut behind the smile. Dolores had to know his feelings for her, even though he'd never put them into words. That was an error he could remedy, and soon.

Meanwhile, if she seemed too enchanted with the gringo, there were things that he could do.

I'm sure you'll be the first to let me know, Cesar had said.

And so he would be.

Yes indeed. He'd be the very first.

4

The lieutenant was nervous, with excellent reason. He knew word of his failure had preceded him, and now he would be forced to give a full accounting of himself. He knew enough of human nature and of politics within the *federale* ranks to understand that blame must have a focus. Nothing ever simply happened in the service. If results were beneficial, someone wanted credit. If they weren't, someone must take the blame.

This time, it would be him.

Lieutenant Cruz knew his superiors wouldn't accept responsibility for the escape and the resultant loss of life. Why should they? He had been in charge and proud of it, prepared to bask in the glory of caging and hanging Cesar Zapata. Now that the plan had blown up in his face, he was prepared to face the consequences.

But he couldn't help trying to mitigate the damage, plead his case just once before the dark cloud settled permanently over his career.

"Lieutenant Cruz?"

He had been waiting for the summons, but it still surprised him. Bounding from his chair as if it were red-hot, he spun to face a slightly older version of himself. Same uniform, same rank, same rigid bearing. But the officer who stood before him didn't look as if he was about to mount the scaffold.

"Sí?"

"Captain Ruiz will see you now. This way."

Cruz trailed his escort through tall doors, into the office he had only visited on two occasions previously. He had thought about the room—obsessed about it really—on the long ride to Durango, picturing the tall windows with Ruiz's desk in front of them. The way light pouring through those panes blinded the person sitting opposite Ruiz and drove lancets of pain into his skull.

It was all part of the theatrical procedure, Cruz supposed. He had the shakes already. Why not have the headache to go with them?

Cruz's escort left him stranded in the office, closed the double doors behind him, and was gone. Cruz clicked his heels and stiffened to attention, staring at a point above the desk. He couldn't see Ruiz behind the desk, but that wasn't important. At the moment, every ounce of his attention focused on the snap of his salute.

"At ease, Lieutenant. Sit."

The voice came from his left, surprising Cruz. He didn't flinch, and counted that a bonus as he dropped his arm, proceeding to the single straight-backed chair before Ruiz's desk. It was as cold and hard as he remembered, but the window's glare seemed doubly harsh.

Ruiz's footsteps circled him, proceeding slowly toward

the desk. Cruz fought an impulse to follow the man with his eyes.

"I've tried to understand what happened to your prisoners, Lieutenant, but it still eludes me. Since I must explain it to the governor this afternoon, perhaps you would be kind enough to tell me what went wrong?"

"Yes, sir. We had three prisoners at San Filipe, all condemned and scheduled for execution this morning. Shortly after three o'clock yesterday, a gunman tied the local padre up inside his church and stole a cassock. First, the jailers thought he'd come to hear confessions from the prisoners, and by the time they saw he was a gringo, he'd already pulled a gun."

"Gringo, you say?"

"Yes, sir."

"Proceed."

"One of the guards opened the cell. The gunmen put them in and took the others out. One of the prisoners, Guillermo Calderon—"

"The thief?" Cruz interrupted.

"Yes, sir. Calderon panicked and ran out through the front door, to the street. Two of my men were there and intercepted him."

"Shot him, in fact."

"Yes, sir. He was a fugitive."

"Of course. Go on."

"While that was happening, the others left through the back door and rode south, out of town."

"Horses were waiting for them at the jail?" Cruz couldn't see the captain's face, but he could almost hear the frown he wore.

"The jailers had their horses tied in back, sir. We assume the gunman brought his own."

"A safe assumption. Does it not seem strange to you that he would bring only one horse?"

"Sir, I'm not sure—"

"If he planned to liberate one of the prisoners, much less all three, would he expect them to run after him on foot?"

Cruz started blinking rapidly and fought to make it stop. "No, sir," he said at last. How had the simple thought eluded him so far?

"Proceed."

"When I was summoned to the jail, I organized a party to retrieve the fugitives."

"You did not lead it personally."

"No, sir. But—"

"And the pursuit did not go well."

Again, "No, sir. My men killed the Apache, but there must have been an ambush party waiting. None of them returned alive."

"So, we have two dead felons, eight dead officers—and no Cesar Zapata?"

"At the moment, sir, but—"

"Do you suppose the governor will be amused by this performance?"

"No, sir."

"Nor do I. I'm honestly not sure what I can say to make him think you've done your best. A thing like this is damaging to all of us, and all the more so to the man responsible."

"Yes, sir."

"Perhaps, if you were able to retrieve Zapata *and* inflict real damage on the rabble he presumes to call an army, there might be a measure of . . . forgetfulness about this episode."

"I understand, sir."

"Do you? I sincerely hope so, for your own sake. If you were to fail a second time, so soon after the last, it would be most unfortunate."

"Don't worry, sir."

Despite the glare behind him, Cruz imagined he could see the captain's wolfish smile. "I'm not worried, Lieutenant," he replied. "Not in the least. Dismissed."

It was a short walk from his office to the state capitol building, but Captain Elaminio Ruiz Valdez took his time. The sun was punishing, and he did not intend to stand before the governor reeking of sweat and guilt.

Despite what he had told Lieutenant Cruz, Ruiz *was* worried. Not for Cruz, but for himself. The governor was volatile at times, and while he rarely raised his voice, he was relentless in assessing blame and penalizing those who cast a shadow on his own career. If that were not enough, he spoke directly to and for Porfirio Diaz, the most feared man in all of Mexico. A whisper there could place Ruiz in mortal jeopardy, unless he talked fast enough to place the blame squarely on Cruz.

And even then . . .

The capitol rotunda was a shady vault, all stucco, tile, and marble. A few short paces from the sunbaked street outside, the temperature dropped ten degrees. Ruiz waited a moment, dabbing at his neck and forehead with a freshly laundered handkerchief. The walk had not been long enough for him to sweat through his dress uniform, but Ruiz stooped to swipe the pale dust from his spit-shined boots.

Ready.

The marble staircase echoed to his footsteps. On the second floor, he turned left, following an ornate balcony halfway around the building to the suite of offices his master occupied. The governor's receptionist was male, mid-twenties, stern of countenance.

"May I help you?"

"I have a two o'clock appointment with His Excellency."

The receptionist kept Ruiz waiting while he checked his book, dragging a finger down the page to find his name. Ruiz despised the little weasel, but he didn't let it show.

"This way, Captain."

He knew the way, but there was protocol to follow. Just as he had kept Lieutenant Cruz waiting, then called him like a servant, now it was his turn.

The inner office of Governor Lazaro Neron Constanzo was twice the size of Captain Ruiz's living quarters. Some might call it opulent, but Ruiz was more concerned with the expression on Neron's face than the artwork on his walls. The governor was frowning, standing with his feet apart and hands thrust in his pockets.

It was never a good sign.

"Your Excellency, Cap—"

"Leave us, Ramon."

"Yes, sir."

"It's a bad business, this, in San Filipe," said the governor.

"Yes, sir. I have the details, if you'd care—"

"I know the details, Captain. Three convicts escaped from custody and killed eight *federales* in the process. I assure you that the president will not be pleased."

"No, sir, but two of the escapees were recovered."

"Killed, in fact."

"Yes, sir. Resisting capture."

"And the worst of them escaped. Cesar Zapata is at large once more because your people couldn't hold him, even with a noose around his neck."

"My staff is working on a plan to rectify the situation, sir, I promise you."

"Are you a man who keeps a promise, Captain?"

"Yes, sir!"

"Good. I plan to tell the president that we can deal with our own riffraff in Durango, and we don't need any special help."

"Of course, sir."

Ruiz knew the kind of "special help" Diaz would send if he lost patience. It would be an inquisition, starting from the top and working downward, wreaking havoc as it went. There was a chance that none of them would be in office when the new broom finished sweeping through their lives.

And some of them might not survive.

"Zapata and his bandits are a blight upon this territory, Captain. He's a sharp thorn in my flesh. Remove it swiftly, with a minimum of damage, and you may go far. Fail me, and I can promise you there'll be nowhere to hide."

"I understand, sir."

"As I knew you would." The governor turned toward his desk, took several steps, then glanced back at Ruiz. "Are you still here?"

Governor Lazaro Neron Constanzo was not a man easily worried. He would celebrate his fiftieth birthday three weeks hence, which made him a remarkable survivor in the tumultuous realm of Mexican politics. The fact that he had not only survived, but also risen through the ranks to reign over Durango as its governor, spoke volumes for his personal tenacity and ruthlessness.

It was a stepping-stone, of course, in his view. Every civil servant's goal was to land a choice assignment in Mexico City, close to the trough where the pickings were choice. The danger of working so close to Diaz and his notorious, explosive temper was offset by the potential for enrichment through *mordida,* the time-honored trickle-down system of graft.

He wasn't doing badly in Durango, granted. Squeezing tax money from peasants, skimming his share off the top before he sent the rest on to Diaz, was a game he had learned to play well and with relish. But it held no more surprises for him, no more fresh rewards.

There was only so much he could steal from impoverished farmers, only so many women to choose from in the state capital's high—or low—society. Before he'd even settled in Durango, Neron had already been planning to move on. Move up. But all his plans could still be ruined, dashed to pieces on the ground, if he grew careless.

Cesar Zapata should be dead by now, already rotting underneath the desert sun. It would've been a grave blow to the revolutionary movement in Durango, and a feather in Neron's cap when he sought promotion from Diaz. Zapata's escape was worse than a setback. It was a reversal of Neron's best-laid plans, an obstacle to his dreams.

But obstacles could be shifted or demolished, couldn't they?

He'd give Captain Ruiz another chance to do it right, and if the captain failed it would be *his* head on the chopping block. A charge of treason was the easiest of all to prove in Mexico, where paranoia filtered downward from El Presidente's office, spreading far and wide like a subversive virus. No man could be trusted absolutely in the present system. It was not whether a subordinate would stab him in the back, but rather when and where the ambush would occur.

If Captain Ruiz failed to bag Zapata by week's end, Neron intended to "discover" evidence detailing his collusion with the rebels. Neron wouldn't have to forge a document, since most peasants and farmers were illiterate. He'd only need a witness, maybe two, who would accept a few crumbs from his table in return for testimony that would compromise Ruiz.

Simple.

And if the witnesses themselves should disappear after Ruiz was gone, who was there to complain? There was no peasant shortage in Durango. They would not be missed by anyone who mattered in the scheme of things.

Neron was not anticipating failure. He sincerely hoped Captain Ruiz would get it right this time and rid his state of the man some traitors already called Cristo Segundo.

Second Christ.

Like all great thieves of his acquaintance, Neron was a deeply religious man when it mattered—on holy days, at public gatherings, when it was time to take the oath of office. In that respect, Zapata's nickname was a blasphemous outrage. At a deeper level, it disgusted and infuriated him to see a filthy peasant elevated to such stature in the eyes of people who could only serve one master faithfully. Neron was meant to be that master, held the title handed to him by Diaz that gave him near-omnipotent authority of life and death within the state, and yet the people turned to some unwashed pretender who could barely write his name.

For that, they would be forced to pay.

What could he tax next that was not already taxed?

Before he pondered that decision, though, Neron knew he must plan for the event of failure if Ruiz should let him down a second time. He must have someone waiting in the wings, ready to step in at a moment's notice with a new plan and a warrant to arrest Ruiz.

There were legalities to be observed. Neron was not a savage, after all. And as befitted his reputation for meticulous planning, he had an officer in mind.

Neron picked up the telephone. It was a new addition to his office and it only reached the waiting room, but he regarded it with something close to awe. The future was upon him, and he meant to ride that wave to greater things.

Three quick taps on the lever for attention, and the tiny voice of his receptionist replied, "Yes, sir?"

"I want Captain Montoya, from the post at Peñón Blanco. Get him here as soon as possible."

"Yes, sir!"

Neron replaced the earpiece with a smile.

He felt better already.

"I need a fresh approach, Sergeant. Some way to draw the rebels out and bring Zapata with them. Any thoughts?"

The stripes on Carlos Villa's sleeve were new, but he already felt their weight. No officer had ever asked for his opinion on the weather, much less a decisive point of strategy. He wasn't sure if he should play the game or flee the room in fear.

He heard himself say, "One thing, sir."

Lieutenant Cruz stepped closer. "Yes? I'm listening."

"If they were angry, sir—"

"Angry? They hate me as it is."

"Angry enough to want revenge, sir. Maybe then they

would expose themselves. Maybe Zapata would be with them . . . sir."

"Something specific, eh? A prod to move them, or a lure to draw them out?"

"Perhaps, sir."

Cruz smiled. "And why not both?"

Now Villa was confused. Instead of showing it, he simply said, "Yes, sir! Why not?"

"It's brilliant, Sergeant! I'm a genius." Strutting up and down the little room, Cruz pinched his chin, frowned deeply. "What we need's a target now," he muttered. "Something we can strike with no risk to ourselves that will so enrage Zapata that we force his hand."

"Sir, if I may—"

"What is it, Sergeant?"

"There is a village where Zapata spent time as a child. . . ."

Cruz took the bait. "Does he have family?"

"I doubt it, sir. But maybe friends."

"Where is this village?"

"North, sir. Thirty miles, I think. Sangre de Maria."

The lieutenant's eyes narrowed. "How do you know this, Sergeant?"

Villa blinked and swallowed hard. The facts were common knowledge, but he couldn't ask Lieutenant Cruz why he was ignorant. "It's just something I heard, sir."

"Heard? Heard *when*?"

A sudden inspiration came to him. "Last week, sir. I informed Sergeant Aguirre."

"Aguirre?" It was the lieutenant's turn to blink and grind his teeth. A dead man was immune to punishment and couldn't contradict Villa. When he regained total control, Cruz asked, "It's thirty miles, you say?"

"About that. Yes, sir."

"If you leave tonight, you could be there for breakfast."

"Yes, sir."

"Perfect. That will be our prod. As for the lure, we need something Zapata can't resist. Something that every revolution needs."

When Cruz resumed his pacing, Villa thought it might be safe to offer one more small suggestion. "Sir?"

"I'm thinking, Sergeant!"

"Yes, sir."

"Something that will draw Zapata out, just when he's furious and reckless. Something he believes will hurt us, even as it helps his cause."

"Gold, sir?"

"Don't be ridiculous! The governor won't give us any gold to bait the rebels."

"Sir—"

"What *is* it, Sergeant?" Cruz was angry now.

"They only have to think it's gold, sir. Boxes filled with sand would do as well for bait."

Cruz blinked again, and then his dark face broke into a smile. His teeth were small, a child's teeth in his beaming face, and very white.

"I like it. What's more, I believe Captain Ruiz will like it too."

"I hope so, sir."

"How soon can you be ready, Sergeant?"

"Ready, sir?"

"Ready to *ride,* man! What have I been saying?"

"To the village, sir?"

"Sangre de Maria. How large is the place again?"

"Twenty or thirty families, I think, sir."

"Not many men of fighting age. That's good. Take thirty

men. Handpick them. I want an example made of these traitors. Any apparent rebels should be liquidated. As for property and women, I leave that to your discretion."

"Yes, sir!"

"And the bait will be prepared when you return."

"One thing, sir."

"Yes?"

"How will Zapata know about the bait, sir?"

"Ah. Leave that to me, Sergeant. You don't think I could hatch this plan without having some way to see it through, do you?"

"No, sir!"

"That's all. Dismissed."

Outside, where he could breathe again, Villa knew that he'd been handed the opportunity of a lifetime. It was his to make or break, win or lose. He only had to spill a little blood, and it was all within his grasp.

Sangre de Maria. *Mary's blood.*

Where better to begin?

The traitor always had mixed feelings when he met Captain Ruiz. There was a risk of being followed, being seen, which would mean almost certain death, and so he worried. At the same time, though, he found the cloak-and-dagger business quite exciting. It was thrilling to hold secrets from his fellowmen, pass by them every day on ordinary business, knowing that they couldn't pierce his mask.

It made the traitor feel *special.*

And there were physical rewards, of course. Each time they met, Captain Ruiz provided money "for expenses," doubtless knowing that the pesos would be spent on alcohol and whores before the traitor crept back to the comrades he betrayed. Still, when else would a lowly peasant taste such pleasures, hiding in the mountains with a pack of fools who reckoned they could change the world?

The traitor didn't feel he was betraying anyone. Instead, he helped himself—and wasn't that what God asked every man to do?

He never met Ruiz twice in the same place. Their meetings always took place in Durango, meaning that he had to manufacture some excuse for staying overnight, but they did not meet frequently. Tonight would be the third time in nine months, and he had volunteered to mingle with the *federales* to find out what they were doing to recapture their lost prisoner.

It was enough to make him chuckle as he stepped into the small cantina, crossed the public room, and climbed a flight of stairs to reach the private rooms above. No one downstairs gave him a second glance, assuming he was there to meet a whore.

Not yet, he thought. *Right now, I* am *the whore.*

Which didn't bother him at all.

He chose a numbered door, knocked softly, and obeyed the summons from within. Captain Ruiz was out of uniform, as always when they met. The false mustache was new and made the traitor smile. It didn't change Ruiz's look so much as make him comical, a clown.

"Please, sit," the captain said. Forced courtesy. "Tequila?"

"*Sí, Jéfé. Gracias.*"

He received the liquor from Ruiz and sent it scorching down his gullet in one swallow. Smiled as it began to warm his gut.

"I need to know about the jailbreak," said Ruiz, "and why you didn't warn us."

He'd expected this, but even so, the traitor felt sweat creeping underneath his arms. He tried to blame it on the stuffy room, but couldn't quite deceive himself. If Captain Ruiz thought the traitor had betrayed him instead, the penalty could be severe.

"It wasn't planned, *Jéfé*. Zapata's people didn't break him out. They were afraid of *federales* waiting for them."

Ruiz frowned, glaring. "If that's the case, who did it then?"

"A gringo." As he spoke the words, the traitor saw Ruiz stiffen. The captain knew something, but not enough to satisfy him yet.

"Why would a gringo help Cesar Zapata?"

"That's the funny—er, the strange part, *Capitán*. The gringo didn't know Zapata. Never heard of him, it seems. He went to fetch an Indian and let the others go as well."

"He came for the Apache?"

"*Sí.*"

"And how do you know this?"

"Zapata told us."

"So, he's back in camp?"

"He is." The traitor didn't worry over that point. He'd convinced Ruiz that an assault upon the rebel mountain stronghold would be futile, costing countless lives without result. Unlike some of the tales he spun, it was at least approximately true.

"And have you seen this gringo?" asked Ruiz.

"*Sí, Jéfé*. He is with the others now."

"Describe him."

"Tall. Not fat or thin. Dark hair." The traitor nearly giggled as he added, "No mustache."

"An ordinary man, is he?"

"To look at, *sí*. But he's a gunman. Cesar says he killed

eight *federales* in the desert. Charged them by himself after they shot the Indian and dropped them all."

"You say there was no ambush party waiting?"

"No, *Jéfe*. The others were resigned to losing Cesar. I could see Duarte puffing up next morning, ready to take charge as soon as they had time to grieve."

He watched the captain ponder that, trying to make the information useful. If he couldn't think of anything, perhaps the traitor would suggest some possibilities. It wouldn't be the first time that he'd earned a bonus by displaying his initiative. In fact—

"This gringo. Does he have a name?"

"Zapata calls him Matt. Matt Price."

Ruiz frowned over that a while, then said, "I have a plan. Zapata will expect some information from you, yes?"

The traitor nodded, wishing he could ask for more tequila.

"Perfect. When you return to camp, tell him a gold shipment is coming to Durango from the mines in Sinaloa, stopping overnight before it moves on to Mexico City. Three wagons, along the Presidio road. Can you do that?"

"*Sí, Jéfe.*"

The traitor could do that, and more. As he received his money and departed, counting it, he was already thinking of excuses to avoid joining his comrades on the raid, from which he was convinced none would return alive.

Captain Ruiz despised the traitor, as he did all turncoats, but the man had served him well so far. When he was gone, Ruiz relaxed, considered peeling off the stage mustache, then left it glued in place. It was a silly affectation, but it helped to get him in the spirit of the covert work he'd done tonight.

He hadn't disclosed the upcoming raid on Sangre de Maria, because he didn't want Zapata and the rest of them forewarned. The traitor always went to find a bottle and a woman when they finished, as Ruiz knew from having him followed on other occasions, but he might break the pattern if innocent lives were at stake. Ruiz didn't think so, but why tempt Fate?

Trust no one, and you cannot be betrayed.

Ruiz checked his mustache in the cracked mirror, then descended to the ground floor and slipped out the back, unseen. He moved along the alley, one hand on the small revolver in his pocket, ready if he met some drunken thug along the way. His destination was a small adobe building in the vice district, where his face was recognized by the proprietor and no one else.

The owner was Chinese. He was at least fifty years old and might've been a hundred, from the look of him. Ruiz had no idea and didn't care. The Chinaman met him with something like a smile and led Ruiz past dangling strings of beads that rattled as they passed, into the dark recesses of his lair.

Oil lamps were mounted on the walls at intervals, their wicks turned low enough to light the way without revealing much of the surroundings. Ruiz didn't need to see the other customers to know what they were doing, laid up in their cribs that reeked of incense and of something stronger, sickly-sweet and perfectly intoxicating.

In his youth, Captain Ruiz had been a drinker, and he still enjoyed it on occasion, but he'd found a more delightful vice of late, to calm him after days like this when everything went wrong. Some claimed that opium was an addictive substance, but Ruiz ignored them. He could leave the pipe alone, if he so chose, but why on earth should he?

Already, when he hadn't even reached his bunk, Ruiz could feel the sweet sensation of defying gravity. He didn't walk so much as he floated along in the Chinaman's wake. It was a prelude to the pleasure and forgetfulness he would achieve after he traded cash for one of the long pipes and settled in to let himself unwind.

Ruiz deserved these stolen moments. He apologized to no one for his chosen form of recreation—though, in truth, he'd taken pains to guarantee that no one learned of his occasional excursions. Why court trouble, when he already faced so much of it every day?

Ruiz cared nothing for the peasants who would die tomorrow when Lieutenant Cruz raided Sangre de Maria. Some of them were traitors, and the rest were nothing much at all. If there were any loyal among them, why had they not given up Zapata to the *federales* long ago?

Tomorrow would be a day of reckoning, and not the last by any means. The plan—he thought of it as his, dismissing Cruz from any major contribution to the scheme—was nearly perfect. Rage and greed together would combine to make Cesar Zapata reckless, and this time there'd be no foolishness about a public execution.

Ruiz always learned from his mistakes.

This time, Zapata and his men would be shot down like vermin on the spot. There would be no mistakes.

Ruiz's host produced the pipe, lit it, and left him to his dreams. Within a few short moments, rebels and revenge were all forgotten. He was in a better world, and only wished he never had to leave it for the one outside.

5

Price woke to a medley of noises and smells as the camp came alive around daybreak. He'd slept alone most of his adult life—except for a few weeks in Texas last summer, when he'd been fooled into thinking a man's path could change—and he had trained himself to wake when other living things trespassed upon his private space.

It only took a second for him to remember where he was, but even as he started to relax and tell himself that he was safe, a small voice whispered in his ear.

Says who?

The camp was relatively quiet, for so large a group massed together. Even when a hungry baby started wailing for the nipple, it seemed muted, as if the surrounding trees absorbed and muffled sounds. The clanking noise of cookware sounded distant, but the smell of food was close enough to make his stomach growl.

Price had tried counting heads his first day in the camp,

but he couldn't stick with it for any length of time. Zapata kept introducing him to people, and others came up on their own with cautious smiles, thanking Price for the rescue. He'd thought of climbing on a stump and telling them that it was all a big mistake, but he'd decided not to bother. In another day or two he'd be long gone, forgotten in a week, and who would even care?

Between interruptions, he'd calculated that there were two hundred people in camp, or perhaps a few more. He supposed that made it a village, rather than a camp, except that there were no permanent shelters or other facilities. Everybody lived in tents or lean-tos, which was fine from spring to early autumn, but he wondered what they did for warmth and cover when the snow came.

Not my problem. I won't be here.

About one third of the people he'd seen so far were men of fighting age; the rest were women and children, with maybe a dozen old folks in the mix. His was the only gringo face in camp, which came as no surprise to Price, but it didn't seem to bother most of the others once they got over their initial shock.

One exception to that was Zapata's lieutenant, introduced to Price last night as Rufio Duarte. He couldn't look at Price without frowning, presumably because he didn't trust outsiders and a gringo was the ultimate outsider in this makeshift settlement.

Price guessed there might be something else, though. Once, around the fire last night, he'd caught Duarte scowling worse than usual after Zapata's sister had served Price a second helping from the stew pot. When she'd given him one of her bright smiles for dessert, Duarte had looked as if someone had kicked his favorite dog.

Something to watch there, Price decided, but Duarte

didn't scare him and he didn't plan on chasing any skirts during the day or two that still remained to him in camp.

One thing his mother taught him that he'd never lost: *Fish and houseguests start to smell after three days*. Price reckoned that was true even when there was no real house involved.

He was a trifle stiff this morning, but the kinks worked out while he was rolling up his blanket, placing it atop his saddle. Sleeping fully dressed had its advantages when strangers were around. Price buckled on his gun belt, tied down the holster, then went to see about the roan.

Zapata's men took turns guarding the horses overnight, against the threat of snakes or woodland predators. They didn't give a thought to theft, it seemed, because a thief would have nowhere to go. Price wished it could've been that simple in the world outside, but who would want to spend his life in a box canyon, with a sniper posted on the only entrance?

Price knew this was all supposed to be a temporary setup, but he wondered if the people had deceived themselves. Mexico had been embroiled in one upheaval or another throughout his lifetime, and well before that. He thought about the camp's children, waiting and hoping for a victory they'd likely never see, and wondered whether it was worth the blood already spilled.

The roan seemed glad to see him, pausing in the middle of its grassy breakfast long enough to sniff his shirt and snort in Price's face.

"Good morning to you too," he said.

"You talk to animals, Matthew?"

He turned to find Dolores watching him. She'd closed the gap to twenty feet without him noticing, which told Price he was too relaxed for his own good.

"Sometimes," he told her, "they make better company than people."

"I agree," she answered, smiling. "I've been here three months, and already I've learned to speak with birds and squirrels."

"It would be snakes you have to watch out for," Price said. "Forked tongues and all. Can't trust a thing they say."

Dolores laughed at that, then asked, "Will you join us for breakfast, Matthew? Please? A man needs to keep up his strength."

Price saw the trap, but inched a short step closer with his eyes wide open. "How could I refuse?"

There was no single cook or dining place in camp, except when everyone joined in to celebrate a victory. There had been few of those lately, and families most often took their meals together when they could, while solitary men were either welcomed to their fires or broke off into little groups of three or four together. Dolores had been worried that some other hostess might claim Matthew Price, so she'd been up before the sun, waiting and watching for him to awaken.

"I hope you don't mind venison again after the stew last night." She felt a need to chatter, make him constantly aware of her, as if he might forget that she was walking at his side. "We don't have any ham or bacon at the moment, and—"

"It's fine," he told her, smiling. "Tell the truth, I could get by on coffee till around midday."

"Oh, no! We can't have that."

Dolores wasn't sure exactly why the stranger fascinated her. She knew, of course, that part of it was gratitude. Her brother would be dead now if Price hadn't rescued him, and she'd be facing choices that she didn't want to think about. Whether to leave and head off on her own, with nothing besides her name, and that a strike against her in the eyes of Mexican authorities, or to remain and make the best of a bad bargain. If she stayed, it would've meant humiliation. She'd have had to beg some other family for help, or wed one of the single men.

A man she didn't love, like Rufio Duarte.

Price had changed all that, and while he was a stranger from a strange land, she was not suspicious or afraid of him. Duarte thought he was a spy, Cesar had told her, and she had to laugh at that. Such foolishness. What agent of the beast Diaz would spare her brother's life simply to worm his way inside their humble camp? It was ridiculous.

She understood Duarte's personal mistrust of Price. It was the same way Rufio behaved toward anyone who came too close to her, or to her brother. He had staked a silent claim of sorts to the remainder of her family, and Dolores thought no better of him for it.

"You're from Texas, I believe?" she asked, unable to keep still.

"Most recently. Way back, I come from Kansas."

"How far back?" she teased.

That made him smile. "For you," he said, "I'd guess about two lifetimes."

"You think I'm a child?" Pouting this time.

"I think I'm getting old," he answered diplomatically.

"You're not so old," she said. Then, blushing, she added, "I am not so young."

"How long have you and Cesar been alone?" Price asked, changing the subject.

"It will be five years next month. The army killed our

parents. By mistake, they later said. 'So sorry, there were rebels in the area. Accidents happen.' Then they took our home because the taxes were not paid. Good-bye, good luck, move on."

"Sorry to hear it," Price told her.

"It's all so long ago. Diaz made Cesar what he is today, made all the rebels what they are. If he weren't such a greedy pig, he'd understand and know that he will never be forgiven while we live."

"You've got a lot to carry on small shoulders."

She stiffened, ramrod straight, thrust out her chest. "I'm not so small," Dolores said.

Price smiled. "I see that now."

She blushed again, and for the first time noticed others watching them. A moment later, they found Cesar kneeling by the fire she'd built that morning in the dark, roasting fresh meat on wooden spits.

"Matt, I see Dolores talked you into breakfast."

"How could I refuse?"

"She'll talk your leg off, this one," Cesar cautioned. "Let me know if she keeps buzzing in your ear like a mosquito, and I'll swat her for you."

Dolores faced her brother, fists on hips. "Oh, will you? Just remember who went off with bruises the last time you tried."

"I let you win, *chiquita*, but I think now you're too spoiled for your own good."

"Brothers!" She turned to Price, cheeks flaming with the sunrise. "Do us all a favor, Matthew. If you ever find this one in jail again, please leave him there!"

"Dolores—"

"What?" She rounded on Cesar again. "*Dolores* what?

Go plan a battle, will you? Let me do this now before you ruin Matthew's meal!"

The venison was lean and lightly seasoned, with some kind of rice dish on the side Price didn't recognize. It wasn't what he pictured in his mind when someone mentioned breakfast, but it was a vast improvement over jerky and hardtack. He told Dolores that and sugared it a little, liking how her cheeks flushed just a bit before she turned away.

Easy, one of his mental voices whispered. And another answered, *Never mind. It's nothing.*

But he wasn't sure.

Price hadn't sworn off women after Mary Hudson was murdered back in Texas, but her death had taken something out of him, and there'd been little time for thoughts of anything resembling romance in the time since then. At first, he'd been consumed with tracking down her killers, and when that was done, it didn't seem to matter where he went or who he met along the way. Being alone and on the move was second nature to him anyway. Why fix it if it worked?

But this was good. Price could admit that to himself without surrendering his independence, giving up his advantage. Another day or two in camp wouldn't hurt anyone.

He hoped not anyway.

When they had finished breakfast and the plates were cleared away, Dolores brushing off his bid to help her with the cleanup chores, Zapata started plying him with questions. They were general at first—how long he'd been in Mexico; whether he planned to stay—but Price soon found them turning to specifics, trying to pin down the routes he'd traveled, any troops he'd met along the way. Price was considering a way to head off the questions without insulting his host, but Rufio Duarte rescued him from the dilemma.

Duarte had walked by twice while they were eating, giving off the signals of a man with vital business elsewhere, rushing to fulfill his obligations. Still, Price caught him glancing at Dolores with a hurt look in his eyes, then beaming unadulterated vitriol at Price before he passed on out of range. Now, here he was again, Dolores just returning with the clean plates, but this time Duarte's full attention focused on her brother.

"Cesar," he said, "Mateo has returned. He's coming up the mountain now."

"Alone?" Zapata asked.

Duarte bobbed his head. "He wasn't followed."

"I should hope not. Have the sentries keep a sharp watch anyway. I'll be there soon."

It must've felt like a dismissal, and from the expression on Duarte's face, he wasn't used to it. He blinked once at Zapata, spared a tight frown for Dolores on the sidelines, then gave Price a look that told the gringo this was somehow all *his* fault. Price didn't flinch away from it, eyes locked with his antagonist's until Duarte turned away.

Price knew that game. He could've played it all day long.

"Your friend can't wait to see the last of me," Price said.

"He's like a child sometimes," Dolores said, then realized Price had been speaking to her brother.

"Rufio means well," Cesar replied. "He's spent his whole adult life in the struggle, orphaned like Dolores and myself. He doesn't trust you, Matt. You're a stranger, which means trouble, and you're from El Norte. Washington supports the pig Diaz."

"You'll find I don't have much in common with the U.S. government," Price replied.

"For me," Cesar went on, "you proved yourself by helping me—a stranger—when you could've let me die. I know you're not a spy for Diaz or Neron, because I saw you fight their men after the *federales* killed your friend. Rufio didn't see these things. It's natural that he should worry."

"Just so you're aware," Price said. "I don't want anything to come of it before I go."

"I'll speak to him."

Price shrugged. "No need on my account. I take care of myself."

"Perhaps I'll caution Rufio for his own sake. I'd hate to lose my oldest friend."

Price knew the warning cut both ways. He nodded to Zapata as the rebel leader rose and went to meet Mateo, whoever that was. Price didn't take Zapata's comment as a threat and wouldn't let it worry him. If Duarte had his heart and mind set on a quarrel, there was nothing Price could do about it but defend himself.

Or leave, he thought. *There's always that.*

"Why must you go?" Dolores asked him when her brother was well out of earshot.

Price, bemused, asked her, "Are you a mind reader?"

"Excuse me?"

"Never mind. You understand, the business with your brother was an accident. I wasn't signing up for a crusade."

"Is it so bad here, Matthew? Is there nothing that might change your mind?"

He smiled and took another baby step in the direction of the trap, telling himself it couldn't hurt. "You never know," he said.

•   •   •

Mateo Alcazar was entering the camp on foot, leading his horse behind him, when Cesar Zapata reached the clearing's eastern limit. Duarte was already there, and began speaking to Alcazar while one of the young soldiers led his horse away.

"Starting without me, Rufio?" Zapata asked, closing the gap with measured strides.

"I wasn't sure if you were coming, Cesar."

"Did I not say that I was?"

Duarte frowned, his eyes shifting. "You seemed . . . distracted."

"And you hoped to ease my burden, eh? Thank you for your concern, old friend." Zapata turned from Duarte to the new arrival. "So, Mateo. What news from the nest of vipers?"

Alcazar chuckled at that. "Durango never changes, *Jéfé*. There are still too many *federales*. They still drink too much tequila and forget to mind their tongues."

"Does that mean you have something for us?"

Alcazar was in his early forties, with a hard-weathered face that made him look ten years older. Lean and wiry, he was almost lost inside his baggy clothes, and the serape draped across his shoulder had long since surrendered its vibrant colors to sun and wash water. A straw hat with nicks in the brim cast his long face in shadow.

"There is excitement over your escape, of course. They talk about the gringo who released you and the army that was waiting to ambush their men."

"Army?" Zapata grinned. "A one-man army, that was. Is there more?"

Alcazar's nod was like a nervous tic. "I heard one *federale* talking to his whore. I think he wanted to impress her, so she'd make believe he was a stallion, rather than a burro."

"Never mind the whore, Mateo. What's the news?"

"The pig said he'd been chosen to escort a wagon train, coming into Durango on the day after tomorrow. It will carry gold, he said. A shipment from the Sinaloa mines, bound for Mexico City. Three wagons in all."

"More loot for Diaz," said Zapata.

"Sí, Jéfé."

"Was there any mention of the route?" Duarte asked.

Another jerky nod from Alcazar. "They'll use the Presidio road."

"What else?" Zapata asked.

"That's all, Jéfé. The whore was ready then. She took the pig upstairs. I waited, listening in the cantina, but the others said nothing of gold."

"And what of us?"

Alcazar flashed a crooked smile, revealing gaps where teeth had once resided. "Federales boast that they will have you back in prison soon," he told Zapata, "and the rest of us will all be dead. They mean to hang you and the gringo, so their friends can rest in peace. But none of them seemed to be in any great hurry to lead the search."

"What of the people?" asked Duarte. "Were there only federales in Durango?"

"More than usual," said Alcazar, "but I saw others too. The common people love Cesar Zapata and support the cause. As for the merchants, all they love is money. Nothing changes."

"And your sister? What of her?"

"Juanita?" Alcazar looked somber now. "Her husband's health is failing," he replied. "The accident took something out of him. He can't work, barely walks. Their money's almost gone. I fear there'll be a funeral soon."

"They could join us, Mateo."

"Muchas gracias, Jéfé." The small man almost bowed. "I'm afraid Roberto doesn't travel well or far since he was injured, and Juanita will not leave him."

"No," Duarte said. "A wife's place is beside her husband."

"Maybe when . . . after . . ."

Zapata heard Mateo's voice break. Stepping closer, he placed one hand on the thin man's shoulder. "Anytime she's ready, go and bring her back here with the children. We'll make room."

He could've sworn that Alcazar was on the verge of weeping as the spy reached up to clutch his hand. "I will. Thank you, Segundo Cristo."

"Don't blaspheme," Zapata scolded him. "We're all *compadres* here."

"Of course."

"Go get some breakfast now, and rest after your journey."

"Sí, Jéfé."

When Alcazar had left them, Duarte stepped in closer. "More gold for Diaz," he said. "The bastard never gets enough."

"It's in his nature, Rufio. You wouldn't scold a scorpion for stinging, would you?"

"Scold him? No. I'd crush him."

"As we shall Diaz in time. I think the gold may help us."

"You would take it then?"

"Why not?" Zapata asked, smiling. "It sounds like an adventure. And I have in mind someone to help us crush the scorpion."

"You mean the gringo?" Duarte's face was grim as he

reached out and caught Zapata by the arm. He felt the bitter gall of anger rising in his throat.

Zapata glanced down at the hand clutching his arm, and Duarte drew it back as if his fingers had been scorched. "I mean Matthew," said Zapata.

"You make him sound like one of the disciples, Cesar."

"He's not a gringo in my eyes."

"Oh, no? What is he then?" Duarte challenged.

"He's the man who saved my life when no one else could do it."

"Ah." Duarte felt as if he had been slapped across the face. "That's it then, is it? You blame me because I didn't lead a raid to break you out? Have you forgotten whose order forbade it?"

"The order was mine, Rufio. And I blame you for nothing."

"Yet this Anglo stranger is now your new hero. You trust him with secrets, perhaps with the safety of everyone here."

Zapata frowned. "What danger is he to us, Rufio? What threat to *you* that you hate him so much?"

Duarte had to stop and think this time, before responding. It was never wise to say too much, particularly when the conversation turned to life-or-death concerns.

"He is no threat to me," Duarte said at last, "and I don't hate him. I distrust him, Cesar. There's a difference, and you understood that once. You haven't known this white man three full days, but still you treat him like a brother."

"I've already told you why."

"I know. Because he saved your life." Too late, Duarte recognized the mocking tone he had unconsciously adopted. Desperate to make it right, he said, "Cesar, you know that I would die for you. I've killed men without number on your order."

"For the struggle, Rufio. For freedom."

"Yes! And what does *Matthew* know of that? Where was he when the *federales* killed your parents? When they stood my brothers up against the wall? Cesar, we don't know where he was three days ago, for God's sake! You don't know this man at all."

"But *you* know *me*," Zapata answered. "Don't you, Rufio? You claim to trust my judgment when we plan a strike against Neron, and when we're picking new recruits. You've never challenged me before, when I said this or that one should or shouldn't be admitted to the struggle."

"No, you're right," Duarte granted.

"So, what's changed?"

"You have, Cesar. The other choices you describe were all made using this." Duarte tapped his forehead with a callused index finger. "Those you picked to join us were our own people. We share a common history and common goals. Amigo, you have more in common with Neron than with your precious Matthew. He knows nothing of our people or our struggle."

"Yet he risked his life for mine."

"You've already forgotten the story, Cesar," Duarte jeered. "He risked his life for a filthy Apache, not for you."

"This bigotry does you no credit," said Zapata.

"What, you love Apaches now as well as gringos? What's become of you, Cesar? Did they clip your *cojones* in that prison cell?"

Zapata's move was swift. It put him in Duarte's face before Duarte could recoil, one fist clutching the soft front of his old friend's shirt.

"You're right," he said. "I changed while I was counting down the hours to my death. When they were almost gone, I realized that we must not repeat the errors of Diaz, Neron, and others like them. Our new Mexico cannot be ruled by men obsessed with greed or hatred."

Duarte felt himself trembling. He wasn't sure if it was anger, fear, or some strange combination of both, but he hated the feeling. If he raised a hand against Zapata now, he knew they'd be locked in a fight to the death, and Duarte wasn't sure he could win it.

And there was Dolores to think of as well.

Standing with fists clenched at his sides, Cesar still clinging to his shirt, Duarte answered in a softer voice, "So, you don't hate the pigs who killed your parents now? Would you reward them for their crimes?"

"I'll kill them if I can," Zapata said, "because they have no place in the new Mexico we're building. If they can't or won't change, then they must be weeded out."

"By you and Price?"

"By whoever cares enough to lend a hand. We fight for justice, Rufio, not to become like them."

Duarte almost blurted out his fears, about the gringo and Dolores, but he knew it wouldn't help his case. Quite the reverse, in fact. It would give Cesar one more thing to use against him.

"Perhaps you're right," Duarte said, tasting the words like sour milk. "But you won't blame me if I watch the stranger just in case?"

Zapata smiled, released his shirt, and smoothed the wrinkles with his fingertips. "I would expect no less, amigo. That's your job."

Price was reloading his Winchester when Zapata found him. He had put off cleaning it the night before, but couldn't let it go a second day. As any decent carpenter maintained his tools and kept them sharp, so shooters who intended to keep breathing did the same. The Peacemakers were next, beginning with the one he'd used against the *federales,* but Price made a point to never have his guns unloaded all at once.

Zapata had Duarte with him. Studying the two of them, one smiling and the other sour-faced, Price couldn't tell if they were bringing him good news or bad. Guessing, he figured that Duarte would be smiling if they'd come to tell him that he had to leave.

As they approached, Price finished topping off the rifle's magazine. He had three loaded weapons now, if things went badly, but he wasn't worried at the moment. Cesar wasn't fool enough to try Price by himself without good reason, and Price would've noticed gunmen circling around him through the trees.

Zapata and Duarte reached the boulder where he sat. "Done with your meeting then?" asked Price.

"The first part anyway," Zapata said.

"Must keep you busy, all that planning."

"Cesar has a question for you," said Duarte.

"Oh?"

Zapata didn't look too happy as he shot his friend a chilly glance. "It's true," he said. "The man who just returned has brought us news. An opportunity presents itself. I thought perhaps you might wish to accompany us when we investigate."

Price wasn't sure where they were going with it, only that Duarte had been dragged along against his will. He guessed Zapata thought another shooter would be useful in whatever it was, and had gone against his chief lieutenant's wishes.

"Opportunity, you say. What kind?" Price asked.

"There is a gold shipment from Sinaloa, passing through Durango on its way south, to Mexico City. Neron and Diaz have enough gold, I think."

Price frowned, nodded. He hadn't been expecting highway robbery. "How much gold would it be?"

"Three full wagons," Zapata said.

"You won't get those in here," Price said, remembering his observations on the mountain trail.

"We have friends on the outside too."

"Cesar!" Duarte glared at his companion, as if willing him to silence.

"I've mentioned no one, Rufio." And then, to Price: "Matt, what do you think?"

"A holdup's not the first thing that I think of when somebody mentions revolution," Price replied.

"All armies need support, some more than others," said Zapata. "If I see a chance to help my people and to weaken enemies at the same time, I take it."

"That makes sense."

"Consider it an act of war."

"Speaking of war," Price said, "I'm guessing that they'll have a few guards on the wagon train."

"More than a few, I think." Zapata smiled.

"Does it seem strange at all to you?" asked Price.

"How strange?"

"Well, they were set to kill you yesterday, but you gave them the slip. Now, three days later, comes a gold shipment passing through territory where you're bound to sniff it out and make a move. It strikes me as an odd coincidence."

"You think it is a trap, Matt?"

Price shrugged. "I don't know who you're dealing with or how they think, how smart they are."

"That's right," Duarte said. "You don't."

"But if I had to guess, I'd say the top dog didn't get on top by being blind or stupid. Greedy's one thing, but it doesn't always mean a man's an idiot."

"I have to try it, Matt."

Price considered it. He nodded. "I see that."

"My men are fighters," said Zapata, "but they're not like you."

Price didn't take offense. He saw the truth of it and reckoned it must be some kind of blessing in disguise, that his kind was a limited edition.

"You want to make an ambush work," he said, "you need the right ground for a start."

"We'll have it," said Zapata.

"And you have to make your mind up in advance whether you're playing fair or if you want to win."

"Winning is what we need, Matt."

"Okay," he said. "I'll tag along."

6

The troop of horsemen left Durango shortly after midnight, *federales* grumbling about the lack of sleep although they'd been forewarned. Sergeant Carlos Villa spurred his horse along the line of slouching, muttering figures, hissing threats and orders as he went, reminding them that the lieutenant would be riding with them.

Watching. Listening. Remembering.

That was the part that made Villa himself most nervous. Riding after dark was no great challenge, most particularly on a fine night like this when the desert moon was nearly full. At an easy pace, they should reach their target as planned, just at dawn.

The mission didn't bother Villa either. When he joined the *federales* seven years before, he'd known there would be things about the job that would leave him feeling dirty, that would make his neighbors shy away from him as if he were diseased. He'd known it, and he'd gone ahead because the paychecks were dependable, if not spectacular, and there had been a promise of advancement over time.

Now Villa had advanced, and his first task as sergeant was leading a dawn raid against suspected traitors in the village of Sangre de Maria. He'd never seen the place before, and likely never would again after his work was done. He didn't know the people there, but being labeled a "suspected traitor" was the same as a conviction these days under the beneficent regime of President Porfirio Diaz.

And the sentence for treason was death.

Villa had barely finished silencing his troops when Lieutenant Cruz appeared, already mounted on a jet-black stallion. Cruz wore a pistol holstered on his right hip and a long sword on his left. Villa hoped the sword was merely added as a badge of rank, but it was not his place to ask.

In truth, he didn't want to know—but he would find out soon enough.

He snapped a sharp salute to Cruz. "All ready, sir!"

"Proceed."

They had a half-breed scout to lead the way, since neither Cruz nor Villa could be certain of the route. At some point they would have to leave the road, and it was easy to get lost. The half-breed was a mercenary, serving anyone who paid his going rate. Tonight, it was Lieutenant Cruz. Tomorrow—who could say?

Villa had chosen thirty men to carry out the night's grim work. Leaving Durango, they rode two abreast, with Cruz and Villa at the point, the scout well out in front of them but visible, a shadow that preceded Death and marked those whom it touched along the way.

Cruz didn't speak to Villa as they rode, which spared the sergeant from a nightmare of feigned sociability. Cruz was well known as an arrogant *chingado* who preferred his own reflection in the mirror to companionship from others. Spit-and-polish discipline was his obsession, though he hadn't bothered to inspect the troops tonight. Villa supposed he must have other pressing matters on his mind.

Like saving his career.

By now, the whole state knew that Cruz had lost Cesar Zapata. Even if he hadn't personally set the traitor free, he wore the stigma like a sign around his neck. And if he fell, Captain Ruiz might well go with him.

Would that mean further advancement for a lowly sergeant? Villa didn't think so, but it did no harm to dream.

Their route skirted the mountains, following a course that posed no challenge for the riders or their animals. They weren't in hot pursuit, and there was ample time to reach their destination by sunrise.

Sangre de Maria wasn't going anywhere.

Some of its people never would again.

Villa didn't concern himself with abstract concepts such as Justice. Pondering philosophy was a pastime for rich men, smoking fat cigars and sipping well-aged liquor in their book-lined studies. Sergeant Villa's mandate was to follow orders, and to hope that he would pass unnoticed if and when the wheels of Justice ever turned again in Mexico.

He had prepared himself for the night's work with three shots of tequila, chewing cloves to kill the odor while the liquor did its work. His Colt revolver had been oiled and freshly loaded, but he didn't have a sword. The other troops were armed with carbines that could drop a man at ranges approaching two hundred yards, but Villa didn't think there would be any long-distance shooting at Sangre de Maria.

His was a punitive mission.

And perhaps something else.

Villa was not a strategist, but he could recognize a simple game of tit-for-tat. Cesar Zapata had embarrassed Cruz and those above him. If Zapata was beyond their reach, then someone else would have to suffer in his place. Their punishment might draw him out, or simply raise the level of contempt that a majority of Mexicans felt for their government.

In either case, it wasn't Villa's problem. He was being paid to do a job, and God help any peasant traitors who opposed him.

Miguel Cadiz Hidalgo woke as old men often do, abruptly, clutching vainly at the wistful tatters of a dream. Too late. The images were lost, and in their place remained only a nagging sense of loss.

Something had pulled him from the dream—but what?

His poor eyes sought the shuttered windows and determined that the sun had yet to rise. The tiny house he occupied alone was quiet, like the village street outside. It might've been a dog or a coyote howling, but he didn't think so. Cadiz was accustomed to the normal night sounds of Sangre de Maria and the surrounding desert. At his age, they lulled him to sleep.

Something else.

Cadiz rolled out of bed, slipped his feet into sandals, and moved to the window. It was cold, but he was used to it. Lighting a fire would just distract him, and its sounds might cover whatever it was that had awakened him.

He cracked the shutters, peering through a slit that would only be visible to someone outside if they focused deliberately on his window to the exclusion of all else. Nothing moved in the street outside, as far as Cadiz could see. The shadows were familiar, lengthening as gray light came up in the east.

But there was something. . . .

Cadiz had no desire to go outside, but he could not shirk his responsibility. Sangre de Maria had no mayor, being too small and insignificant to rate a formal government of any kind, but age and reputation made Cadiz the village elder. He was called upon to mediate in minor feuds, greet dignitaries on the rare occasions when they passed through town, and examine strangers with an eye made wary by experience.

It was his job to find out what had roused him and determine if it posed a threat to others in the village. When it proved to be an old man's quirk, he would be thankful and go back to bed.

But in the meantime, Cadiz took his ancient musket from its place beside the door and checked its load. When he was satisfied that it would function to the limits of his vision and his none-too-steady hands, he slipped the crude latch on his door and stepped outside.

Around him, all was still. The other houses showed no lights, and he saw no one on the street. The village rooster wouldn't be awake for half an hour yet, if then. He clutched the musket, feeling silly as he scanned Sangre de Maria for a threat existing only in his mind.

At last, he turned his eyes to the horizon, squinting in the darkness and the distance, seeking anything that would disturb an old man's sleep. Cadiz saw nothing to the north, and only a creeping sunrise to the east. Beginning to relax, he swiveled to the south—and saw a dark blotch moving toward the village from a quarter mile away.

What is it?

Riders.

Even with his failing vision, Cadiz recognized a mounted column. Soon, if the wind shifted, he might even hear the clip-clop of the horses' hooves. He couldn't count the riders from afar, but their formation spoke of military discipline. Soldiers or *federales* then, and both were equally bad news.

Cadiz forgot about his musket, barely conscious of it as he started moving through the village, rapping urgently on doors along the way and warning those who trusted him to solve their problems. There was nothing more for him to do, until he found out what the riders wanted, what would satisfy the man in charge and send them on their way. At least his people would be on their feet, instead of being caught asleep.

Sangre de Maria wasn't large, but it took time to knock on twenty-three plain doors and whisper messages to those inside each small adobe house. By the time Cadiz returned to his own open door, the riders had halved their distance from the village. Cadiz stepped back inside, returned his musket to its place beside the door, then waited on the threshold within arm's reach of the weapon.

He was old, but he had been a fighter once. Another troubled time, another cruel regime. Cadiz remembered his adventures from those times and marveled that he'd managed to survive them. And he wondered what the odds were that he would survive today.

He heard the horses now, and in the first pale light of dawn saw how their hooves raised little puffs of dust as they approached. Cadiz rehearsed imaginary dialogue, anticipating questions, framing answers that he hoped would satisfy the visitors without provoking them.

Knowing that if he failed, there might be hell to pay.

•　•　•

The old man in the street seemed perfectly respectful, but Lieutenant Cruz was not deceived. He knew the peasant class, the way their minds worked, always hiding bitter rage from their superiors. That rage fueled revolutions. He was here to stamp it out.

And send a message in the process.

Yes indeed.

"Buenos dias, Capitán," the old man greeted him.

"Lieutenant," Cruz replied. He was convinced the old man had promoted him as a backhanded insult. "Do you speak for this . . . community?"

"I'm the eldest, *Jéfé,* but I have no title, no authority. There are no rulers here."

Another insult, Cruz was sure of it. He couldn't finally decide, though, whether it was aimed at him, the governor, or possibly El Presidente. Instead of answering, he made a little sniffing sound and let it go.

People were spilling from their hovels, some still rubbing grit from sleepy eyes. Cruz waited for them to assemble, watching carefully for weapons in their hands, then asked their aging spokesman, "Is this everyone?"

The old man turned, blinking, as if surprised to find the others ranged behind him. He went through a show of counting heads, then answered, *"Sí, Jéfé.* That's all."

"No rebel fugitives hiding inside then?"

"Rebels?" Almost wistfully, the old man shook his head. "No rebels here, Señor."

"Then you won't mind if my men search the village." Without waiting for agreement—which he didn't need in any case—Cruz turned to Villa. "Sergeant, if you please."

"Yes, sir!"

Villa barked orders at the men and those in the left file dismounted, handing their reins to the men on the right.

Those still mounted held the horses and kept their carbines ready as the men on foot spread out to search the tiny village house by house.

Where doors were left ajar, the searchers pushed inside. If doors were closed, although unlocked, the *federales* knocked them down. In each small dwelling, once they entered, the manhunters seemed to go insane. Instead of simply peering under beds and checking cupboards, they demolished everything in sight. Gun butts smashed pots and earthen jars as if they thought some Lilliputian fugitive was crouched inside. Clothing was torn from hooks and shredded, trampled underfoot. Bedding was slashed with knives. The legs were wrenched from handmade furniture and used as clubs to shatter window glass and any trinkets that were found.

Firearms of one kind or another were retrieved from thirteen of the twenty-four houses. They made a motley arsenal, strewn in the dust before Lieutenant Cruz's stallion. Nine of them were long guns, some more properly belonging in museums—muskets, shotguns, even an ancient blunderbuss. The rest were pistols, three flintlocks and one revolver dating from the years before El Norte's civil war.

"So many guns," Cruz said. It was a challenge not to laugh as he reeled off a version of the lines he had rehearsed. "You're not just simple farmers after all."

"We farm, *Jéfé*," the old man answered, "but the soil is poor. If we don't hunt for meat, we starve. Also . . ."

Cruz waited, saw the old man grimace. "Also *what*?"

"I was about to say we must defend ourselves sometimes. From bandits and the like, *Jéfé*. You understand."

"I do indeed. You're saying that the governor, His Excellency, and the *federales* can't protect the common people of Durango."

"No! No, sir. I only meant—"

"Subversive propaganda is like poison seeping through the veins of Mexico," Cruz said, interrupting him. "It starts here, in the countryside where rebels breed, then spreads to larger towns and cities like a plague, infecting everything it touches."

"Please, Lieutenant—"

"My job—*our* job—is to find the source and cauterize it, to prevent the spread of more contagion." Shifting gears, he snapped, "Who owns these weapons? Quickly! Raise your hands!"

The old man was first to step forward. "This is mine," he said, stooping as if to lift one of the muskets from the dirt. Cruz nodded, and one of his men swung a carbine's stock into the old man's face. It made a satisfying sound and dropped the peasant on his backside.

Cruz waited a moment, then asked, "Can you hear me, *viejo?*"

The old man spit blood, wiped a dusty hand across his face, and answered, "*Sí.* I hear."

"You are charged with assaulting an officer of the Federal Judicial Police. I will pass sentence after we've had time to talk. As for the rest of you, I'm waiting for a show of hands. Who owns these weapons?"

One by one, men raised their hands. As each identified himself, a pair of *federales* pulled him from the larger group and dragged him to one side. When Villa had a baker's dozen in that clutch, including the old man, Cruz told the rest, "Get back inside your homes and stay there while we question these traitors."

When they were slow to move, Cruz turned again to Villa. "Sergeant!" At a word from Villa, half the mounted *federales* stepped down from their saddles and waded into the villagers, slashing left and right with gun butts, driving them back into their ransacked houses.

When the street was clear, Cruz told Villa, "Sergeant, you may begin."

Interrogating traitors was a relatively simple process. Sergeant Villa had a basic list of questions he would pose to each suspect in turn, applying pressure until he received the answers he desired. In fact, the answers were irrelevant since judgment had been levied in advance, but he would still go through the motions as Lieutenant Cruz demanded.

When the prisoners had formed a line of sorts, Villa paced off its length, regarding each in turn with thinly veiled disdain, and stopped before the last in line. Dawn's blushing light revealed a youth of seventeen or eighteen years.

"Which gun is yours?" Villa demanded.

"It's the shotgun there, for hunting. Look for my initials on the stock."

"I'm looking for a nest of traitors," Villa answered. "Do you know Cesar Zapata?"

"I know *of* him."

"When was he last here?"

The youthful face went blank. "I've never seen him here."

"Where *have* you seen him then?"

"Nowhere! I—"

Scowling, Villa drove his knee into the liar's groin. Before the young man had a chance to fall, two *federales* rushed to club him with their carbines, battering and kicking him when he was curled up on the ground. The other suspects, facing leveled weapons, made no move to intervene.

"Enough," said Villa when he thought the point was made. He moved on to the next in line, pulling the knuckle-duster from his pocket, fingers slipping through the fat iron rings. "How often does Zapata come to visit you?" he asked.

The second man in line, a scarecrow in his forties with unruly hair and a pathetic wisp of mustache, blinked at Villa in confusion. "Visit me? He doesn't—"

Villa put his weight behind the swing, driving his iron-bound fist into the peasant's face. One of the lurking troopers caught him lurching backward, while another slashed his carbine's butt into the scarecrow's stomach. Once again, Villa stepped back and let the soldiers work a while before he called a halt to the beating.

Turning to face Lieutenant Cruz, he said, "They're liars, *Jéfé*, all of them. I think they'll tell us nothing."

"Still, we have to try. Go on, Sergeant."

The old man with the bloody nose was third in line. His level gaze shamed Villa, but the sergeant had his orders. "Make it easy on yourself!" he hissed, then raised his voice to ask, "How does Zapata signal you before he comes to visit?"

"With a choir of angels," said the old man, smiling.

Villa cursed and swung his fist into that mocking smile. He felt the brittle teeth implode. The old man fell before the other *federales* had a chance to beat him down, but they made up for it by stamping on his fingers, elbows, knees.

Sergeant Villa made his way along the line of traitors, questioning each one in turn, dispensing punishment when they defied him, lying to his face. By number six, he had to switch the knuckle-duster from his bruised and throbbing right hand to the weaker left. Four more, and both hands ached. He let the others do the beating for him then, and hoped Lieutenant Cruz would not regard his lapse as weakness.

Only the last two in line made any effort to cooperate. One was a boy of sixteen years, if that. He wept in fear and tried to placate Villa, claiming that Zapata had been in the village only three nights earlier, making inflammatory speeches. Sadly for the youth, Zapata had been locked up on the day in question, waiting to be hanged. Once more, Villa unleashed his men, and watched the sobbing youngster beaten to the ground.

One left, an older man with shifty eyes and a scar on his left cheek that ran from his earlobe to the drooping corner of his mouth. "I've seen Zapata's men," he blurted out before Villa could ask his next question. "They come here sometimes, but they don't bring Zapata."

Villa cocked an eyebrow. "Oh? When do they come?"

"Sometimes when they need food," the peasant said. "Or when they bring us something from a raid."

"Then you admit receiving stolen property?"

The peasant shrugged. "We try to stay alive from day to day."

Behind Villa, Lieutenant Cruz announced, "Today, I think you've failed the test."

Miguel Cadiz was dizzy when a neighbor, Luis Chama, helped him to his feet. His head throbbed from the beating and he wobbled on his feet, hunched over slightly to accommodate the sharp pain in his side. It felt like broken ribs, a hurt remembered from his youth.

Cadiz knew he'd be lucky if he suffered no worse injury today.

When the world stopped spinning, when his eyes came into focus, squinting in the harsh new light of sunrise, Cadiz saw that Chama was bleeding from scalp wounds. Red streamers were bright on his face. Cadiz turned with an effort and looked at the others who'd been found with guns in their homes. Except for Paco Vasquez, every man and boy present was bloodied and battered, a few of them scarcely able to stand. Vasquez, unmarked, stood slumped and staring at his feet, as if the weight of ages rested on his shoulders.

Federales moved among them, shoving, cursing, until they had formed a ragged semblance of a line. The slim lieutenant still had not dismounted from his stallion. He remained above the gritty work of torture, set apart by altitude that let him physically look down upon his victims with disdain. Cadiz imagined that it must feel something like a judge's bench, the thrill of exaltation that derives from holding power over life and death.

"You disappoint me," the lieutenant said when all of them were more or less upright and facing him. "I came in hope of finding loyal citizens, but there are only rebels here. By your own admission, you conspire with traitors like Cesar Zapata to unseat the lawful government of Mexico and plunge the nation into anarchy."

Cadiz knew why Vasquez was so despondent now. The spineless *pendejo* had cracked and betrayed them before the accusers could touch him. A hot rush of fury infused the old man, but he knew he couldn't reach Vasquez before the *federales* cut him down.

No matter.

If Vasquez survived what the lieutenant had in mind for

them, there would be others in the village waiting to repay his treachery.

"El Presidente has been merciful to traitors in the past," said the lieutenant, warming to his lies. "But there is no more room for mercy in the war we fight against this scum. From this day forward, rebels pay the only price appropriate for treason."

Cadiz didn't flinch at the pronouncement of his death sentence. He had lived long and reasonably well, had known his share of women, and regretted very little that he'd done. He felt a twinge of sorrow for the younger ones, but death was part of life, as inescapable as pain and loss.

"Since a communal guilt has been established beyond doubt," the mounted officer proclaimed, "it would be fair and just to execute swift judgment on all present in this nest of treason."

Someone wailed behind Cadiz, a woman's voice he almost recognized, from one of the adobe houses. It distracted him. He tried to pick the face and name out of thin air, but the lieutenant's voice demanded his attention.

"Even now, however," the harangue went on, "El Presidente cannot bring himself to do the things of which he stands accused by liars like Zapata. He will not harm women, even though they suckle traitors. He does not judge children, even knowing that their mothers raise them to betray him and their homeland."

Cadiz wished the windbag would make an end of it. He wondered whether he could reach his musket, aim, and fire its single shot before the *federales* riddled him.

If they were bound to kill him anyway . . .

"As for these traitors," the lieutenant bellowed, glaring at the ragged line of beaten men, "guilty of bearing arms against El Presidente by their own admission, there is no forgiveness. For betrayal of their country and its people, they must pay the price."

Cadiz stepped forward, shrugging off the hand that Luis Chama stretched out to restrain him. No one seemed to notice as he took the first few wobbling steps. There was a ringing in his ears that drowned out the lieutenant's voice. Still unopposed, he reached the line of dusty weapons, stooping to retrieve his musket.

For an instant, Cadiz thought the dizziness would overwhelm him, but he mastered it. The weapon in his hands helped balance him. It gave him strength. He was aware of distant shouting, frantic movement that meant nothing to him now. He raised the musket to his shoulder, thumbed the hammer back, and aimed it at the mounted officer's astonished face.

Miguel Cadiz Hidalgo smiled and squeezed the trigger, barely conscious of the thunder echoing around him from a cloudless sky.

Fear saved Lieutenant Cruz's life. He'd glimpsed the old man's movement from the corner of his eye and turned in that direction, not believing that a simple peasant on the brink of death would dare disrupt his speech by simply wandering away. Almost too late, he realized the old man's purpose, saw that no one else was close enough to intercept him, and Cruz did the only thing that he could think of with a musket leveled at his face.

He squealed and toppled from his horse, tumbling to earth.

He'd never know if the old man's shot would've struck him. Squirming on the ground, dirt in his eyes and on his tongue, Cruz heard reports from several weapons, firing almost simultaneously. Pain lanced through his left leg as the stallion shied and brought a hoof down on his ankle, then turned and bolted from the village.

Cruz was on his feet a moment later, spitting sand and drawing his revolver. He saw the old man's crumpled body with a haze of dust still hanging over it, where several of his men had fired after their target fell. Others were standing with their carbines aimed at the remaining dozen rebels, while a few faced toward the little houses, ready to repel a desperate charge if it should come.

Cruz tried to salvage some vestige of dignity. He found his hat, slapped it against his injured leg, then placed it squarely on his head. He hobbled to the old man's corpse and stood above it, wincing at the sharp pain in his ankle.

"See how traitors die!" he shouted to the other villagers, and bending low, squeezed off a point-blank shot into the old man's head. When he turned back to face the others, there were blood flecks on his dusty face.

"Mata los!" he ordered his troopers. "Kill them!"

Of the dozen condemned still remaining, only the one who had confessed to spare himself a beating tried to flee. He turned and bolted with a cry of panic, traveling no more than twenty feet before two *federales* shot him in the back. The impact of their bullets pitched him forward, sliding facedown in the dust.

The others stood together, several of them cursing Cruz, the rest silent as carbines swung around to cover them. The first volley of point-blank fire cut through them, dropping all but two. One of the pair still standing had a flesh wound in his side, while his companion was unscathed. Cruz aimed his pistol at the nearer target, but he jerked the shot and missed completely, saw his bullet strike a pale adobe wall behind the man he meant to kill.

Raging, Cruz thrust his pistol back into its holster, reaching for his sword. He had it half drawn from its scabbard when the carbines blazed again and dropped the last two rebels in a cloud of scarlet mist.

Cheated, Cruz moved among the bodies, limping as he searched for signs of stubborn life. One twitched at contact with his boot and Cruz struck swiftly, slashing with his blade until the polished steel ran crimson. When he lurched away at last, he found the other *federales* eyeing him uneasily.

"What are you waiting for?" he challenged them. "Destroy this nest of traitors! Burn it down!"

Cruz didn't know if it was possible to burn adobe, but he meant to try. If nothing else, he could destroy whatever pitiful possessions still remained to these ingrates and let them eke their living from the arid land.

"Villa! Where are you?"

"Here, sir."

Wobbling through a turn on his bad leg, Cruz found the sergeant standing at his elbow. How long had he been there? Did it even matter?

"Fetch my horse," he snapped. "The damned thing ran away."

"We have it, sir."

Cruz followed Villa's gaze and saw one of the mounted *federales* waiting with his stallion, reins gripped tightly in his fist.

"Well, bring it over here," Cruz said. "And help me mount. I'm wounded, Sergeant."

For an instant, Villa seemed about to question him, then turned and beckoned for the stallion. It was awkward, mounting on the right side to avoid more pressure on his injured ankle, but the sergeant and another trooper hoisted

Cruz into his saddle. He felt better on his perch, watching the *federales* routing people from their homes a second time. And when the first pale tentacle of smoke snaked through an open doorway, Cruz remembered how to smile.

7

It was a good thing, Price decided, that he had a taste for venison, since it appeared to be a staple on the menu in Zapata's camp. By suppertime on Monday, Price's second full day with the rebels, he had eaten venison five times, with two meals that were mostly beans and rice. He didn't mind so much, because Dolores had a fair imagination when it came to spice and such, but there were moments when Price wished a cow might wander into rifle range, for some variety.

Mealtimes aside, he made a point of keeping to himself as much as possible, without being offensive to his hosts. Dolores seemed to find him wherever he went, and while Price couldn't honestly deny the pleasure of her company, he noted that Zapata's second in command found some excuse to interrupt their conversation any time he found the two of them alone. From the expression on Duarte's face at such times, and the glares he shot at Price in passing, Price concluded that Duarte's interest in Dolores went beyond mere brotherly concern.

Earlier that afternoon, Price had begun to think he'd made an error, signing on to help Zapata take the wagon train, but if he changed his mind now it would mean that he was running from Duarte. Of the two alternatives, he liked the second less.

Duarte didn't frighten him, but Price reckoned he ought to watch his back this evening, on their ride to reach the ambush site, and doubly so tomorrow, if and when the action started. Anything could happen when the bullets started flying, and Price wouldn't make himself an easy mark for backshooters.

"You're very quiet," said Dolores, scooting closer to him as they sat before the fire. Her brother had gone off to see about the horses, and Duarte hadn't popped up yet to make it a threesome.

"Just thinking," Price replied.

"About tomorrow?"

"More or less."

"You shouldn't worry," said Dolores. "Cesar's very clever when it comes to outwitting the *federales*."

"Still, they caught him once."

Even her frown was pretty, Price decided. "*Sí*, but that wasn't his fault. He went to visit . . . friends, and someone told the *federales* he was coming."

"Oh? And who would that have been?"

Dolores shrugged, a nice move in the low-cut blouse she wore. "If we knew that, they would be punished. Cesar will discover them someday, and justice will be done."

"You have a lot of problems with informers then?" Price asked.

"Some of our people are not strong, Matthew. If their

lives and families are threatened, they may help the *federales* out of fear. Some others do it for rewards of gold, tequila, women. . . ."

"So, you've found spies in the camp before?"

"Just one, last spring. Juanito Vega. Rufio caught him sneaking out at night to meet the enemy."

"And he admitted spying for the *federales*?"

"No." Dolores shook her head. "He claimed to have a mistress in a nearby village. Cesar met the woman, a young widow. She denied the whole affair."

"And that was it?" Price asked.

"There was a trial, of course. Given the evidence, the jury naturally convicted him. It's war, Matthew. Cesar didn't want to kill Juanito, but he had no choice. It is the leader's duty to protect his people."

"I see that. You say Rufio's the one who caught this other fellow sneaking out?"

"Another saw him first and came to Rufio. Then Rufio set out to watch him, and was waiting when he tried to leave the camp next time."

"Who was it turned him in to Rufio?"

"I think it was Mateo Alcazar. He spies for Cesar on the *federales* sometimes, and he saw Juanito on the road one night."

Price played a hunch. "Dolores, did the information on this job we've got tomorrow come from Alcazar?"

"I think so. Yes. Is that important?"

"Likely not. I'm just getting to know the people here."

"And will you stay? I mean, after tomorrow?"

"Let's see how it goes."

Dolores bit her lip, then blurted out, "I want to show you something."

"What would that be?"

"I can't *tell* you. Come with me. It isn't far."

"Your brother will be back, and—"

"I won't keep you from your mission." She was on her feet, one hand outstretched toward Price. "We need to hurry."

Price knew there must be a hundred reasons not to follow her, but at the moment they eluded him. Rising, he half expected to find Duarte rushing up to stop him, but Cesar's lieutenant was nowhere in evidence.

Dolores took his hand and led Price from the campfire to the nearby trees. Zapata had decided they would leave tonight and ride by moonlight to the ambush point he had selected for tomorrow's work. It wasn't fully dark yet in the canyon, but the shadows were already long and cool among the trees.

Price kept an eye on landmarks as Dolores led him through the forest. He had no idea where they were going, but it didn't take a mind reader to know Duarte would be furious if he found them out here alone. Price wasn't altogether sure how Cesar would react either, but he'd had some experience with girls and their protective brothers. If Zapata turned against him, Price knew he'd be lucky if the penalty was just expulsion from the camp.

But still, he trailed Dolores through the trees, enjoying how her hand felt holding his.

Five minutes later, they were standing in a forest glade where no trees grew within a fifty-foot circle. The place was overgrown with ferns that stood waist-high to Price, and in the middle of the clearing was a solitary boulder, placed as if it might've fallen from the sky.

"This is my secret place," Dolores said, turning to face him, still holding his hand. "I come here when I want to be alone."

"Okay, I'll leave you to it then."

"No, wait!" Her fingers tightened on his hand, refusing to let go. "I don't mean that."

"What do you mean?" Price asked.

"I want to be alone with you."

"Dolores—"

"Don't answer now," she said, blushing. "I know we don't have time tonight, before you go."

"I reckon not."

"But later . . . when you're back to stay. . . ."

"I don't know—"

She surprised him, rising on tiptoe to silence Price with a kiss. He responded without trying, without thinking through it, and an endless moment passed before she stepped away.

"You go back first," Dolores said. "It's better that no one sees us together, yes? If you can find the way."

"I might just manage."

"And you won't forget my secret place?"

"There's not much chance of that," Price said.

Twelve riders waited in the moonlight for Zapata's signal. With himself, it made thirteen, but he had never fallen prey to superstition. There were no unlucky numbers in Zapata's world, and black cats held no mystery. The only evil power scheming to destroy him was based in Durango and Mexico City, where Governor Neron and President Diaz worked night and day to crush the people's revolution.

But Zapata had a rude surprise in store for them.

He was about to pick their pockets, and if Matt Price was correct about the shipment being staged to trap him, then Zapata would surprise them twice. He'd beat the trap *and*

take their gold. A double victory that would repay his enemies for nearly killing him.

Except for Price, the riders all had friends and family to
see them off and wish them well. Dolores had already
kissed Zapata's cheek and warned him to be careful, take
no foolish chances. Now he saw her standing off to one
side, by herself, watching the horsemen. Was it his imagination, or did she have eyes for Price?

Zapata frowned at the idea. She could do worse, he realized, in terms of strength and courage. Still, Price was an
Anglo of uncertain background, with a demonstrated pen-
chant for attracting trouble. They had not discussed why
Price was traveling alone in Mexico, breaking Apaches and
their cellmates out of prison, but he guessed that they
would have to talk about it soon.

If Price decided to remain and join the struggle.

If Zapata wasn't just imagining the way his sister
watched the Anglo's every move.

But that could wait. Tonight, a journey fraught with danger lay before them, and a battle waited at the journey's
end. Some of the riders ranged before Zapata might not see
another moonrise. When the final toll was counted, even he
might be among the fallen.

But Zapata didn't think so. Even shunning superstition
as he did, the rebel leader had begun to think his life was
charmed. It seemed that Fate had chosen him to play a role
in history, and only when he'd run the course ordained for
him would Death be granted leave to pluck him from the
fold. It might be no more than a childish fantasy, but in Zapata's mind, if faith meant anything at all, it had to start
with those who took unpleasant duties on themselves and
sacrificed their futures for a sacred cause.

He moved along the line, his bay mare stepping proudly

as Zapata passed from one man to another, making sure that all were ready for what lay ahead. Duarte flashed a smile and turned as if to share it with Dolores, but Zapata saw that she had slipped away into the night. Matt Price, in turn, nodded without comment. The others, mostly young but all well-blooded, were prepared to ride.

Zapata led the way into the narrow canyon, trusting moonlight and the mare to keep him from the stony walls pressing so close on either side. When they were through and on the open desert, he would send a scout ahead of the main party, but he thought it was important that he lead the party out of camp.

Zapata hoped he wasn't leading any of them to an early grave.

Four hours out, they stopped to rest the horses for a bit, some of the riders smoking behind cupped hands. Price took the opportunity to stretch his legs after the first break of their long, silent ride. The moon, one night past full, made the desert an alien landscape, leeching from the arid land and thorny plants whatever color they possessed. The landscape had a graveyard look about it, lacking only tombstones to complete the picture.

Time enough for those tomorrow, Price thought, and wondered whether one of them would bear his name.

It was a gamble, riding with Zapata and the others on a mission that meant nothing to him. Price had questioned his decision to participate, recalling the experience he'd suffered at the hands of *federales* several weeks before he ever heard Zapata's name. That time, they'd nearly hanged him for a crime committed by the killers he was stalking, and only Gray Wolf's last-minute intervention had saved Price from being the guest of honor at his own necktie party.

But that debt was paid, and Gray Wolf was dead. Why was he riding with Zapata and the others now, against another group of *federales* whom he'd never met, and who'd done nothing in the world to inconvenience him?

The answer Price kept coming back to was the same.

Why not?

His life in Mexico, since Price had finished with the bloody job that brought him there, came down to drifting aimlessly and waiting for the next event to overtake him. He was going nowhere, and he had the rest of his life to get there. However long that might be.

Zapata had invited Price to his mountain stronghold, and Price had accepted because he had nowhere better to go. Likewise, he'd agreed to join the ambush party because it was something to do.

But was that all of it?

He walked his roan a little distance from the others, watching out for sidewinders, and scanned the eerie black-and-white horizon as if seeking answers there. Whatever Price had hoped to find, night's shadows had concealed it well.

All right. He hadn't *only* joined the raiding party out of boredom. There was something in the way Zapata talked about his people and their struggle that attracted Price and made him think that helping them wasn't the worst thing he had ever done.

Not even close.

And then there was Dolores.

Price knew better than to fall for her. It would be worse than foolish, and . . .

Racing hoofbeats announced Zapata's scout returning at

a gallop. That could only mean bad news, and Price was back with his companions by the time the horseman reached them. Rapid, muted Spanish passed between Zapata and the scout. Price couldn't catch it all, but he picked out a few stray words—village, Maria, *muerto*.

Death.

When he was finished with the scout, Zapata moved among them, speaking urgently. "The *federales* have attacked Sangre de Maria," he announced. "They torched the houses. There were executions. We will stop there first, and see what may be done."

Price didn't know Sangre de Maria from any of a thousand other villages in Mexico, but it clearly mattered to Zapata and he was along for the ride. They mounted and Zapata led them on a new course, veering off their former route of travel ten or twelve degrees to the northwest. Riding several yards behind Zapata and Duarte, Price made no attempt to overtake them or inquire about the change of plans.

As far as Price could see, they had simply postponed one appointment with Death to keep another. It was all the same to him.

They pushed the animals a little faster now, but there was no safe galloping across the desert moonscape. The scout had pushed his luck and then some, bringing back bad news, but thirteen of them racing through the night was bound to mean lame animals and riders thrown. Better to take their time and get it right, knowing the damage was already done.

Price smelled Sangre de Maria half an hour later. Or rather, he smelled what was left. Wood smoke was wafted to them on the night wind, but there wasn't very much of it.

From that alone, Price guessed that they were too late to make any difference.

And he was right.

A guard of sorts was posted on the southern approach to Sangre de Maria. Price pegged his age around eleven years and noted that his only weapon was a hoe. The little sentry challenged them, then waved them on after Zapata had identified himself. Passing the boy in moonlight, Price couldn't decide if he was frightened, furious, or simply numb.

The smell of smoke was stronger as they neared Sangre de Maria. Strictly speaking, Price could tell the *federales* hadn't burned the village down, but they had done the next best thing. Each of the small adobe homes bore soot and scorch marks at the edges of their vacant doors and windows. People huddled over small fires, next to humble buildings they'd once occupied, as if the stench of roasted memories prevented them from going back inside.

A few of them, women and old folks for the most part, rose and came to meet Zapata when they recognized him. In their hands, Price saw, they carried any kind of makeshift weapon they could salvage from the ruin of their simple lives.

Duarte waited for Zapata to speak first. It was the leader's right, and besides, all the words he could think of to utter were curses. Trembling with rage, Duarte reined his gelding through a tight half circle, scanning the shadows as if they might offer a target.

Nothing.

Duarte turned back and forced himself to listen as an old man with a rusty hatchet in his fist related to Zapata what had happened. *Federales*. Accusations. Beatings. A confession. Executions. Fire, to purge Sangre de Maria of its treason to El Presidente.

"Who was the informer?" asked Zapata.

"Paco Vasquez." As the old man spoke the name, he spit into the dust.

"Where is he? Did the *federales* take him with them?"

"No. They shot him with the rest."

The old man nodded toward a long, low mound of earth that marked a common grave. Duarte pictured the survivors digging with the same tools used to till the soil and raise crops that were barely adequate to feed themselves. The same tools that they brandished now, too late, as paltry weapons.

"Who were they looking for?" Zapata asked. Duarte guessed the answer in advance, but still he waited, listened.

"Any friends of yours," the old man answered. "This is all for you."

Duarte found his pistol, let his hand rest lightly on its butt. This was the moment that could transform silent mourners into howling members of a lynch mob. One wrong word could tip the balance, and the riders would be forced to finish what the *federales* had begun.

Zapata swung down from his saddle to face the old man. They were three feet apart when he said, "Will it help you to kill me? Then do it. Whoever can bring back their loved ones by spilling my blood, here I am! Strike the blow! There will be no reprisal. I offer my life for the pain you have suffered, and promise revenge on the cowards who murdered our people because they're afraid to face me."

No one moved for a moment, and then the old man dropped his hatchet, extending his hand to Zapata. As Zapata clasped that bony hand in both of his, the old man answered, "Avenge them, my son. Make them suffer as we have, a hundred times over."

"I promise you that," said Zapata. "We ride even now to a battle. By midday tomorrow you'll have blood for blood. Who can name the commander in charge of the party who did this?"

"A bastard lieutenant named Cruz," said the old man. "I've seen him before, in Durango."

Duarte caught Zapata's sidelong glance and read his old friend's mood. "I know him," Cesar told the villagers. "Three days ago, he had me caged in San Filipe, but he didn't hang me fast enough. I tell you plainly that he did this thing because I shamed him. Is there no one who will strike me down for causing you such pain?"

"None here," the old man answered for his people. "*You* strike him for us."

"You have my word. If Cruz still lives when next the moon is full, my life is yours in payment of this debt."

"You will not find us here," the village spokesman told Zapata. "We are leaving at first light."

"Where will you go?" Zapata asked.

The old man shrugged. "Away. This ground is poisoned for us now."

"Then let me shelter you," Zapata said. "It is the very least I owe you for your loyalty."

"What shelter do you have?"

Zapata called out to his men. "I need a volunteer to take these people back to camp." Mateo Alcazar was first to raise his hand. "Wait here for dawn," Zapata ordered, "then lead them back to the canyon. Their lives are my responsibility—and yours."

"*Sí, Jéfé,*" Alcazar responded. "But the mission—"

"You have more important work to do. Don't fail me."

"No, Jéfé."

Zapata next ordered the riders to surrender half the rations they had packed to eat while traveling and waiting for the wagon train. None grumbled at the order, and Duarte noted that Matt Price was one of those who moved the fastest to divest himself of food. For some reason he couldn't name, the simple act of charity increased Duarte's dislike of Price.

They spent the best part of a gloomy hour in Sangre de Maria before riding on. Duarte didn't glance back at the village as he left. The dead were buried, and they would be mourned. His task was vengeance, and he craved the chance to settle scores against his enemies.

Both old and new.

Price saw a kind of resolution in his fellow riders as they left Sangre de Maria that he hadn't seen before. When they were chosen by Zapata for the raiding party, his companions had been laughing, slapping hands, and making macho noises for their audience in camp. Once they were on the trail, compelled to silence by Zapata's order, Price had thought that some of them seemed ill at ease. Whatever might've bothered them before, though, had been wiped out by their meeting with the homeless villagers.

Price guessed that any hope of mercy for the *federales* riding with the shipment they were set to intercept had been discarded now.

So be it.

Price knew—and Zapata must've known—that there was barely one chance in a million they would find the village raiders riding shotgun on the gold wagons tomorrow. Something else he knew was that it didn't matter, one way or the other. Symbols counted heavily in wartime, and the *federales* they waylaid tomorrow would be picking up the tab for something done by others, for a common cause.

Price was concerned about the timing of the village raid, more so because its leader was the same lieutenant who had tried to hang Zapata three days earlier. That wouldn't be co-incidence, and it encouraged speculation that the gold shipment might be a trap. At this point, though, he realized Zapata didn't care. The rebel leader wanted blood.

And that could make him dangerous to friends, as well as enemies.

There was still time to split from the pack and ride off his own way, skip the show altogether, but Price wasn't in a running mood. Granted, the villagers in Sangre de Maria were strangers to Price, and he couldn't really claim to feel their loss. On top of that, he'd seen so much death since he entered Mexico a few weeks earlier that it had lost some of its impact.

Still, there was something that kept him in line, north-ward bound. Price couldn't put his finger on it, but he guessed that it was equal parts of stubbornness and curios-ity. He'd never been a quitter, never run from a fight even when it seemed he might lose.

And then, there was Dolores.

Careful, the inner voice warned him.

Price didn't need a DANGER sign to know he was walk-ing on treacherous ground. Cesar Zapata's feelings and Duarte's opposition were the least of it in his mind. Price had cherished two relationships with women in his life, and both of them had suffered for it. One was dead, the other married to a man who'd never walk again unless the Lord decided it was time to work a miracle.

It didn't help that neither circumstance was truly Price's

fault. His first love had abandoned him because she couldn't stand the violence in his world, and Price had played only a small part in the course her life had followed after that. His second had been murdered when Price wasn't there to help her, and the sweet taste of revenge had long since soured on his tongue.

Cesar Zapata's war contained an element of vengeance too, but Price knew there was also more at stake than simple vengeance. In his mind and heart, Zapata fought for something larger than himself, and if he was deluded in believing he could win, that only made the struggle more heroic.

Or more foolish.

Price tried to see it from the bright side, picturing the rebel force victorious, but he still didn't know what that would mean to him. He shared no common history or culture with Zapata's people. When the smoke cleared, win or lose, he'd still be just another gringo killing time south of the border, thinking up excuses not to cross the Rio Grande.

You're headed north right now, the inner voice reminded him. *Why not keep going?*

Not so fast.

He'd volunteered to help Zapata do a job, and he would see it through. Tomorrow, after it was done, he could decide which way to point his roan.

If he was still alive.

The moon had set behind them, and the eastern skyline had begun to show a hint of dull light when Zapata raised a hand and brought the column to a halt. A quarter mile ahead, Price saw the jut and thrust of rock formations that reminded him of a fortress gone to ruin, falling in upon itself. Some force beyond human imagining had marked this land, leaving his race to pick and scratch about the surface like a swarm of ants.

"The road lies there," Zapata told him, pointing into darkness. "Just beyond the rocks and down the slope."

"High ground and cover," Price replied. "You can't beat that, unless your targets have it figured in advance."

"You still think it's a trap?"

"It's got a funny smell about it."

"Maybe that's your fear," Duarte said.

"You know the *federales* best," Price answered. "Maybe they're too dumb to bait a trap and make you reckless going into it, by killing folks you care about. Maybe they won't stake out the best place on the road to jump the shipment. What do I know? It's a wonder that you haven't beaten them by now, as stupid as they are."

"Listen, *gringo*—"

"He's right," Zapata said. "We need to scout this place while we have time."

"That's all I'm saying," Price replied.

"Will you come with me, Matt?"

"Cesar, let someone else—"

"No, Rufio. I don't ask anyone to do what I won't do myself."

"Then let *me* come with you."

"I need you here, in case Matt's right and we do not come back. In that case, take the others home. Forget about the gold. You understand?"

"Of course," Duarte answered stiffly. "It shall be as you command."

Zapata dismounted and handed his reins to Duarte. Price followed his example, but chose another hand to watch his roan. He drew the Winchester, knowing it had a live round in the chamber, and set off across the desert at Zapata's side.

Ten cautious minutes later, standing in the shadow of that tumbledown fortress, Price wondered if his caution might've been excessive. Maybe he'd given the *federales* too much credit. Maybe—

Scraping sounds and muffled voices put him back on full alert. Someone was definitely on the rocky point above them, and if they were talking, Price assumed there must be more than one. How many guns would *he* have sent to meet an ambush party in the middle of the night?

Enough to do the job.

Zapata flashed a smile at Price and squeezed his shoulder, then pointed to the left and led the way around the rock formation, taking care to make no noise along the way. Price literally followed in his footsteps, conscious of the danger that the slightest sound would pose for them right now.

Zapata seemed to know the rock pile's layout. In another moment, they were climbing slowly, inch by quaking inch, between two slabs of granite that resembled giant dominoes. The voices, still above them, were a little clearer now. Price thought there must be three or four, but didn't want to bet his life on it.

Too late, he thought. *The bet's already laid.*

Another moment, and they reached a lip of rock that overlooked a pit of sorts, the courtyard of Price's fantasy fortress. Zapata pushed his hat off, let it dangle by a cord against his back as he wormed forward, peering down into the drop. This close, Price could make out some of the dialogue: an argument about whose turn it was to play lookout.

Zapata wriggled back to join him, leaned in kissing-close, and whispered, "*Federales*. Five of them, but none on watch. Maybe they are a little stupid, eh?"

Price shrugged in answer, getting ready for the part he knew was coming. There would be no turning back, and they couldn't afford to let their enemies finish the squabble. It was time to strike, before another sentry took his post and found them lurking in the dark.

Zapata tapped his own chest, pointed to the right, and raised a finger. Price supposed it meant one minute, and he nodded. As Zapata crept away, Price edged up to the rocky lip and took his first look at the men he'd come to kill.

The pit was larger than he'd thought, almost a giant bowl. They'd built a small fire at the bottom, knowing it would be concealed from any riders on the flats. Price saw no horses and supposed these five had been dropped off by others, waiting to be picked up when their work was done.

Bad luck, he thought, and cocked the Winchester.

It was too dark to read his pocket watch, but Price was counting seconds from the time Zapata crawled away. At fifty-five, he'd picked a target. He framed the dusty tunic in his sights by firelight, with his index finger taking up the trigger slack.

Waiting.

Price fired on sixty, and another gunshot sounded from the rocks beyond him, like an echo of his own. Below, two *federales* crumpled to the stony ground. The three remaining scrambled for their carbines, one running straight through the fire in his haste, trailing sparks from his heels.

Price caught the runner turning, weapon in his hands, and shot him in the chest. Pumping the rifle's lever, swiveling about, he found another mark just as Zapata's third shot brought the *federale* down and finished it. Below him, blood pooled on the firelit stone and Price saw only death.

Zapata waited for the echoes of their gunfire to subside, then whistled shrilly in the night. It must've been a signal that Duarte recognized, because a moment later there were horsemen circling around the rock pile, brandishing their rifles in salute.

Price waited for Zapata where he was. The granite underneath him was no colder than his heart.

"So you were right," Zapata told him, grinning. "And we start off with a victory, before we even see the gold."

"So far, so good," Price said. "Let's see what happens when the sun comes up."

8

Sunrise enhanced Price's first estimation of the desert rock pile as a natural fortress. Four narrow passages extended from the central slaughter pit at odd angles, like spokes on a badly bent wheel. A man could squeeze through any one of them if he turned sideways and was careful not to breathe too deeply, and three of the four rose to natural parapets, fifteen to twenty feet tall. On top, the stone was relatively flat and smooth, weathered for centuries, and shaded through the morning hours by jagged rocky walls.

The fourth passage led downward to a smaller pit where sunshine rarely kissed the stone. Zapata had his riders dump the *federales* there, after they stripped two of the cleanest uniforms. He asked for volunteers to wear the perforated clothes, explaining how he hoped to lull the gold train's escort and increase their margin of surprise. Ten hands went up in answer to his call, leaving Zapata to select two men who'd fit the tunics well enough to pass.

When that was done, Zapata chose the youngest of the rebels present for a job nobody wanted. Since they couldn't hide twelve horses where they were, the chosen one would take the animals a mile back from the road and guard them in a stand of old mesquite they'd passed the night before, on their approach. The small oasis had a stream, and there was probably enough dry grass to keep the horses happy through midday. Price kept his saddlebags and watched them go, led by a youth who looked as if he'd been excluded from a Christmas feast.

That left eleven shooters armed with rifles on the rock pile, most of them with handguns on the side. Price didn't know how many *federales* would be riding with the wagon train, but since they'd left five at the route's most likely ambush point, he guessed headquarters was pulling out all stops. He wouldn't be surprised to see five guards per wagon, and it could go to twice that many.

Maybe more.

Their two advantages were cover and surprise. The enemy had tried to shut them out, barring Zapata's rebels from the granite sniper's nest and maybe picking off a few while they were at it. Price gave his opponents credit for the plan, but they'd used soldiers who were short on discipline and none too bright to start with. If the *federales* in the pit had left a sentry posted overhead last night, there was a good chance they'd still be alive.

That was the problem when the stakes were life or death. Most players didn't get a second chance.

Price wondered how long they would have to wait before the next phase of the killing started. All they'd gathered from Zapata's eavesdropper in town had been the shipment's date and chosen route. Price still suspected treachery—it would've been bizarre, in his view, if the shipment *hadn't* been a trap—and he didn't believe the five men killed last night were all of it.

Zapata's adversaries wouldn't want to miss a second time. They wouldn't stake their hopes on five unmounted *federales,* sitting in a rock pit halfway between Sinaloa and Durango. Price imagined they would stake out other points along the route of travel, guard the shipment well, and maybe hold a little something extra in reserve.

The more he thought about it, with the desert sun steadily climbing, the more Price wished that he was somewhere else.

Back in the mountains with Dolores, for example.

At her secret place.

At half past ten o'clock, by Price's pocket watch, one of Zapata's sharp-eyed lookouts sounded the alarm. Squinting away to westward, Price picked out a tiny smudge on the horizon that could be a desert whirlwind or a troop of riders traveling his way. Unless they pushed their animals at killing speed, Price guessed he had an hour left, maybe a little more, before the new arrivals were within range of his Winchester.

Price was examining potential moves and calculating angles when Zapata joined him on his perch, making the rounds and checking on his men. "You see them, yes?" he asked.

"I see something."

"It is the gold. I feel it."

"This could still go sour," Price reminded him.

Zapata flashed a smile. "You always see the worst, eh?"

"It cuts down on rude surprises."

"Something troubles you," Zapata said.

"You mean besides the fact that we're on foot and we don't know how many guns we're facing?" Price wanted to raise the subject of Mateo Alcazar, Zapata's spy in *federale* land who'd volunteered to leave the raiding party at Sangre de Maria, but he wasn't sure how to broach the topic without implicating Dolores. And what would it achieve in any case? He had a vague suspicion, stacked against Zapata's knowledge of his men that came from months or years of interaction under pressure.

"Something else, I think," Zapata prodded him.

Price frowned and shook his head. "I need to think about it for a while. I'll let you know."

"As you prefer," Zapata said. "Until then, good hunting!"

Price watched him go, then turned his eyes back to the road.

Waiting.

Sergeant Hernando Obregon Martinez knew he should be honored that he'd been selected for the plum assignment of his thirteen-year career, but he was suffering from an acute state of anxiety. It wasn't every day that his superiors entrusted him with such a monumental task, and Obregon couldn't help wondering if they had planned for him to fail.

Of course, he knew they didn't want the *plan* to fail, but Obregon was only part of it, a cog in the machine. He recognized that fact of life and took it in his stride from day to day, but this assignment was so critical—so unexpected— that he was oppressed by nagging doubts.

He knew this much: Cesar Zapata had been captured and condemned, then he'd escaped from custody and murdered several *federales* in the process. Theoretically, that should've outraged Obregon, but all those years in uniform had taught him to think first about himself. A plan had been devised to remedy the problem and destroy some of Zapata's rebels in the process, whereupon the brass had chosen Obregon and dropped him in the midst of it all.

And the question that nagged him was—why?

He was a veteran, of course, who'd hunted bandits, rebels, and Apaches in his day. Headquarters knew that Obregon would follow orders without asking questions, and would keep his mouth shut afterward. Perhaps they simply trusted him to see the job well done.

But why then did he feel like bait?

Of course, he *was*. That much had been explained to him last night. He was to lead a team of twenty men, escorting three wagons from Sinaloa to Durango along the Presidio road. Each wagon bore a heavy wooden crate, whose contents were unknown to Obregon. The wagons also held surprises for the rebels who, he was assured, were waiting to relieve them of their crated burden. If the escort and surprises weren't enough to cancel any threat, Captain Montoya had told Obregon that reinforcements would be waiting at key points along his line of march, positioned to deny the enemy any substantial hiding place.

It sounded fine, until his little wagon train was in the middle of the wasteland, easily a half day's ride from any settlement he knew of, with no help in sight. To make it even worse, a solitary vulture had been following his party for the last five miles, circling a hundred feet above them as if it expected Death to overtake them on the highway.

Obregon's tired eyes picked out the landmark he'd been watching for, less than a half mile farther east. He recognized the rock pile from his other trips along this road, though distance now reduced it to the size of a man's fist. He should find *federales* there, guarding the highway and ensuring that Zapata's raiders didn't spring upon him from concealment.

For the time being at least, Obregon reckoned he was safe.

Impulsively, he craned his neck and glanced skyward, seeking the vulture. For a moment, Obregon thought he was seeing double, then he realized that there were two birds circling above his party now. The scavengers wheeled effortlessly overhead, keeping their distance from each other, both watching the progress of potential meals below.

Mouthing a silent curse, the sergeant focused on his short-term goal. Five hundred yards to reach the rock pile, and he might stop there to have a word with the sentries, find out if they'd seen any trace of Zapata's raiders. Maybe the damned rebels would be smart enough to recognize a trap and save themselves this time.

It meant that Obregon would have no part in bringing back Zapata's head, but there was something to be said for peace and quiet too.

He glanced back at the covered wagons, saw his riders slumping in the heat, and snapped at them, "Look sharp there! We've got company ahead, maybe an officer."

He doubted that was true, but the suggestion got results. His troops stiffened, finding the ramrod in their spines, recapturing the best part of their military bearing. Granted, they still had a dusty, wilted look about them, but that was inescapable on long rides through the desert.

At a hundred yards, he saw a lookout standing on the rock pile, watching their approach. The vision of a friendly uniform encouraged Obregon to risk another glance into the cloudless sky.

Three vultures now.

Obregon tried to spit, a gesture of contempt for evil omens, but his mouth was dry.

Damned birds. To hell with them.

At thirty yards, he raised a hand in greeting to the sentry, and the gesture was returned. A second man in uniform appeared beside the first, and Obregon lifted his hand again. A simple courtesy.

With no response.

No, that was wrong. The lookouts had their rifles shouldered, as if ready to fire a salute.

But why, the sergeant wondered, were both weapons pointed at his face?

Cesar Zapata saw the leading rider blasted from his saddle and cursed his impetuous soldiers. The first shot was meant to be his, not from any sense of honor or entitlement, but rather because Zapata had feared this—a premature start to the fighting before the wagons and their escorts were properly positioned.

The men he'd placed in uniform had disobeyed his order and they'd suffer for it when the work at hand was finished.

First things first, he thought, and sighted on the driver of the leading wagon. He could stop that one at least, before the others turned and bolted out of range.

Before Zapata had a chance to fire, the driver lashed his team forward, bringing his wagon closer to the rocks. Zapata didn't know if it was courage or stupidity, but either way it worked to his advantage. He had the *federale*'s sweaty face framed in his rifle sights when the stranger surprised him again, turning to grab a dangling rope or cable on his left and pull on it with all his strength.

Almost too late, Zapata realized his target was about to

leave the driver's seat, leaping for cover behind the wagon. Zapata tagged him with a hasty shot, well left of center, but the power of his .44-40 slug was still sufficient to take his man out of the fight. As the *federale* toppled over, he clung to the rope in his left hand, dragging it with him—and as he fell, the whole right side of the covered wagon's canvas top flew upward like a curtain.

Zapata had only an instant to focus on what had been hidden inside—before the shiny Gatling gun exploded with staccato thunder, strafing right-to-left across the rock face with a spray of bullets. One man stood behind the gun, cranking its handle, while another crouched beside him, ready to reload the piece at need.

Zapata ducked behind a granite outcropping as bullets spanged and ricocheted around him. When he dared look out again, he saw that the flaps on the other two wagons were drawn back as well. The third wagon in line carried another Gatling gun, already firing at his men among the rocks. The middle wagon held three *federales* armed with pump-action repeating shotguns, who were also firing rapidly into the crags.

Above and to his left, Zapata heard a cry of mortal pain. He turned as far as possible in that direction, without revealing himself to the shooters below, and saw one of his uniformed sentries rebound from the slab as he fell, ragdoll limp, to the dry earth below.

That meant one less to scold for insubordination, and it wouldn't matter in the slightest if the *federales* killed them all.

Zapata cursed himself for letting his enemies draw him into an obvious trap. Price had warned him, and while Zapata recognized the wisdom of the Anglo's words, he'd still been convinced that no task was beyond him. He could defeat any force thrown against him and still take the gold for his people.

What gold?

Inside the first wagon, Zapata saw a bulky wooden crate. The Gatling gunner's comrade crouched behind it, passing up fresh magazines when one was spent and had to be replaced. The crate bore no markings, as far as Zapata could tell, but if it *was* filled with gold—

A bullet cracked the granite near Zapata's face and stung his cheek with jagged shards. He felt blood flowing from the cuts and knew that he must focus on the moment if he wanted to survive.

The two surviving wagon drivers had retrieved pump shotguns from beneath their seats and joined the battle, firing with the rest into the crannies where Zapata's men were huddled. Sighting on the closer of the two, Zapata drilled him with a bullet through the chest that spun him from a crouch and dropped him sprawling in the dust beside the wagon.

He pumped the lever action on his rifle, sought another target, and began to pray that this would not be his last day on Earth.

Price didn't fear the Gatling guns as some might, but he'd seen them work before and knew what they could do. One of Zapata's men had toppled from the heights already, crumpled on the stony ground below, and more would die unless they took decisive action now, before a troop of *federale* reinforcements galloped in and made the odds worse yet.

He caught one of the shotgunners reloading, hunkered down so that only a portion of his head was visible above the wagon slats. It was enough. The slug that killed him sprayed the next shooter in line with blood, and as that *federale* recoiled, dabbing at his eyes, Price made it two for two.

He had to duck back under cover then as several weapons sprayed the rocks around his nest. A couple of the shots were close, but neither one drew blood. Price figured it could only help to draw fire from Zapata's men, and the increase in rifle fire responding to the *federales* told him some were taking good advantage of the moment.

But he wasn't sure that it would be enough.

They still had cover and a fair supply of ammunition, but the *federales* had them both outnumbered and outgunned. Ten of the enemy were mounted, free to ride at will around the rock pile and seek ways of creeping up behind them, while Zapata's raiders were pinned down, enjoying only limited mobility within the confines of their granite bastion.

At the moment, though, it felt less like a fortress than a cage.

One of the mounted *federales* rode in close to fire his carbine at the rocks, then wheeled away. Price fired in haste and almost missed him, but his bullet struck the rider's hip and knocked him from his saddle. Not a killing shot, by any means, and by the time Price finished ducking more incoming rounds, his wounded mark had wriggled underneath the nearest wagon, out of sight.

Damn it!

The wagons were all taking hits, and a couple of horses were down in their traces, but the *federales* were hanging in there, fighting back with grim determination. There would be no quarter asked or offered, after what Zapata's men had seen the night before, at Sangre de Maria, but Price still

worried that they were being held in place while some
larger force swept down upon them from the desert.

If that happened, they were dead.

But if his hunch was wrong, they had a chance.

The Gatlings had to go, first thing. Price lined up on the
closer of the wagons, but he couldn't get a clear shot at the
federale on the big gun's crank. Instead, he hit the loader
with a slug that hit below one upraised arm and came out
on the other side, mangling both lungs as it went through.

That *was* a killing shot, and as the Gatling gunner saw
his comrade fall, half-turning to discover what had happened, Price levered another round into his rifle's chamber.
Squeezing off before he had a decent chance to aim, firing
on instinct more than anything, he saw his target stagger
backward from the tripod-mounted gun, raising one hand to
clutch his throat.

What there was left of it.

Life doesn't tarry long when oxygen is cut off from the
brain and blood is spouting from an inch-wide exit wound
that's clipped a major artery. Price didn't have the medical
credentials to pronounce an instant death, but it was close
enough. The *federale*'s eyes were blank and glassy as he
tumbled backward from the wagon, out of sight.

The other Gatling gun swung back toward Price, its six
barrels spinning and blazing, while the other *federales* laid
down covering fire. Price squirmed backward, against the
granite slab that still might prove more dangerous than
helpful, if he caught a bad-luck ricochet. Around him, rifle
fire still echoed from the rocks, and while he had no way of
accurately counting shots, it seemed to Price that there were
fewer friendly weapons firing than there had been moments
earlier.

Pinned down, and whittled down, their chances for sur-

vival—much less anything resembling triumph—seemed
to dwindle by the moment. They needed to seize the initiative, carry the fight to their enemies—and that meant going
down among them on the flats.

Price reached into his saddlebag and spent a moment
topping off the rifle's magazine. He also took the backup
Colt and wedged it down underneath his belt, in back.

He was as ready as he'd ever be.

Cursing the certainty that there could be no other course
of action, Price began to scramble down the rock pile, toward ground level.

Rufio Duarte rapid-fired his lever-action rifle at the *federales* ranged below him, fear and fury mingling to subvert
his aim and send most of his bullets flying wide of their
mark. So far he'd dropped one rider, wounded another's
horse, and peppered two of the wagons without doing any
significant damage. He was embarrassed and frustrated, not
to mention worried that the ambush might become his own
death trap.

The crisp *snap* of his rifle's hammer on an empty chamber surprised Duarte. On top of everything else, he'd forgotten to count shots as they were fired, and now he
recoiled as a spray of bullets from the second Gatling gun
found his crevice, chipping pieces from the rock.

"Jesus Cristo!" he muttered, fumbling in a leather pouch
for cartridges while ricochets whined overhead. His rifle
held eleven rounds, but Duarte's hands were trembling and
he twice dropped cartridges, scrambling to pick them up
before they rolled away and out of reach.

The battle showed no signs of letting up, as far as he
could tell. Why would it? Both sides were committed—

federales to the goal of wiping out their enemies, and rebels to survival, now that they were stranded on the rocks without their horses.

How long would it be before another troop of riders came to seal the trap and make it permanent? Duarte hated to admit it, but the gringo had been right this time. Perversely, that fact made him hate Price all the more, as if the gringo was somehow responsible for Cesar's poor judgment.

It would be Price's fault somehow if they were killed on this adventure. If Duarte never again saw Dolores in this life, he knew that he'd go to his grave blaming Price. It was irrational, he realized, but such is life.

Crawling back toward the aperture he'd chosen as a sniper's nest, Duarte wished he could have one clear shot at Price before he died. He reckoned it would be the next best thing to having a free shot at Governor Neron or El Presidente himself.

It wouldn't be that easy, though. The enemies that he could see were down below him, and they seemed to have no shortage of fresh ammunition as they fired into the rock pile. From above, Duarte heard another gargling cry before a body hurtled past his niche. Another of his comrades gone, but he had no idea which one.

Rage conquered fear and carried him the last six feet to open air. His altitude and the location of his targets forced Duarte to expose his head and shoulders when he fired. It was a risky proposition, but he had no choice if he intended to participate in the engagement. His *compadres* probably wouldn't have noticed if he'd crawled away to hide somewhere, but Duarte still had to live with himself—for a short time at least—and his honor compelled him to fight.

He was about to drop another horseman from the saddle, when he glimpsed a furtive movement from the corner of one eye. Below and to his left, someone was moving at ground level, closer to the granite face than any *federale* had progressed so far.

Craning his neck, enticed by curiosity beyond all fear of being picked off by his enemies, Duarte saw Matt Price creeping along the shadowed base of the rock pile. The *federales* hadn't seen him yet, distracted by their duel with enemies above.

Duarte understood what Price was doing, and a fleeting surge of admiration drowned in bitter gall. The gringo couldn't wait to be a hero in Zapata's eyes, and to the others. To Dolores.

Duarte couldn't get a shot at Price from where he lay, without exposing two thirds of his body to the shooters who would gladly kill him. He'd let the *federales* do it, when they noticed Price. And if Price proved too much for them, perhaps there'd be another chance for Duarte to drop him without being blamed.

Gritting his teeth, Duarte turned to face his other enemies, and caught a horseman galloping almost directly toward him, carbine raised to fire at someone on the rock pile. Duarte shot him in the stomach, smiling as the *federale* somersaulted backward off his horse's rump and landed facedown in the dirt. He wasn't dead yet, squirming from the stark pain of his wound, but Duarte knew he wouldn't rise to fight again.

He felt better already. Killing helped.

Now all he needed was to see Price fall before the hostile guns, then find a way out of this mess for Cesar and himself. Dolores would be waiting for him, even if she didn't know it yet.

But he would take it one step at a time.

•   •   •

Price wasn't sure exactly how he'd come this far, but he was running out of time. One of the *federales* had to spot him soon, and he would be as good as dead once the alarm was raised.

Unless he hit them first and hit them hard.

Do it!

He came out of the shadows firing his Winchester, barely taking time to aim. His first shot swept a *federale*'s saddle clear and sent the bay mare galloping for safety. Next, he saw one of the drivers crouching in his wagon's shadow, angling toward Price with a long-barreled pistol. A shot to the face put him down, and Price swung toward the rear Gatling gun.

Its gunner had finally seen him, but bringing the weapon to bear took some muscle. Price watched it swivel toward him, rapid-firing with his rifle as he ran, but he was headed for the middle wagon, where the shotgunners were startled into fleeting immobility by his appearance on the scene.

Price spun and shot the nearest of them in the groin, then grabbed a handful of the wagon's tailgate, leaped, and rolled into the bed. The wounded shotgunner was covering himself with one hand, bloody-fingered, while he tried to bring the pump-gun back on target with the other. Price kicked the gun away and drew a quick bead on the man behind him, but the panicked Gatling gunner beat him to it.

Price stayed low and hugged the wagon bed while thunder pealed above him. Bullets ripped into the *federale* who had been about to blast him, tearing bloody rents in his blue tunic, sweeping him away. Price caught his shotgun as it fell, and used his first shot on the only man still standing in the wagon. Aiming was superfluous at that range with a scattergun. The buckshot spread enough to take his target's face off as the dead man spilled backward, out of the wagon.

Price pumped the shotgun's slide-action as he turned and rose, facing the last wagon in line. He had a fraction of a second before the Gatling gunner overcame the shock of his mistake and self-preservation compelled him to fire.

He squeezed the shotgun's trigger, pumped the slide, and fired again. A cloud of red mist marked the spot where his target had stood when he fired the first blast, but the shooter was down.

Price was aware of gunfire from the rock pile and from several points around him, at ground level. Turning from one wagon load of corpses to another, he saw horsemen racing toward him, brandishing carbines and pistols. The nearest, on his left, was squinting down the barrel of a Colt when Price squeezed off and slammed him from his saddle with a tight pattern of lead.

He heard the other Gatling gun resume chattering, some new gunner at the crank, but Price had closer enemies to deal with at the moment. Dropping to his knees, he heard the nearest horseman's carbine shot hiss overhead, even as Price took up the shotgun's trigger slack. Instead of cursing when the hammer snapped on a dry chamber, Price reversed the weapon, lurching to his feet again, and swung it like an ax into his mounted adversary's path.

The wooden stock shattered on impact with the *federale*'s skull, and Price received a sharp blow from the carbine's barrel to his ribs that dropped him on his backside. Another rider was upon him, leaning out to fire his Colt at point-blank range, but someone on the rock pile hit him with a long-range rifle shot that spun the blue-coat from his mount and left him laid out in the sand.

Price found his Winchester, confirmed a live round in

the pipe, and lined up on the new Gatling gunner as he rose. His shot was true, but half a dozen other rifles had the same mark in their sights at the same time. Price watched the *federale* twitching through a jerky little dance of death before his knees buckled and he went down.

He jumped down from the bullet-riddled wagon, seeking cover, and was suddenly confronted by the man he'd hammered from the saddle moments earlier. The *federale*'s jaw hung at a crazy angle, leaking blood, and one eye was already swollen shut, but he was on his feet and fumbling with the holster at his hip. Price turned, raising his rifle as the grisly figure lurched in front of him—and then the *federale*'s damaged head exploded, spewing any final plans he might've had into the dust.

Tracking the shot, Price saw Duarte staring at him over rifle sights, up near the stony crest. He raised a hand in thanks, and saw the rebel's handsome face convulse into a grimace.

Silence had descended on the battlefield. Price glanced around him and discovered only dead men on all sides, riderless horses breaking for the open desert and safety. When he was sure no one was playing possum, waiting for a chance to plug him in the back, Price climbed into the nearest wagon's seat and stepped over to reach the bed.

He meant to let Zapata crack the wooden crate so many men had died for, but a ragged line of holes along one end showed where a burst of Gatling fire had come too close for comfort. There was something odd about the damage, though, and Price bent closer to discover what it was.

In other circumstances, he would probably have laughed.

The ruptured crate was bleeding sand.

9

It was a long ride back in daylight, beneath a clear sky and the unrelenting sun. Cesar Zapata wished the trek was over, but he still had far to go and ample time to think about his choices.

He'd left camp the night before with twelve riders, reduced to eleven after he sent Mateo Alcazar back with the people from Sangre de Maria. Today, his party had six mounted men and one assigned to drive the *federale* wagon he had commandeered. Crowded into that wagon were two Gatling guns, with other captured arms and ammunition, plus three corpses and a wounded comrade who would likely die before they got him back to camp. Five horses without riders walked beside the others, seeming lost.

There'd been no gold, of course. Zapata blamed himself for not anticipating that. Price hadn't mentioned it, but neither had he seemed surprised when Duarte and Zapata cracked the boxes one by one, revealing only sand and rocks inside. None of Zapata's men had challenged his decision, even after it was proven wrong, but they were silent now, escorting guns and bodies through the wasteland.

Zapata tried to find the bright side of the business, for his own sake. There were twenty-five fewer *federales* in the world today, nearly double the tally from Sangre de Maria, against four friendly losses. His fighters also had new weapons to defend their stronghold, and perhaps to use against Neron or Diaz in some future battle that could prove decisive. Most strategists would've called the engagement a triumph.

Why did Zapata feel as if he'd lost?

The bastard Cruz had laid his trap, baited with fairy gold, and Zapata had blundered into it despite advance warnings. Aside from the losses he'd suffered, it meant that he must reevaluate Mateo Alcazar's sources in Durango.

Alcazar.

What was it Price had asked about Mateo, just last night? Something about Juanito Vega, hanged for selling out the struggle after Alcazar had seen him on the road at night, without official leave from camp.

He still remembered Vega twitching as he strangled, with the rope around his neck. Zapata had prepared the noose himself, and slapped Juanito's horse to make it run and leave him kicking empty air. As leader of the rebellion, he'd refused to dump the dirty work on someone else, but he'd insisted that the whole camp watch and learn the price of treachery.

That night, he'd wept in secret for Juanito's soul and for his own. Today, Zapata wondered if he'd been wrong all along.

If *he* was the one who was lost.

Duarte rode up on his flank, frowning, to say, "It's not your fault, Cesar."

"Whose is it then?"

"It's war, amigo. People die. We hope that more of them are *federales* than our own."

"Will that console their people, Rufio?"

"It should. They died fighting for Mexico, and none were left behind."

"Small comfort," said Zapata.

"But a comfort, all the same."

For whom? Zapata swallowed it, unspoken.

"Think of what we can accomplish with the new weapons, Cesar. That pig Neron will know he made a serious mistake."

"You think so?"

"Absolutely! First, he'll have to tell El Presidente how he lost so many weapons. Think of what the *federales* will be thinking next time they come hunting for us, knowing that we have their Gatling guns."

"One thing is certain. They'll be coming."

"Let them! We can handle anything they throw at us."

"I wonder."

"Why so glum, Cesar? It's not the first time we've lost soldiers."

"It's the first time that I've felt their lives were thrown away for nothing, Rufio."

"Nothing? You mean, because there was no gold? The guns—"

"I *mean* because I led our men into a trap, despite a warning, and they paid the price for it in blood."

"What warning? You don't mean the gringo surely. Cesar—"

"If not for Matt, we wouldn't have your precious guns right now. We might not even have the wagon for our dead.

I didn't charge the *federales,* I didn't see *you* down there, fighting hand to hand."

"Is he your new lieutenant then?"

Zapata frowned. "Sometimes I wonder what you're thinking, Rufio. I made a critical mistake that cost three lives, more likely four, and you behave as if it were a children's game."

"I guess you'd rather have me sobbing like a woman, eh, Cesar? Would that be helpful?"

"If you want to help me, find out who deceived Mateo. If he *was* deceived."

It was Duarte's turn to frown. "What are you saying?"

"Maybe nothing. Just find out. First thing, as soon as we get back to camp."

"All right," Duarte said, wheeling his horse away. "I will."

Zapata reached for his canteen, hoping a sip of tepid water might remove the taste of failure from his mouth.

"How could this happen, Sergeant?" asked Lieutenant Cruz.

The sergeant stood before him at attention, boots and uniform still dusty from the hard ride to Durango. When he spoke, there was the bare suggestion of a tremor in his voice. "I don't know, sir. When we arrived, they were already dead."

"What, *all* of them?" Cruz couldn't make his reeling mind digest the fact.

"Yes, sir. I mean, it took some time to find them all. The hidden bodies and—"

"Start over," ordered Cruz. "From the beginning."

"Yes, sir. My detachment left Sinaloa three hours behind

the wagons, as ordered. We were told keep our distance, take our time, and not let anybody know the shipment had an escort."

"I drafted the order, Sergeant. I'm aware of what it said."

"Yes, sir. I thought—"

"Get on with it!"

"Yes, sir. We followed orders, staying well behind the wagons. It was slow and hot. At half past eleven came shooting in the distance. We rode for it and found the place too late. That's all, sir."

"All?" Cruz clenched his teeth to keep from cursing at the sergeant. "I don't think so. Describe for me *exactly* what you found."

"Yes, sir." The sergeant closed his eyes briefly, as if to view the scene more accurately in his memory. "We found two wagons with the horses still in harness. One horse had been wounded, and we finished it. The drivers and their escort, twenty men, were all around the wagons. Dead, sir. We retrieved some of their horses from the desert, but the rest . . ." His dry voice trailed away.

"Tell me about the men," said Cruz. "How were they killed?"

The sergeant blinked at him. Cruz saw him looking for the trick inside the question. "They were shot, sir."

"Shot from *where*?"

"We reckoned from the big rocks on the north side of the road, sir. There were markings on the boulders, where the escorts fired up into them. But still . . ."

"Yes? *What?*" Cruz fought an urge to leap across his desk and shake the man.

"Sir, I thought some of them were shot up close. If you know wounds, sir . . . well, they have a different look."

"You think the rebels were among them then?"

"I don't know, sir. It's what I saw."

"You mentioned twenty men. What of the rest?"

"We found them later, sir, searching the rock pile. There was blood. I hoped some of the rebels had been wounded, but the men we found were ours. The uniforms were stripped from two of them."

"And did you find them?"

"Sir?"

"The *uniforms,* damn it!"

"Yes, sir! Beside the rock pile and the road, not too far from the wagons, sir."

"What did you make of that, Sergeant?"

"I didn't understand it, sir."

Idiot.

Cruz kept from shouting with an effort. "You found two wagons. The shipment started out with three. What else was missing?"

"Guns, sir."

"I see." Cruz felt as if a nest of snakes was squirming in his gut.

"We checked the bodies and the horses we could find, sir. The rebels took their weapons. Also, in the wagons that were left, we counted many cartridges from shotguns and a Gatling gun, but there were no guns left."

Perfect. Not only had Zapata and his men escaped, killing two dozen *federales* in the process, but they'd also made off with an arsenal including heavy weapons. Cruz felt suddenly light-headed. Concentrating on his balance, he sat down and leaned back in his chair.

"And can you tell me where the stolen wagon went, Sergeant?"

"No, sir."

"You didn't try to follow it?"

"We did try, sir, but there were sandstorms and I thought . . . I only had a dozen men, sir, and they'd just killed twenty-five."

"You were afraid."

"Sir, in my judgment it was more important to alert headquarters and—"

Cruz raised a hand to silence him. "Enough, Sergeant. Where are the bodies and the two remaining wagons now?"

"We brought them with us, sir. It took a bit more time."

"Of course. And you're exhausted, I suppose?"

"Well, sir—"

"That's most unfortunate. You have one hour to get cleaned up and prepare a new patrol. Choose twenty men, the best remaining in Durango."

"Yes, sir!"

"Sergeant—what is your name again?"

"Rodriguez, sir."

"Sergeant Rodriguez, you are ordered to retrace your steps and find that missing wagon and the men who took it. You will not return without it, is that clear?"

"Yes, sir!"

"I don't care if it takes a week or the rest of your life. Understand?"

"Yes, sir, Lieutenant!"

"Go, then. Leave me."

Normally, Cruz could improve his mood by punishing subordinates, but this was different. He had to brief Captain Ruiz before someone else beat him to it, and the full responsibility for the disaster ultimately rested on his shoulders. There was no more time to waste.

Leaving his sword behind, Cruz left the tiny office and went out to meet his fate.

•   •   •

Rufio Duarte didn't understand the change that had been wrought in his old friend by one engagement with the enemy, but as he rode south toward the hidden canyon and their camp, his mind was busy searching for a way to blame Matt Price.

Before the gringo joined them, Cesar had mourned the fighters who fell in their struggle, but he had also shared Duarte's recognition that sacrifice was a necessary part of war. In the not-so-old days, Duarte told himself, Zapata would've celebrated that capture of powerful weapons from their mortal enemies, without wallowing in useless grief over four dead rebels.

It was the stranger from El Norte who had made him soft, Duarte thought. And yet, Price clearly wasn't soft himself. Although Duarte hated to admit it, Cesar was right in saying that they might not have the guns—indeed they might be dead—except for Price charging the enemy alone and killing nearly half of them himself. Duarte wondered, briefly, whether it was simple jealousy that made him hate the gringo, but he instantly dismissed the thought as foolish.

Price was *dangerous,* a foreigner who stood for everything Duarte hated about Mexico. His country had been ruled by Spaniards and Frenchmen in turn, had lost nearly half of its territory to the United States in a war of outright imperialism, and now it was ruled by brutal pigs who thought first and last of themselves, with never a care for the poor folk they trampled in their rush to the trough.

Matt Price was part of that somehow. Duarte felt it in his very bones, but proving it to Cesar would be difficult, perhaps impossible.

He'd tried to solve the problem when the opportunity was offered to him, lining up his shot as Price was fighting with the *federales* at close range. Only a trick of Fate had spared the gringo then, pushing another man between Duarte and his chosen target. Thus, ironically, the bullet meant for Price had saved his life and killed a *federale* in his place. A heartbeat later, Price had captured Duarte with his eyes and there had been no second chance to cut him down.

But did he *know*?

That prospect troubled Duarte more than he was willing to admit. Although a killer in his own right, the survivor of a dozen battles greater than this morning's skirmish, Duarte recognized that he might not be Price's equal if they fought a private duel. There was something in the gringo's manner, in the way he risked his life and killed without compunction, that made Duarte shy away from overt challenges.

But if Price knew the rifle bullet had been meant for him that morning, why had he said nothing, done nothing afterward? Duarte understood why such a man would not involve Zapata in a private quarrel. That might seem unmanly, even under military discipline. But would he hesitate to call Duarte out and face him privately?

Duarte shook his head in silent refutation of the question, then glanced up to see if anyone had caught him in the act. If so, the nearest riders gave no sign. Returning to his private thoughts, Duarte knew that Price was not afraid of him. Although he wanted to believe the worst about the gringo, Price would never be mistaken for a coward.

Maybe he was foolish then. Perhaps he thought Duarte meant to save him with the near-miss shot that claimed a *federale*'s life instead.

Perhaps.

But in his heart, Duarte didn't believe that either.

And that disbelief was further cause for worry. If his

supposition was correct, Price knew Duarte had meant to
kill him and he must be planning some revenge for the attempt. Maybe he thought a private fight between them
would be too much, with the battle smoke and smell of
blood still lingering upon them. Surely, Cesar would've
stepped between them in that moment, trying to restore the
fragile peace.

But Price could always watch and wait, biding his time.
And in the meantime, he could work his gringo magic on
Dolores, slowly stealing her away from family and friends,
her very heritage itself.

Duarte fumed as fear and jealousy of Price combined
to hone his hatred, giving it a shiny razor's edge. He had
to think about the best way to employ that weapon, using
it to Price's detriment without endangering himself.

And something told him he was running out of time.

No problem, Duarte thought.

He had the will, and he would find a way.

Captain Ruiz listened in stoic silence as Lieutenant Cruz
detailed the ruin of their plan. He thought of it as theirs,
now that the scheme had failed, though he'd have gladly
claimed all credit for himself in the event of a successful
resolution.

Now that it was spoiled, Ruiz wished he could disavow
the plan entirely, blame it all on Cruz or someone else, but
it was too late to protect himself with simple sleight of
hand.

He needed something else, and quickly, if he meant to
salvage his career, perhaps even to save his life.

Cruz finished speaking, and tense silence lay between
them for a moment. The lieutenant plainly didn't know

what to expect from his superior, but he seemed braced for anything.

When Ruiz spoke at last, his voice was brittle, crisp and sharp as broken glass. "You're telling me," he said, "that we've lost twenty-five men, two Gatling guns and other weapons, with a quantity of ammunition, and we have nothing at all to show for it. Is that a fair summation?"

"Sir, we have Sangre de Maria."

"Ah, yes. I forgot the thirteen peasants executed as a lure to draw the rebels out. In that, at least, it seems you were successful."

"I, sir?" Cruz blinked rapidly, as if trying to parse the moment and determine when responsibility had shifted to his shoulders. "But—"

"Don't be concerned, Lieutenant. I've no doubt that Governor Neron will understand how these things happen. One moment, triumph is within your grasp. The next—"

Ruiz opened his upraised hands to simulate the flight of good intentions on their way to Hell. He stopped short of smiling at Cruz. It would've been too much, and in fact he had nothing to smile about.

Tormenting Cruz in private was one thing, but Ruiz knew where Neron would place most of the blame. He was already thinking past this moment toward his coming confrontation with Durango's governor, imagining what he would say to keep the ax from falling on his own neck.

And if that wasn't possible, Ruiz would still do everything within his power to take Cruz with him when he fell from grace.

It pleased Ruiz to see the slightly dazed expression on his subordinate's face and hear the tremor in his voice as Cruz replied, "Sir, is there nothing I can do to make it right?"

"The loss of twenty-five good men is difficult to overcome," Ruiz answered. He had no idea if the dead *federales* were good men or not, but their slaughter proved they weren't good enough soldiers, as if that mattered. "Still, if you could reach out for Zapata and deliver him to me, it would be helpful. I'll accept his head, Lieutenant. Can you do that?"

"Capitán—"

"I understand, of course. No doubt the governor will sympathize with your predicament."

The doomed lieutenant's shoulders almost slumped as he replied, "Yes, sir."

"You'll be informed of Governor Neron's decision," said Ruiz. "Dismissed."

"Yes, sir." There was less spring than usual in the salute Cruz offered him. Ruiz returned it with a calculated air of boredom, as if Cruz no longer mattered in the larger scheme of things. As if he'd ceased to be, for all intents and purposes.

The office door closed softly, leaving him alone. Ruiz was unable to hold his smile beyond another second, losing it completely as he pictured what might lay in store for *him* when he delivered the bad news to Governor Neron.

And even now, Ruiz wondered if it would come as a surprise.

He thought Neron had been spying on him, nearly took the suspicion for granted after their last conversation. Neron's last words returned to haunt him now: *Fail me, and I can promise you there'll be nowhere to hide.*

Ruiz knew he'd be easy to replace. There was no shortage of up-and-coming officers who would do anything within their power to replace him at Neron's right hand. Ruiz suspected some of them were plotting to embarrass him, and they would not ignore this opportunity to do him harm.

Self-preservation would require a swift and certain strategy for victory, and that eluded him. His only asset at the moment was a traitor whom he couldn't reach without endangering the rebel and himself. It might be worth the gamble, though, if he could pull it off.

Frowning, Captain Ruiz addressed the full-length mirror mounted on the backside of his office door. Rehearsal of important statements did no harm, and it might do a world of good.

"Your Excellency," he began, "I am afraid I have bad news."

Price kept to himself on the ride back to camp. It wasn't hard to do, since one of the remaining riders had been sent ahead to scout their trail, two others flanked the wagon with their friends inside, and the party's two leaders rode in silence that verged on hostility.

Price had a fair take on Zapata's mood, but he was less sure of Duarte. On the surface, Duarte seemed pleased with the mission's outcome, and he'd even congratulated Price on a job well done, but his heart wasn't in it. His words rang hollow, and Price guessed that Duarte would've been happy to see him stacked in the wagon bed, with the other casualties.

That thought took him back to the rock pile and the shot that had probably saved him from joining that bloody cargo. The shot was Duarte's, but why had he fired it? And where was he aiming?

Price couldn't swear the Mexican had tried to kill him and brought down a *federale* by mistake. If he'd been certain of it, he would've returned fire at the time and settled it, once and for all. Instead, he'd have to watch his back as long as he was in Zapata's company, until Duarte made another move.

Why would Zapata's sidekick want him dead?

Price knew that killing didn't always need a reason that was well thought out. He'd seen men killed for winning card games, even when they didn't cheat, or simply for the looks they gave another man. In Duarte's case, he guessed there was some kind of jealousy at work, maybe embarrassment that Price had been the one to liberate Zapata from his prison cell after Duarte had claimed it was hopeless.

And then, there was Dolores.

Price knew there was more than platonic friendship behind Duarte's attentions to Zapata's sister. He hadn't seen Dolores do anything to encourage those feelings, but he hadn't been in camp that long. There might be history between them, or it might just be Duarte's yearning for Dolores that made him regard Price as an enemy.

Whatever the cause, Price knew an enemy when he met one, and Duarte could be dangerous. Price couldn't prove he was a backshooter—not yet—but there were other kinds of trouble Duarte could stir up if he tried. Price knew he'd have to watch his back and watch his step around the rebel camp, if he decided to remain there.

They had nearly reached the canyon when Zapata called a halt, breaking the silence that had shrouded most of their return trip. Stopping by the wagon, he spoke softly to the wounded man who lay beside the corpses and received no answer.

One more for the worms, thought Price.

"The wagon will not pass," Zapata said. "We must unload it here. The dead, we tie across their saddles. They will have an honored place to rest. One of the Gatling guns will be dismantled. We can pack it into camp with ammunition and the other small arms. Rufio, you take the wagon and the other big gun to the caves and hide them well."

"Cesar—"

"Just do it. Please. There's no one else."

Duarte nodded, mollified, but he still shot a sour glance at Price. It wasn't difficult to read his thoughts. Duarte didn't want Price riding back to camp—back to Dolores—in his absence, but he didn't trust a gringo with the knowledge of a hideout where Zapata stashed his surplus weapons either. He had created his own dilemma, and now he was stuck with it.

Price welcomed the respite, however brief it might be, but he resolved to stay alert when Duarte returned to camp. And in the meantime, he'd be thinking through his options for the future. Riding with Zapata wasn't a permanent choice. He was simply passing through.

But where was he going?

Price reckoned he needed an answer to that one, before Duarte or anyone else tried dictating his future. For the moment, he was part of an uneasy team.

And they were nearly home.

"You bring me more bad news, Captain. I see it in your eyes."

"Your Excellency—"

"Let me guess," Neron said, interrupting him. "Your brilliant plan to stop Cesar Zapata and his traitors failed. Again. Is that your message, Captain?"

"Sir—"

"May I assume you've killed a few of them at least? Perhaps enough to make them think twice about challenging the power of the state? Can you at least tell me that much, Captain?"

"Thirteen rebel supporters have been executed, sir. I think—"

"Rebel *supporters*? You mean peasants, I assume."

"Traitors, Your Excellency. They provided aid and comfort to the enemy. My men discovered weapons in the village and—"

"You shot them, eh?"

"Lieutenant Cruz made that decision, sir, after the prisoners confessed to dealing with Zapata."

"A decision then. You said his name was Cruz?"

"Yes, sir."

"I'll make a note of it," Neron replied. "There was more to your plan than a raid on some backwater village, if memory serves."

"Yes, sir. I hoped to trap Zapata and his men."

"What has become of that hope, Captain?"

"There was a skirmish on the Presidio road, sir. Unfortunately, the rebels escaped."

Neron pinned the *federale* captain with a glare. "And how many men have you lost?"

Ruiz seemed to shrink as he replied, "Twenty-five, Your Excellency."

Neron already knew the answer, having been tipped off by an informer in the ranks before Ruiz arrived. Still, there was no need to pretend outrage as he advanced upon Ruiz.

"Did you say twenty-five? All dead?"

"Yes, sir." Nearly a whisper.

Leaning close enough to smell a faint trace of tequila on Ruiz's breath, Neron asked, "Is there more you have to say?"

Indeed there was, as he well knew.

"Your Excellency, in the skirmish, certain weapons were . . . misplaced."

Neron affected an expression of astonishment. "Misplaced? Do you mean *captured*?"

"Stolen, sir. The rebels—"

"Took them after wiping out your men. Of course, I understand. These would be carbines and pistols, I take it?"

"Not entirely, sir."

"What else?"

"There were shotguns."

"A trifle, eh?"

"And two Gatling guns, Your Excellency."

The governor locked eyes with his subordinate, letting the captain squirm before he said, "Am I to understand, Captain Ruiz, that you gave Cesar Zapata the gift of two Gatling guns?"

"I gave him nothing, sir. He—"

"Simply *took* them, eh? After he killed your men. All twenty-five of them."

Neron turned his back on Ruiz, stalked back to his desk and the telephone standing upon it. He palmed the earpiece and jiggled its hook until his secretary answered.

"Yes, sir?"

"Send him in," Neron commanded, then cradled the handset without waiting for an answer.

Seconds later, a door opened to his left and a *federale* officer entered the office from Neron's private waiting room. He advanced a half dozen paces into the governor's presence, then snapped to attention with a crisp salute.

"Your Excellency!"

"Thank you for joining us, Captain. Please stand at

ease." Neron turned to Ruiz and asked, "Are you acquainted with Captain Manuel Montoya de Cozar?"

"By reputation only, sir," Ruiz answered.

"It was his reputation that impressed me," said Neron. "I've asked him to assist you in resolving this Zapata problem. I assume you don't object?"

"No, sir. Of course not."

"Good. Captain Montoya, I'm afraid the situation has degenerated since our last discussion. The traitor Zapata has killed—how many men was that, Captain Ruiz?"

"Twenty-five, sir."

"Incredible! Twenty-five dead, and now it seems that we've *misplaced* two Gatling guns, along with other weapons."

Captain Montoya frowned. "It seems . . . unusual, Your Excellency."

"We're agreed then. Something must be done to remedy the situation."

"Absolutely, sir."

"I knew it. With cooperation, anything is possible. I take it, Ruiz, that you won't mind working with Montoya."

"No, Your Excellency."

"Good. And for a fresh perspective on this business, I am placing him in charge."

A flush of color tinged Ruiz's cheeks, but he did not reply. Neron had half-expected some objection, was prepared to demote or dismiss Ruiz on the spot, but the captain's quiet desperation robbed him of that pleasure.

For the moment.

"Captain Ruiz has certain resources you may find useful, Montoya. Granted, they haven't served him to the best advantage yet, but perhaps in new hands they'll prove useful."

"Yes, sir."

"I look forward to good news in the near future," Neron told both men. "Should that not be the case . . . but why be negative? I wish you both good luck this one last time. Dismissed."

10

The banquet was part wake, part celebration. Someone had procured a steer somehow, and it was roasting on a spit in the middle of camp while various women prepared the side dishes. Price had attended the funeral service beforehand, understanding most of what was said about the struggle's newest martyrs. Zapata made a speech extolling sacrifice, and widows shrilled their grief beside four open graves.

Price stayed to watch the holes filled in, and counted simple markers in the forest graveyard. There were seventeen so far, and he assumed there had been others lost in situations where their bodies couldn't be retrieved. Another thirteen in the village where the *federales* had come calling yesterday, and thirty-three that he was sure of on the other side since he had noticed Gray Wolf's picture on a poster back in San Filipe.

So much killing, but the country never seemed to tire of it. Across the Rio Grande, a fraction of that killing would've roused the populace to arms, with deputies and vigilantes scouring the countryside. Price wondered why it was so different in Mexico, if life was held more cheaply there, or if the people simply had greater capacity for suffering.

The worst of it was that he had begun to feel at home.

Zapata's men had mounted their new Gatling gun a few yards from the barbecue pit, captured small arms stacked around it, so the people could see what they'd purchased with blood. Later, Price supposed, the big gun would be carried to a point where it could guard the camp's narrow approach, further insurance that no enemies could pass that way.

The weapon was a symbol of security, but they were not secure. Price knew a siege party could seal the camp's exit as surely as Zapata's sentries barred intruders from the camp. Zapata and the rest must know it too, but in the days Price had been with them, no one had expressed the notion.

Returning from the cemetery to the banquet, Price wondered if that was part of the arrangement. Maybe tyrants needed rebels after all. Without them, would the strongmen lose their grip and slowly fade away?

Dolores found him in the crowd and led him to the serving line. Some of the men made room for them, and that left Price embarrassed. Stories of that morning's battle had already made the rounds, inflated by tequila and the common tendency of soldiers to exaggerate, and somehow Price had come to be a hero in the telling of it.

But he didn't feel heroic.

Truth be told, he felt like an impostor at the feast.

Killing came easily to Price. It always had, but that was nothing to be proud of, nothing that demanded celebration. He'd known shooters who were haunted by the ghosts of men they'd killed, but Price had never shared that handicap. He wasn't superstitious, and whatever fear of Hell he'd learned in childhood had long since been swept away like gun smoke on the wind.

If there was any Hell at all, Price reckoned people built it for themselves and walked its arid roads from day to day.

"You should be proud, not sad," Dolores told him.

"Proud of what?"

"You fought a great battle today. The victory is yours."

"I did my bit, that's all."

"You are too modest. Cesar told me of your bravery, how you saved the others."

"The four men you just planted might not see it that way," Price replied.

"They were soldiers," she reminded him. "They knew the risk. And now, they're heroes of the struggle too."

"Is getting shot what makes a hero?"

"Sacrifice for others is the mark of heroism. Some fall in the battle; others live to fight another day."

"It gets old, though," Price said. "The fighting."

"But you still go on."

"I wonder why sometimes."

"Is there perhaps something you'd rather do?"

"In life, you mean?"

Her hand found his, squeezed lightly, then withdrew. "I mean tonight," she said.

Price saw her smile and glanced around them, half-expecting Rufio Duarte to be watching from the sidelines. When he wasn't there, Price asked, "What did you have in mind?"

That smile again. "Do you recall my secret place?"

He nodded. "I'm not likely to forget it."

"Give me ten minutes," she instructed him. "Then follow."

"I'll be there."

Dolores left him, moving through the crowd. Price stepped out of the serving line, no longer hungry, if he ever had been. When he tried to find Dolores once again, she had already disappeared.

Trouble, he thought. And then: *So what?*

Price had already risked his life that day, with nothing much to show for it but stolen guns and bodies in the ground. This time, at least, he could look forward to a tangible reward.

This time, it might be worth the risk.

Duarte had been careful not to let Dolores and the gringo catch him watching them. He kept his distance, pausing here and there to speak with others and accept congratulations for the morning's victory. Avoiding Cesar wasn't difficult, but keeping track of Price required a measure of finesse.

He'd seen Dolores seek out the gringo, had been expecting it, caught in a fever of anticipation mixed with dread. Duarte felt her need for Price, a cruel inversion of his own craving for Dolores, but he wasn't certain if the gunman shared her feelings.

Did it matter?

Price was only human, after all. What man of flesh and blood would spurn the offer of such beauty for the taking?

When they stepped into the serving line, Duarte shadowed them. He had already filled a plate, one of the first served in accordance with his rank, though he had little appetite. The argument with Cesar, still unmended, was a part of it. Watching Dolores with the gringo finished any taste he had for food.

Duarte still went through the motions, though, eating and smiling at his comrades in a parody of celebration. Here and there, he was aware of other women watching him. Duarte was a prize catch in the camp and knew it well enough, but he had eyes for only one among them.

One who might betray him if she found the opportunity.

He watched Dolores and the gringo talking, wished that he could read their lips. She smiled sweetly enough to break his heart, but Price was solemn, unresponsive.

Could the gunman be that foolish?

Was Duarte worried without reason?

No.

Staring while someone jabbered nonsense in his ear, he saw Dolores take the gringo's hand. A fleeting touch, but Duarte felt it like a knife blade twisting in his gut. And when Dolores left the serving line, he had no doubt that Price would follow her.

The confirmation came a moment later. Price stepped out of line before the women had a chance to serve him, glancing after Dolores though he moved in another direction.

All part of the game.

Duarte saw it clearly, felt he could predict each move the would-be lovers made. Rising, he left his plate and his companions without explanation. He took his cue from Price, plotting a parallel course through the camp without seeming to follow. Duarte didn't know where Dolores was going, but Price would find her.

And when he did, Duarte would have both of them.

What then?

He hadn't thought beyond verification of his worst sus-

picion. Imagining what they might do, what he might see,
Duarte raged inside—but how should he react?

It was a simple thing to let the jealous rage consume
him, guide his hands, but peril lay in that direction. Price
was dangerous enough, but if Duarte harmed Dolores by
mistake, he would be faced with Cesar's wrath as well. Unless . . .

It only took a moment to devise the plan. A witness
would solve everything, at once confirming Duarte's accusations and providing backup if it came to killing with the
gringo. All he had to do was choose the right man for the
job.

He saw Price moving with a purpose now, heading for
the outskirts of the camp. There was no time to waste if
Duarte meant to carry out his scheme. Glancing about, he
saw one man standing alone, sipping tequila from a pocket
flask.

Duarte swerved to intercept him. "Quickly!" he commanded. "Come with me."

"What is it?" asked Mateo Alcazar.

"No questions. Come! You'll find out soon enough."

Dolores was accustomed to visiting her secret place at any
hour of day or night—whenever she felt troubled, lonely,
or afraid—but this night it was different. She couldn't
swear that no one else had ever seen that clearing in the forest, but Dolores herself had brought no person there except
Matt Price. Their first kiss underneath the trees had been
magical, all the more so because she'd made the decision
and seized the initiative.

Tonight, she planned more of the same.

Much, much more.

Dolores wanted Price as she had never wanted any other man within her very limited experience. She had been kissed before, not often, but the rest of it was still a mystery. She knew the mechanics, of course, but it sounded so clinical when explained by a parent or priest.

Dolores wanted to explore the mystery herself, and she was counting on Matt Price to be her guide. She recognized the deadly sin of lust, but she was also mindful of the contradiction. If it weren't for lust, there'd be no human race, no civilization, no—

What?

Dolores paused for a moment on her secret trail and listened to the forest around her. At age nineteen, she was already jaded enough by the pain she had suffered in life to question whether such a thing as *civilization* even existed. And if it did, what were its benefits to any but the filthy rich who made the rules? If life in Mexico was civilized, she thought her people might be better off living in trees and caves like jungle animals, without a government of laws that favored tyrants and oppressed the poor.

Dolores caught herself before the silent rant went any further, recalling her delicious errand with a new thrill of excitement. For tonight, at least, she could forget about the revolution, politics, and power. She could focus on a primal need that burned within her, nurtured like a trembling candle flame until it suddenly blazed hot and strong.

But was she ready?

Yes!

Dolores had no doubts on that score. Most respectable Mexican women were married at her age, many already with children to fill up what passed for free time. Dolores didn't crave a husband or a family—not yet at least—but she had definitely reached the point where she desired a man.

And not just *any* man.

She could've picked and chosen from the single men in camp, she realized. And maybe from the married ones as well, though none of them appealed to her and there'd be hell to pay from that. So far, she'd used her brother's name and reputation as a shield against potential suitors, satisfied to watch and wait until the Perfect Man appeared.

Was Price that man?

Dolores wasn't sure, but she was anxious to find out. Anxious, and then some. Moving through the moonlight, she increased her pace, hoping that Price was close behind her, feeling as she did, eager for her initiation into womanhood.

What did she know of Matt Price really?

He was brave and didn't flinch from battle. He had saved her brother's life, when none of Cesar's faithful comrades thought it could be done. He was a handsome man, within his limits. And when she had kissed him, he'd returned the kiss with cautious passion that aroused her to a fever pitch.

It was enough to know for now.

What could be said about him that would change her mind? He was a gringo from El Norte, but she didn't care. He was a killer, but the same was true of Cesar, Rufio, and every other man in camp. There was a time for killing, as the Bible said. And in the Mexico Dolores knew, that time was now.

Price wasn't just a killer, though. Dolores knew such men, within the struggle and opposing it. Their souls were deadened by a lifetime of experience, or were they simply born without the burden of a conscience? Either way, Dolores didn't sense that deadness in Matt Price. For all he'd suffered, seen, and done before Dolores met him—even before she was born—she still knew he was capable of feeling, caring.

Did he care for her?

Enough, perhaps, to guide her on a precious journey of discovery, revealing things she'd only heard about in giggling whispers from her peers, or in stern lectures from her elders. Possibly enough to make her feel alive and beautiful and wanted.

One moment, she was moving like a shadow through the looming trees; the next, her secret place lay silvered by the moon in front of her. Dolores stepped into the glen and felt renewed, empowered, as if moonlight by itself could banish any fears.

It felt like coming home.

Dolores had no timepiece, but she knew Price should be on his way to join her now. It wouldn't be much longer. When he appeared, should she immediately fling herself into his arms, or was there something to be said?

Trust him, she thought.

She'd chosen Price as much for his presumed experience as for his courage or the angle of his jaw. She guessed he must know how to please a woman, or at least to please himself, and maybe it was all the same. Perhaps it all came down to pleasing one another without calculation or design.

Dolores crossed the clearing, soft ferns brushing at her skirt and legs, until she reached the boulder at its center. She would await her lover there, and be the first thing that he saw by moonlight, after passing through the darkness.

•   •   •

Price had no trouble following the trail. He'd always had a certain skill for navigation, landmarks, and the like. More so when he was amply motivated, as tonight.

He knew the way, all right.

But was he walking into trouble?

Price had thought about the risks while he was easing out of camp and picking up the shadowed forest track. Cesar Zapata was the most obvious, with Duarte running a close second, but Price knew he couldn't afford to overlook Dolores herself. Not that he *planned* to overlook her, but he had to think about her feelings and the danger lurking there.

Dolores behaved like a worldly woman of experience, but Price assumed that most of it was bluff, a pretense seasoned with some measure of excitement. He'd known women who could make a cowboy blush without half trying, and Dolores wasn't one of those.

Not even close.

The forest had a chill to it this evening, cooler even than the desert down below. The altitude would do that, and the trees that kept the soil and rock beneath his feet from soaking up much heat by day. Price hadn't worn his jacket, coming from the fires in camp, but he supposed he wouldn't need it.

One way or another, he'd keep warm.

And afterward? What then?

It was a fine line, knowing when to leave. He couldn't simply cut and run next morning, even if he wanted to. But then again, if he stayed on too long it carried implications of a settled life, or something like it.

What did "settled" even mean for the Zapata family these days? They lived in hiding, tried to stay one jump ahead of *federale* justice, and each morning's sunrise had to be at least a bit of a surprise.

Price hadn't meant to join the revolution when he trailed Cesar Zapata home, and he wasn't committed to it now. That morning's skirmish had done more to sour him on staying than to make him put down roots. But he had nowhere else to go just now, no pressing need to hit the road, and if Dolores wanted him . . . why not?

It never crossed his mind that he was preying on a child. She wasn't that by any means. Dolores had survived more hardship than most women twice her age, at least back in the States. To Price, the difference in ages mattered less than what they'd seen and where they'd come from, moving toward this point in time.

He saw a moonlight glimmer through the trees before he reached the clearing. Caution made him take it slowly, planting each step carefully to make a minimum of noise. Price didn't mean to scare Dolores, but if there were other parties in the neighborhood, he likewise didn't mean to be surprised.

Reaching the tree line, Price could see she was alone. There'd been no reason to suspect a trap, but he was still relieved. As he relaxed, his hand fell from the pistol grip where it had come to rest, instinctively, a moment earlier.

Price moved into the clearing, feeling each step as he took it, like a stride away from something that he couldn't quite identify, toward something that he barely recognized. It was a strange sensation, not entirely pleasant, but he followed where the footsteps led.

Dolores saw him, rose, and came to meet him, tall ferns whispering around her as she ran. She leapt into his arms with staggering enthusiasm, trusting Price to catch her, and he managed it somehow. Their lips met, and Price felt hers open, offering a tongue that flicked and teased him.

Gravity took over then, and Price surrendered to it, cushioned by the ferns and softening the impact for Dolores with his body. Soft and hard together, that would be, and the alarm bell ringing in his mind was muffled by a sound of yearning that emerged from her and him and both of them at once.

Danger, a small voice whispered in his ear, and then Price lost it in the sweet sound of Dolores saying, "Yes, oh, please. Yes, yes!"

The night seemed to conspire against Duarte as he hurried through the forest. It was difficult to travel silently and still keep up a decent pace on unfamiliar ground, more so with Alcazar behind him, almost stepping on his heels. Duarte already regretted his selection, hissing curses when his backup stumbled on the trail, but there'd been no time for a better choice.

He'd quizzed Alcazar earlier, in accordance with Zapata's order, and reported back to Cesar that the man's answers seemed satisfactory. It was coincidence, Duarte thought, that Alcazar had met Juanito Vega on the road the night Vega had slipped out to betray them. Even so, Mateo wasn't Duarte's favorite soldier in the camp, no one he'd choose as a companion for the evening.

And now, he feared they might be lost.

How could he spend so much time in the mountain camp, hunting the woods around it in an endless quest for game, and still not recognize the trail beneath his feet? It seemed impossible, and yet the sounds of celebration from the camp were fading in the background, while the brooding silence of the nighttime forest drew Duarte ever onward, folding him within itself.

Nothing to fear, Duarte told himself. If they were truly

lost, he'd simply have to wait for daylight and retrace his steps to camp. It meant a loss of sleep, some physical discomfort, but it wouldn't kill him. There was nothing in the woods that Duarte feared.

Except Matt Price.

And where was *he* right now? Where was Dolores? Were they rutting like a pair of animals while Duarte wandered through the forest at his wit's end, searching hopelessly?

He'd seen Price leave the camp, moments after Dolores slipped away, and he had marked the place where he last saw the gringo's back. A certain pine tree with a scarred trunk was his landmark, and he hadn't wasted any time to speak of with Mateo Alcazar, just commandeered his services and went from there. Not rushing it, of course. He didn't want to overtake the gringo prematurely, catch him answering a call of nature without any evidence of dalliance.

That wouldn't do at all.

Duarte needed proof before he . . . what?

He still hadn't devised a plan of action, stoked on rage at Price and righteous indignation at Dolores's betrayal. Personal experience had taught Duarte that he really *did* see red when fury gripped him, in the heat of battle, but he hadn't reached that state of agitation yet. He had to verify his worst suspicions first, grind salt into his self-inflicted wounds, before he faced Price man-to-man.

Or rather, man-to-*men,* if Alcazar had nerve enough to help him. His accomplice, lurching in the dark and wheezing out tequila fumes, still didn't know their errand. It was better that way, Duarte thought. Less time to worry about consequences while they traipsed through darkness, looking for a man to kill.

Duarte was about to call a halt and try to get his bearings, when a sound like muffled voices captured his attention. He couldn't make out the words, but conversation meant at least two people, somewhere up ahead.

Mateo heard it too. *"Quien es?"* he inquired.

"Quiet, you fool!"

Duarte crept along the trail now, as if he was stalking tasty game and only had one bullet left, one chance to satisfy his gnawing hunger. If he missed, or if he made a sound and spooked his prey before he was prepared to fire, it would be wasted effort. Worse than useless.

Duarte knew he should've brought Zapata with him, as a witness to his sister's degradation and the gringo's treachery, but finding Cesar and convincing him to leave camp in the middle of the night would've ensured that Duarte lost the trail. This way, at least he had a chance to interrupt before Price took advantage of Dolores.

Or was it the other way around?

Was that what really galled Duarte when he saw the two of them together? Knowing that the gringo was her own free choice?

No matter. When his work was done tonight, that choice would not exist.

The clearing took Duarte by surprise. After the darkness of the woodland trail, a veritable blaze of moonlight marked the place where nature or some accident had swept an oval patch of trees away and left the ground to lesser growing things. It was the kind of place where deer might come to feed, and Duarte made a mental note to try it when his turn next came to fetch meat for the camp.

Assuming he was still alive by then.

He felt a chill of apprehension now, this close to facing Price, and when he glanced at Alcazar, the smaller man's blank stare did nothing to increase Duarte's confidence. Duarte raised a warning finger to his lips, demanding silence from his tipsy second, then crept forward to the tree line, one hand on the pistol at his hip.

He scanned the clearing, half-afraid of what his eyes might see, yet craving it. A glimpse of flesh perhaps. Dolores in the gringo's arms, straining against him as they—

Nothing.

There was no one in the clearing. Nothing but a field of gently stirring ferns before him, with a boulder planted in the middle of the clearing. Duarte blinked, confused. The muffled voices *must* have come from this point.

Recklessly, he stepped into the moonlight, Alcazar closing behind him. Duarte heard his voice crack as he called into the night, "Dolores! Price! Where are you?"

And the disembodied answer came back from his left.

"Right here."

Price rose out of the ferns to find Duarte and another man inside the clearing, near the southwest tree line. Duarte wore a pistol on his right hip, while the other seemed to be unarmed. Price knew he couldn't take that part for granted, but Zapata's chief lieutenant had his full attention at the moment.

"So, gringo," Duarte said, "you've lost your hat."

"Just looking for it," Price replied. "You want to help?"

"Maybe another time. I'm looking for Dolores."

"Did you try the camp?"

There'd been no time for strategizing, but he'd hissed an order to Dolores when they heard Duarte's voice, gripping her arms and staring hard into her frightened eyes until she nodded acquiescence. At the moment, she was creeping silently away from Price, concealed by ferns, making her way to cover and the trail back into camp.

Duarte missed a beat, confused, but then regained his confidence. "I saw her come this way," he said.

"Sorry I missed her," Price replied.

"I *know* she's here!"

Price shifted to his left, drawing the hostile eyes along with him and farther from Dolores. "You've been hitting that tequila," he suggested. "Maybe munching some peyote buds."

That got a laugh from Duarte's sidekick, quickly stifled by a glare. Price still saw no sign of a weapon on the second man, but Duarte's hand was twitching near his holster.

"You think this is funny, gringo?"

"I think you've got problems," answered Price. "But frankly, I don't give a damn."

"You should," Duarte said. "My problem is *your* problem now."

"You think?"

"Damned gringos come into our country, act like royalty, insult our women. In your arrogance, you think there'll be no consequence, no day of judgment."

"I was never much on Scripture," Price informed him. "But from where I stand, you'd be the one insulting Cesar's sister. And she isn't even here to watch you make a fool out of yourself."

Duarte hesitated, looking all around the clearing for Dolores. Price hoped she had reached the trees by now, that she would keep her word and go straight back to camp, instead of hatching some half-assed attempt to rescue him.

Duarte shouted at the night again. "Dolores!"

"She can't hear you, Rufio."

"Where is she, gringo?"

"Safe in bed, for all I know."

Price recognized Duarte's companion now. He was Mateo Alcazar, the same one who'd brought word of the supposed gold shipment, and the one whose accusation had resulted in a young man being hanged for treason to the cause. He didn't look so fierce and cunning in the moonlight, barely even steady on his feet, eyes darting rapidly from Price to Duarte while he clutched a flask of courage.

"It was a mistake for you to stay here," said Duarte.

"Maybe you should take that up with Cesar."

"He *believes* in you. His mind is clouded. I must show him that you're just another Yankee bandit, worthless to our people and the struggle."

"Think you're up to it?" Price asked.

"I'm not afraid of you, gringo!"

"Prove it."

II

Dolores Zapata felt as if she was trapped in a nightmare, one of those agonizing dreams where every move requires inhuman effort against hopeless resistance, while some hideous danger rushes closer, unhindered by any sort of obstacles. Time slowed to a crawl, while only her enemies seemed free to move at normal speed.

And it was nearly true, except time wasn't crawling. *She* was. Matthew Price had ordered her to flee the clearing, staying out of sight, and hurry back to camp. She would obey him, even though she'd rather stay and fight beside him, for she recognized that Price knew best in certain areas.

Like killing.

She had recognized Duarte's angry voice, though Price had pinned her down, prevented her from seeing Rufio or being seen by him. Her snail's-pace crawl across the clearing to the tree line was another part of Price's strategy. However foolish it might seem, he would deny that she was with him, thus preserving the honor she'd been on the verge of casting to the winds, even if it should cost his life.

That thought almost prevented her from going on, but then Dolores remembered the stories she'd heard about Price, his reckless courage and deadly marksmanship when he was outnumbered. If two dozen *federales* couldn't kill him, what hope did Rufio Duarte have?

She heard them talking, back and forth across the clearing, but her mind would not translate their words coherently. Her name was mentioned more than once, almost an epithet on Duarte's lips, but Dolores concentrated on holding her course through the ferns, proceeding slowly enough that their thrashing didn't betray her, yet covering ground all the time.

She had an urgent mission now, and nothing short of death would stop her from completing it.

There *would* be death tonight, she feared. As if the funeral before the feast was not enough for one day, now Duarte was determined to force a killing confrontation with Price for her sake. Dolores was convinced that she'd done nothing to encourage Rufio, certainly not to that extent, but guilt gnawed at her nonetheless. Tears stung her eyes and left tracks on her cheeks.

In front of her, some unseen creature slither-skittered through the ferns, retreating from her outstretched hand. Dolores grimaced, then forged on, less frightened of a hidden snake or scorpion than of the drama being acted out behind her, in the moonlight.

She must reach Cesar and tell him what was happening, beg him to intercede before it was too late. But first, she had to reach the trees, where she could rise and run back into camp.

Braced for the sound of gunfire, she was breathless by

the time she reached the tree line, as if she had run a mile instead of crawling thirty yards. The woodland shadows welcomed her, sheltered Dolores as she sprang erect, lifted her skirt knee-high for running, and began to race downhill.

Would Duarte hear her? The idea no longer worried her. If it distracted him from Price, so much the better. Let Duarte turn and chase Dolores back to camp, if that was what it took to halt the duel.

And failing that, don't let him win.

Dolores wasn't sure to whom she had addressed that plea. She didn't think God would concern Himself with gunfights spawned by common jealousy and spite. According to the padres, He allowed the massacre of helpless peasants for some reason simple men could never understand. Dolores guessed that was supposed to build her faith, but all it did was make her doubt the wisdom of the priests and Him they served.

It seemed like hours since she'd left the camp, following the trail to her secret glen in a perfect fever of excitement. Dolores felt as if the celebration should be finished and the fires damped down to glowing coals, but she could still see bright flames burning in the camp as she approached. Dolores fell once, tumbling head over heels, but she came out of the roll like an acrobat and ran on, desperately searching for her brother as she reached the settlement.

He wasn't hard to find, surrounded by well-wishers who ignored his silence, taking the occasional weary smile as assent to whatever they were saying. Dolores pushed past them and clutched Cesar's arm, spinning him around to face her.

"Cesar! You must come with me at once!"

"Dolores?" He squinted at her in the firelight, as if her face was unfamiliar to him. Cesar touched her forehead, near the hairline. She felt sudden pain and saw his fingers come back smeared with crimson. "What has happened to you?"

"What? Nothing! I fell. Come with me quickly!"

"Where?" he asked her. "Why?"

"Just follow me, for Mary's sake, before they kill each other!"

"Who?" Cesar demanded.

She was almost sobbing as she spoke the names.

"Matthew and Rufio. Now hurry, *please*!"

Moonlight was easy on the eyes, compared to high noon's glare. Price didn't need a hat to shield his eyes, yet he felt strangely underdressed without it, as if he was on a military post and his superior had caught him out of uniform. Still, it would make no difference in the end.

The gun was all that mattered now, and his ability to use it under pressure.

Price did not keep score on battles won. He had no running tabulation of the men he'd killed, although the number for his recent busy days was locked into his short-term memory. It didn't seem to him that one or two more bodies mattered greatly, but he had a fair idea that killing Rufio Duarte might stir up a hornet's nest.

Assuming he could get it done, that is.

He'd never seen Duarte fight, except the briefest glimpse with long guns in that morning's skirmish, and Price still wasn't sure if the Mexican had scored or missed with his critical shot. One way made him a lifesaver; the other, a mortal enemy. But whichever it was, Price meant to be the one who walked away from this showdown.

"Be sure you want to do this," he advised Duarte.

"Gringo, I will give you one more chance. Confess!"

"I don't see any padre's collar on your neck."

"Indeed! You can't claim sanctuary here. Admit the truth."

"And what would that be?"

"That Cesar Zapata welcomed you into his home, and you've betrayed him. That you treat his sister as you would a whore."

The near-miss truth of that stung Price, but he was not prepared to argue bedroom etiquette with someone bent on killing him.

"You've got a wild imagination, Rufio," he said. "You reckon Cesar will appreciate you spreading dirt like that?"

The question made Duarte hesitate, but only for an instant. "You don't fool me, gringo," he answered. "Cesar will forgive his sister, and he'll thank the man who helped preserve her honor."

"How's that work?" asked Price. "By calling her a whore?"

"Just tell me where she is, and you may live."

"I wouldn't if I could," Price told him. "But the truth is, I don't know."

"Then *die!*"

They drew together, and their two shots hammered back and forth across the clearing. Price was dead on target, but he hadn't counted on his target *moving*. More precisely, at the moment when he drew and fired his pistol, Duarte had leaped sideways, to his left, and dropped from sight amongst the waist-tall ferns.

The move had saved Duarte, but it also spoiled his shot. Price heard the bullet pass somewhere above him, to his left, while he was pivoting to cover Duarte's backup. This was when the second Mexican would pull a hideout gun, if it was coming, but Price saw him running for the trees, arms raised above his head with nothing but a flask in hand, and let him go.

With that decision made, Price dropped into a crouch that covered him from prying eyes. Ferns wouldn't stop a bullet, but at least he was on equal footing with Duarte now.

Price didn't move at first, waiting to see if his opponent would betray himself with careless noise. Strangely, however, though the clearing had seemed nearly silent while he huddled with Dolores—almost like a vacuum—now it was alive with whispers from the night breeze stirring tender fronds. For all Price knew, Duarte might be creeping toward him at that very moment, closing for the kill.

He moved, using sufficient caution that he didn't make a racket or beat down the ferns to leave a trail. This wasn't Price's style of fighting, but survival instincts helped him to adapt. He wouldn't risk a shot unless he had a target, and until that happened—

Duarte seemed to read his mind. The thought had barely formed in Price's head before a shot exploded and a bullet sizzled through the ferns, off to his right. It wasn't placed exactly where he'd been a moment earlier, but it came close enough to let Price know he wasn't dealing with some greenhorn who could barely load his gun.

Careful, he thought. This was a game that only one shooter could win, but both could lose. He'd seen contests where the combatants took each other out and left an empty field, but futile gestures weren't his style.

If there was trouble waiting for him with Zapata, Price would face it in due time. But first, he had to walk out of the clearing with his life.

•　•　•

Cesar Zapata didn't know exactly what was happening, except that it involved Dolores, Rufio Duarte, and Matt Price. Zapata's first glimpse of his sister in the firelight had been shocking, with her face tear-streaked, blood leaking from a scalp wound, and her blouse torn on one side, across her breast. Protective instincts flared at his first sight of her and swiftly turned to rage, but for the moment it was rage without direction.

He had balked in camp, demanding to know how she'd injured herself before he would move from the spot where she'd found him. "I fell running back," she replied. "Now please hurry, for God's sake!"

There'd been no time to ask her where she had been running *from*, or *why*, before Zapata let her drag him toward the forest. He couldn't deny her urgency and knew, despite his frequent teasing, that Dolores wasn't one to manufacture crises in a bid for personal attention. If she said that Rufio and Matt were at each other's throats, Zapata took her at her word.

But why?

He leaped to the most logical conclusion, and it didn't help his mood. If Matt and Rufio were fighting, and Dolores knew about it—if she'd been a witness to it—then Zapata knew the most likely source of their quarrel. It wasn't unheard of in camp, a blood feud over sex, but for all his worldly realism, it still galled Zapata to think of his sister as any man's plaything.

He still didn't know her part in the trouble, which man she had chosen—if either—and there was no time to ask as they ran through the trees, pursuing a trail strange to him. The first gunshots rang out moments later, spurring Zapata on to greater speed, making him wish he'd brought more men along to help.

For all the drama of her entry to the camp, Dolores hadn't raised a great commotion. There'd been no shouting or histrionics, simply urgent words exchanged and help demanded from her brother. The three comrades whom he'd been speaking with when she arrived were following Zapata now, but otherwise his exit from the camp had gone largely unnoticed.

Not for long, he thought.

The gunfire would be heard in camp, though not immediately placed as to its source. Someone would try to find him, and when that failed, someone else would probably remember that they'd seen him running off into the woods, after Dolores. How long would it take to organize and arm a search party?

Too long, if Rufio and Matt were truly bent on killing one another.

Duarte had despised Price from the moment he arrived in camp, Zapata knew. It hadn't been a secret. Every look and every word he spoke, to or about Price, had betrayed Duarte's enmity. At first, Zapata had supposed it was a case of simple jealousy, arising from the adulation Price received for spiriting Zapata out of prison and for gunning down so many *federales.* Now, he saw, there had been more behind Duarte's festering dislike for Price than simple damage to Duarte's reputation as a warrior.

Women, Zapata thought. They were the blessing of a soldier's life, and yet the bane of a commander's.

But when had Dolores become one?

He called her a baby, to taunt her, but others had seen he was wrong. How many others? Zapata couldn't face that question at the moment. It was foreign territory, fraught with pitfalls, and he had enough trouble to deal with at the moment in his own backyard.

Where *were* they, damn it?

Gunfire helped renew his focus, and Dolores seemed to know where they were going, even though the trail was unfamiliar to Zapata. He blamed that on the darkness, stubbornly refusing to believe that he could occupy the same site for a year or more without knowing its every yard of ground by heart.

There had to be a limit to his blindness, after all, or he would be unfit to lead.

"How far?" he asked Dolores, feeling nearly out of breath.

"Not far," she answered. "Hurry!"

Duarte had expended four rounds from his six-shooter, but there'd been ample time for reloading between his wild shots. Price strained his ears, hoping to hear the metallic sounds of a revolver's extractor rod or fresh shells sliding home inside the cylinder, anything to mark Duarte's position, but the night breeze and rustling ferns cheated him.

He knew more or less where Duarte had been when he squeezed off each shot, but close didn't count in a gunfight and the Mexican wisely kept moving. Muzzle-flashes would've marked a target Price could use, but sound alone was treacherous, particularly in the darkened echo chamber of a forest clearing, where each new blast in turn reverberated from surrounding trees.

Price had to flush his adversary out into the moonlight for a killing shot, but how? If they'd been creeping through dry grass instead of fresh, moist ferns, he might've set a fire—and it might just as easily have blown back in his face. Creeping around the glade was a colossal waste of time and energy; the odds of Price meeting Duarte accidentally were virtually nil.

But what was left for him to try?

He could stand up and make a target of himself, but that would only get him killed.

Unless . . .

If he could shave the risk to an acceptable degree, while tempting Duarte to reveal himself, it just might work. One glimpse, one pistol flash, was all he needed now.

And if he failed . . . so what?

Price hadn't planned on finishing his life in Mexico, but the plain truth was that he hadn't planned much of anything since Mary Hudson's death in Texas. Revenge had consumed him at first, but only yawning emptiness remained when he had paid that bloody debt. If he died here, what difference did it really make?

Dolores.

Price shrugged off that fantasy. He knew there'd be no picket fence or cactus garden in his future. That had been ordained the first time he strapped on a gun and stepped into the street to face another man. Shooters took lives; they didn't build them.

So it was, so it would always be.

Amen.

But if he had a chance to walk away this time, why not?

Duarte's fifth shot settled the debate. It missed by thirty feet or more, but it gave Price a general fix on the man and told him something about Duarte's preparation. The Mexican was either down to one shot now, or he'd reloaded and was one down on his second six. Whichever, Price was ready with a full cylinder, and he knew there'd never be a better time to try his plan.

He bolted upright, hesitating for a heartbeat as the

moonlight found his face, then started running east to west across the clearing. There was no stealth to it, quite the opposite in fact. Price wanted Duarte to think he was spooked beyond reason and running for cover. It was the only way to bring him out of hiding and give Price a shot.

If it worked.

Price couldn't watch the whole clearing at once, so he focused on the quadrant where he thought Duarte's last shot had originated. If he was mistaken, it could cost his life. Hell, even if he had it right, the next shot Duarte fired might bring him down. If he—

The muzzle-flash was closer than expected, flaring like a short-lived red-orange blossom in the moonlight, there and gone. Price heard the bullet crackle past his head and felt its passage on his nape.

That close.

There might've been another, but he fanned two rapid shots into the darkness where the flash had marked his target. At the same time, he pitched forward, dropping underneath Duarte's line of sight. Price didn't try to crawl beyond the point where he had fallen, dreading any further noise now that he knew his would-be killer was so close at hand.

Instead of further shots, though, what Price heard out of the darkness was a gasping, wheezing sound. He recognized a lung shot without seeing it and knew he'd gotten lucky. Duarte wasn't dead yet, but unless there was a surgeon stashed in camp Price didn't know about, his adversary wouldn't see another sunrise.

Duarte must've known it too. Price heard him scuffling to his feet, an awkward effort, and he called out to the night, "Gringo! I think you've killed me. Why not be a man and finish it?"

It was a fair question, but Price was disinclined to answer, since his voice would offer Duarte a target. Instead, he rolled away—slowly, gently, letting the breeze wipe out his tracks—until he reached a point some thirty feet to Duarte's left.

It wasn't perfect, but it could've been a great deal worse. Price could've been the one lung-shot and dying on his feet, instead of crouching in the dark with four live rounds still left in his six-shooter.

How many did Duarte have, and how well could he use them?

Let's find out.

"Where are you, gringo?"

Price rose silently, repeating what he'd told Duarte at the start. "Right here."

Duarte spun to face him, almost losing balance, but he didn't have a prayer. Price shot him in the chest and watched him drop, thrashing the ferns a bit before he shivered out and finally lay still.

Behind him, breathless from the run, he heard Dolores call his name.

Dolores saw Rufio spin to face Price, clutching his chest with one hand as he turned. The blood on his fingers was jet-black by moonlight. Before she could enter the clearing, flame burst from the muzzle of Matthew's revolver, followed by a thunderclap that hammered Duarte to the ground.

Dolores felt as if the bullet had been aimed at her. She couldn't breathe, felt suddenly light-headed, as if she was on the verge of losing consciousness. One slender arm outstretched, she braced herself against the nearest tree, holding her rib cage with the other hand almost as Rufio had done. It seemed amazing to Dolores that her heart still beat inside her, that she was alive.

The moment passed as Cesar and the other men surged past her, trampling the ferns to reach Duarte's body. He was dead, of course. Dolores didn't need to hear Cesar pronounce the words as he rose from the corpse. The others hadn't drawn their weapons yet, but they were facing Matthew in a semicircle, screening Cesar with their bodies. Price still had the pistol ready in his hand.

"You've killed my oldest friend," Cesar told Price. His voice cracked as he spoke.

"In self-defense," Price said, "if that means anything."

"You say he came for you?"

"That's right."

"He came for *us*," Dolores interjected, stepping up to join the men.

"Dolores—"

"No, Matthew. It is the truth," she said. "Cesar, Rufio followed us from camp. He tried to kill Matthew from jealousy. I think he would have killed me too."

Cesar brushed past his men. The others seemed confused now, lost somewhere between anger and surprise, though none of them let fingers stray far from their guns. As for Cesar, he demonstrated no confusion. There was only anger on his face as he confronted Price.

"You brought my sister here? How did you even find this place?"

"It's *my* place," said Dolores as she stepped between them. "*I* brought *him*, Cesar."

"I don't believe you. You are—"

"What?" she challenged, interrupting him. "A child? Wake up, Cesar."

Zapata recoiled from her as if she'd slapped his face.

Her heart went out to him, but still Dolores stood her ground. Cesar spoke past her, to Matthew. "You say Rufio called you out?"

"He called and drew," said Matthew. "I suppose you heard the shooting, on your way up from the camp."

"Sounds don't say who shot first. Dolores, did you see Rufio draw his pistol?"

She was ready with the lie, but Matthew cut her off. "She didn't see it," he replied.

"Then," Cesar said, "we only have your word for who drew first."

"Or you could ask the fellow who was with him," Matthew said.

Dolores blinked at that. It was her turn to be surprised. She hadn't seen a second man, heard only Rufio and Matthew as they quarreled.

"Who else was here?" Cesar inquired.

"I didn't catch his name, but he was with us on the ride last night. You picked him out to guide the villagers back here, if you recall."

Cesar frowned and said, "Mateo Alcazar."

Behind Dolores, Matthew said, "That rings a bell."

More people were arriving in the clearing now, perhaps two dozen in a group, with more coming along behind them. Dolores wished them away, but she had no magic powers. It saddened her to have her secret place exposed and trampled, stained with blood. Now it was lost to her forever, and she wouldn't even have the memories she'd planned to make with Matthew in the moonlight.

She faced her brother squarely. "So, you see? It wasn't Matthew's fault."

"I'll soon find out." To those who'd followed him from camp initially, Cesar said, "Find Mateo Alcazar. Quickly!"

"*Sí, Jéfé.*"

Dolores watched the three shove past the new arrivals, while Cesar chose more at random, ordering that Rufio be carried back to camp.

"Let's all go back," he said at last, "and find out what Mateo has to say."

The trial was short, as such things went. Price was a bit surprised when Alcazar admitted what he'd seen. He'd half-expected that the Mexican might cook up a story against him, but Alcazar told it straight, relating how Duarte had picked him out to follow Price from camp, and how he hadn't seen Dolores in the clearing.

"What? She wasn't there?" Zapata pinned his sister with a glare.

"I *was*," she countered from the sidelines, "but he couldn't see me. I was lying on the ground."

That didn't help Zapata find his smile, but it sent murmurs rippling through their audience. "Go on," Zapata growled at Alcazar.

The rest was simply told. Duarte's challenge, the response from Price. When they slapped leather, Alcazar— armed only with a flask—had hightailed back to camp.

"You didn't come to me," Zapata said, his tone accusatory.

"No, *Jéfé*, I'm sorry. It was an affair of honor. Private business, I supposed."

"You were mistaken." Angrily, Zapata raised his voice to make it heard throughout the camp. "There is no private killing here! The *federales* take enough of us al-

ready. If we turn upon ourselves, there'll soon be nothing
left!"

Another murmur from the crowd, this one agreeing with
their leader. Price stayed quiet, waiting for the verdict. If it
went against him, should he use his pistol? Where would he
begin?

Turning to Price, grim-faced, Zapata said, "I find no
fault with you for killing Rufio. He should've come to me
with his concerns about Dolores, but he challenged you instead. The fight was fair."

Price stood and waited for the rest. Somehow, he knew
Zapata wasn't finished yet.

"That said, I've lost my oldest friend and second in command. The struggle has one less warrior tonight, because of
Rufio's mistake. I don't know yet who will replace him, or
if anyone is worthy. Go to bed," he told the crowd. "There's
no more cause for celebration here."

Price waited, sensing the dismissal wasn't meant for
him. Zapata would have more to say, words meant for him
alone. Dolores lingered with them, as the others drifted off
to tents and bedrolls.

When they were alone, Zapata said, "Dolores, I'm aware
that you are not a child. You've grown into a woman while
I played war games."

"Cesar—"

"You've grown to be a woman and you're free to make
your own decisions, but I still command this place. I won't
permit you to become a laughingstock before my very eyes
and thereby weaken my authority."

"Cesar, what are you saying?"

"You must go, Dolores. In the morning, I'll arrange an
escort. You'll be taken to the convent at El Salto."

"*Convent?* Have you lost your mind? I won't become a nun!"

"Dolores, it's a convent, not a prison. If you choose to leave at any time, you're free to make your own way in the world. You simply can't stay here."

"It's exile then. Is that your answer?"

"You'll be well protected at El Salto, if you choose to stay. With any luck, the struggle may be over soon."

Zapata didn't sound convinced, and Price could see Dolores wasn't buying it. "Exile," she said again. "For what? Because I love a man?"

"Ah, love." Zapata turned to Price. "Is that what you feel for my sister, Matt?"

Price saw already where the lie would lead, as certain as tomorrow's dawn. "I didn't come here looking for a wife," he said.

"But have you found one?"

Dolores watched him, hope and hurting mingled in her eyes. He thought of Belle and Mary, knowing there could only be one answer for the life he led.

"No," Price said. "I haven't."

"Then it's settled. Go to bed, Dolores. You need rest before tomorrow's ride."

She turned and fled, sobbing. Price reckoned that he'd taken one more step toward Hell. "I'll be away by dawn," he told Zapata. "You don't need to worry that I'll follow her."

"Go if you must," Zapata said. "But if you should decide to stay . . ."

"Is that an option?" Price inquired.

Zapata heaved a weary sigh. "Rufio was . . . well, Rufio. His passion was extreme in all respects and sometimes overshadowed logic. I'm as much to blame as anyone,

Matthew. I knew or should have known the way he felt about Dolores. What I didn't see in time was her feeling for you."

"For what it's worth, Cesar, we only kissed."

"I take your word for that," Zapata said. "If I thought you were lying, I'd kill you."

12

Breakfast was sparse and hasty Thursday morning, as if all the folk in camp had lost their appetites. Price figured some of them had hangovers, but most wore somber faces without wincing at the slightest sound or cringing from daylight. Some of the somber looks were aimed his way, but overall, Price didn't feel as much hostility as he'd expected from Zapata's people.

And he wondered why.

As far as Price could tell, Duarte hadn't been despised by anybody in particular, yet no one really seemed to blame Price for his death. Their story would've made the rounds last night, he guessed, before most of the campers fell asleep, and maybe they'd decided that Duarte brought the end upon himself.

Or maybe they were simply used to violent death.

The solemn atmosphere, Price finally decided, was primarily about Dolores, rather than the prior night's fireworks. When she left her tent, a little after sunrise, there were older women lined up waiting with advice, religious medals, various keepsakes. Dolores smiled, accepting each in turn, until Price was reminded of a queen blessing her subjects.

He had fallen asleep around three in the morning, still undecided about his next move. Whatever it turned out to be, Price was keeping his word. He wouldn't trail Dolores or attempt to stay in touch with her. Last night had served to verify one of his darkest fears.

A gunfighter's affection was the kiss of death.

So what?

He'd done all right so far, riding a lonesome road, and if some people didn't call that living, what did they know? Burdened with their spouses, children, homes, and daily jobs that didn't smell of dust or gun smoke—who were they to judge a rootless vagabond, whose best friends in Creation were his horse and the Peacemaker on his hip?

Price watched Dolores make a circuit of the camp, moving away from him. He reckoned that was for the best, since he'd prepared no speech and didn't have a parting gift to offer. It was likely she despised him anyway, after he'd given Cesar the wrong answer to the marriage question, and he figured that was also for the best. There'd be no yearning, in that case, for some imaginary future that could never be. She'd hate him for a while and then forget him, move on with her life to find a calling or a man who wouldn't come to her with bloody hands.

All for the best.

But what about the rest of it?

Zapata had offered him Duarte's position, second in command, but Price hadn't come into camp seeking a cause, any more than he'd come seeking a wife. He sympathized with the oppressed, had risked his life and spilled the blood of enemies on their behalf, but they would never truly be *his* people. Duarte had been absolutely right on that score anyway.

Price was a gringo. An outsider. Even in his homeland, he had been a misfit, better on his own than in the company of others. Price knew that he had no business telling Mexicans or anybody else to risk their lives for causes that he barely understood.

He had no trouble killing *federales,* granted. Several weeks ago, a troop of them had tried to execute him for another shooter's crime, and no encounter since that time had altered his opinion of the brutal, thieving types who served El Presidente. Still, that didn't make him a revolutionary.

He was just another shooter with a grudge.

It should've been an easy thing for him to leave, and yet . . .

Dolores had nearly finished her slow walking tour of the camp. Tracing the path in front of her, Price saw her brother waiting with four other men, all holding horses by their reins. The animals were saddled, loaded up with trail gear. Three of the selected escorts Price knew only slightly from the camp.

The fourth man was Mateo Alcazar.

Price frowned at that, nearly got up to ask Cesar what he was thinking, but he didn't make the move. These were Zapata's people, and he had no right to second-guess the leader's call.

If I was second in command . . .

He thought about it, watching as the others helped Dolores mount her horse. Her skirt got in the way a bit, but still she didn't ride sidesaddle. Price guessed that she could keep up with the boys, if there was any hard riding ahead, but he wished them a carefree trip and hoped El Salto wouldn't be too hard for her to take.

A convent didn't suit her, but Price had nothing better to offer. If any trace of God remained in such places, maybe He would help Dolores find the life she wanted and deserved.

Or maybe it was all just make-believe.

Price watched the other riders mount, a brief exchange between Dolores and her brother. Cesar shook his head emphatically and led the small procession toward the canyon's narrow exit. Almost out of sight, Dolores turned for one last look at Price across the camp.

Her eyes glimmered, whether with tears or anger, Price couldn't have said to save his life.

Dolores scarcely felt the sun's heat or the animal beneath her as her party crossed the desert, following a rough southeastern course. El Salto was a full day's ride from camp. It would be dark before they reached the settlement, unless they camped tonight and pushed on in the morning.

Either way, Dolores didn't care.

She had been numb throughout the sleepless night, surprising herself when the first rush of tears gave way to a hollow, dead feeling inside. Duarte's death was part of it, she supposed, though in truth she hardly missed him at all. The wounds that bled her dry had been inflicted by her brother and Matt Price. Rejection by her almost-lover was the first cut, deep and deadly. It had torn her heart, leaving her soul exposed for all to see and mock. Cesar had finished it, his banishment order severing her last family ties and condemning her to solitary exile.

That was justice in a man's world, she supposed.

Long live the revolution!

Her sudden, bitter laughter surprised Tomas Ochoa, riding beside her on the dusty trail. Ahead of them, Pepe Esparza and Fabian Muñoz had the point, while Mateo Alcazar brought up the rear.

"Are you all right, Señorita?"

"You've known me half my life, Tomas. Please call me Dolores."

"*Sí*, Señorita Dolores. I have water, if you want some."

"I have water too. I'm very well equipped for going out alone into the world."

"You're not alone," Ochoa said. "Your brother wouldn't do that."

"Wouldn't he?"

"He's worried and upset, that's all. About Rufio and the gringo. Give him time. When things are back to normal, he will bring you home again."

"Normal?" Dolores almost laughed again. "I don't know what that even means. Can you explain it to me, Tomas?"

"Normal," he told her, "is how things were meant to be. Some men are born to do great things, while others scratch the soil. Your brother has the mark of greatness on him, Señorita."

"Cesar?"

"You don't see it because you're too close, and you have the same blood. There is greatness in you too, I think."

"Now you're just being foolish."

"Perhaps. But I knew from the first time I saw your brother, heard him speak before a dozen families at Tepehuanes, that he could be great. His name's already known outside Durango. Someday he'll be known in all of Mexico."

"No doubt for being shot or hanged."

"We all die in the end," Ochoa said. "It's what we do with life that matters."

"All this time, Tomas, I never knew that you were a philosopher."

Ochoa blushed, smiled warmly—then pitched forward, tumbling from his saddle with a grunt of stunned surprise. Dolores heard the shot a fraction of a second later, turning in her saddle toward the sound.

Mateo Alcazar was leveling his rifle for another shot, squinting along its barrel from the shadow of his wide-brimmed hat. At first, Dolores thought he meant to kill her too, but then she realized that he was aiming past her, toward the point where Fabian and Pepe were reacting to the first explosive sound.

She hadn't known that Alcazar could fire so rapidly or with such accuracy. Truth be told, she'd rarely given him a thought at all. Now, as she watched dumbfounded, he shot Pepe from the charging roan and swung his piece around to cover Fabian, pumping the lever-action, squeezing off a third and final shot.

Mateo was beside her in another moment, even as Dolores tried to flee. He grabbed her reins with one hand, while the other brought the rifle down to prod her ribs, beneath her breast.

"So clever, these three and your brother," he declared. "Thinking I wouldn't know they planned to kill me on the trail."

"Are you insane? Why would they—"

"Never mind!" snapped Alcazar. "I see and hear more than they think. This time, I change the rules and it's *my* game."

Dolores realized that she'd been wrong as they were riding out of camp that morning. She had thought her life could get no worse, but that was a mistake. Instead of being exiled to a convent, she'd become a madman's hostage, caught up in his homicidal fantasy. She feared that it would be the death of her, and there was no one left to help.

"We're going for a little ride," said Alcazar, smiling. "Relax, Princess. You may enjoy it, after all."

"Your brother thinks I'm foolish, Señorita. He mistakes me for a sheep who'll go to slaughter without fighting back. Today he'll learn how very wrong he is."

Mateo Alcazar was smiling as he spoke, guiding his horse northeastward. The rope around the woman's waist, secured to his saddle horn, prevented her from fleeing. That, and the conviction that he'd kill her in a heartbeat, rather than allow her to escape.

Her voice was tentative. "You wouldn't let me ask before . . ."

"Ask now."

"Why do you think Cesar would wish you dead?"

"It isn't what I *think*," he sneered. "It's not some *fantasy*. I saw him talking to the others."

"Others?"

Alcazar felt his impatience mounting with the desert temperature. "The *others*, Señorita. Pepe. Fabian. Tomas."

The men he'd just killed.

"You *saw* them talking? Did you hear what they were saying?"

"I don't need to hear it," he replied. "Why would your brother meet with three of them and leave me out, unless he had some message I wasn't supposed to hear? What would that be, do you suppose? It's not my birthday, Señorita. No surprise party for old Mateo."

"But I still don't understand," she said. "You've been with Cesar a long time. Why would he want to kill you now?"

His shrug was an extension of his horse's rolling gait. "He knows about me, I suppose." The crooked smile came back. "It took him long enough."

"What does he know, Mateo?"

"Are we down to first names now, *Dolores*? Maybe you prefer a forceful man. God knows you haven't spoken to me in the past two years, except in serving lines."

She couldn't answer that. It was the truth. Instead, she asked again, "What does my brother know? What have you . . ."

When she stopped there, in mid-sentence, Alcazar knew she had worked it out. "You're quicker than Cesar," he said. "Of course, you had the hints."

"You're a traitor!" she spit.

"I'm a realist, Dolores. I support the winning side."

She tried another tack. "Cesar will listen, if you talk to him."

"Ah, yes. The way he listened to Juanito Vega, I suppose."

"But you accused Juanito?"

"What was I to do? I was afraid he might have seen me with . . . my contact. As it turned out, he knew nothing, but I couldn't take the risk."

"You let him die."

"Was I supposed to plead his case? Who would believe it? Better him than me."

"You bastard!"

"Sticks and stones." He feinted with the rifle, jabbing it toward her face, and snickered when she flinched away from him. "See what I mean? Besides, I didn't hang

Juanito. Duarte and your brother wanted blood. They wanted an example for the others."

"Traitors die," she said.

"Not always. Some grow fat and prosper. Have you met the governor? El Presidente?"

"It says much about you that you rank yourself with them."

"I told you, I support the winning side."

"And when they lose, you'll stand with them against the wall."

"Perhaps. Or maybe I'll just fade away."

"When Cesar understands your treachery, there won't be anywhere to hide."

"You overestimate your brother's influence, Dolores. He's a tadpole in a tiny pond. Soon, he'll be swallowed by much bigger fish."

"And I suppose that you'll be leading them?"

"Not leading," he replied. "Advising them perhaps. Guiding."

"You would betray your friends and countrymen—for what, Mateo? How much do the *federales* pay you?"

"We negotiate, Dolores. I suspect you'll bring a decent price."

"What do you mean?"

"Exactly what you *think* I mean," he answered. "Cesar took the bait for fairy gold. What would he do to keep his only sister out of prison?"

"Nothing! He won't be that foolish."

"Maybe not. It's true that you and Rufio left him in San Filipe, where the *federales* would've hanged him. Maybe he'll remember that and say good riddance, but I doubt it. I think he's a gentleman."

"Where are you taking me?" she asked.

"To meet my friends. We should be there sometime to-morrow morning. In the meantime . . ."

"What?" She sounded frightened now. He liked it.

"They won't mind if you've been used a bit. It might even give them ideas."

Dolores bolted then, but Alcazar kept a firm grip on his animal and braced against the jolt. When it came, Dolores squealed and vaulted backward from her saddle, tumbling painfully to earth. Her horse kept running, trailing dust behind it as it fled.

"I guess you walk from here," said Alcazar. "Or I can drag you. Either way."

Slowly, as if each movement caused her pain, Dolores struggled to her feet. She wiped dust from her face but didn't bother with her clothes.

"I hate you," she informed him.

"I don't mind. To me, it's all the same."

"You're nothing but a pig."

"You'll be my sow. Let's find a sty."

He spurred his horse to a canter, forcing Dolores to run. After a hundred yards or so, she fell. He dragged her then, another few minutes, until she begged for him to stop.

"What is it now?" he asked.

"I need . . . I need. . . ."

"Your needs will all be met, Dolores." Squinting in the glare, he found what he'd been looking for. "I see a place where we can stop and take our midday meal, Dolores. Water, shade, a little rest."

"Please, I . . ."

"See, we're making progress. You can work on 'thank you' in a little while. Now, on your feet! We're wasting time."

•   •   •

Sergeant Hector Rodriguez was nearly convinced Lieutenant Cruz had given him a hopeless task. He'd taken his patrol back to the ambush site, found wagon tracks, and followed them as best he could—until they disappeared on rocky ground. It was a guessing game from that point onward, and he'd never been much good at puzzles, even as a child.

Still, his orders were explicit, unequivocal. He could not return without the wagon and its contents, preferably with the bodies of the men who'd stolen it. Lieutenant Cruz was crystal-clear in that respect.

"I don't care if it takes a week or the rest of your life."

And it very well might, Rodriguez thought, at the rate they were going. Having lost the wagon's tracks while riding southward, he'd sent scouts in three directions—south, east, west—to look for any further traces of its passage. They'd returned at dusk with nothing to report, closing the first day wasted on his quest. Their camp was cold and cheerless, beans and salty biscuits, with coyotes howling in the night.

Sunrise comes early in the desert, and they'd wasted little time on breakfast. While the coffee brewed, Rodriguez lectured them again on what he knew. A wagon filled with weapons couldn't simply disappear. It couldn't levitate. There must be signs to follow, if they used their eyes and wits. Incentive was the key, and he reminded them that there would be no more tequila, no *muchachas,* nothing but the long dry search until they found what they were seeking. Then, and only then, were they permitted to go home.

"What if we never find it?" asked a private named Rapalo.

Rodriguez answered with a question of his own. "How many biscuits did you bring?"

"We can't work miracles," the youngster said.

"Not sitting on your ass and whining anyway. Forget the coffee," said Rodriguez. "We're already late."

They searched with no particular design in mind. Because the wagon had initially gone southward from the skirmish site, Rodriguez was inclined to carry on in that direction. There were hiding places in the mountains to the east, he knew, but searching them would literally take forever, and it offered little prospect of success. Westward, meanwhile, the bandits were more likely to encounter government patrols, and there was no real sanctuary in the desert.

Southward then, while hoping for the best.

And if they couldn't find the wagon, if it simply wasn't possible—what then? Rodriguez didn't plan to search indefinitely, endlessly. That would be madness.

But he'd need a good excuse for quitting, if he meant to go back empty-handed and avoid a court-martial. It wasn't just his stripes at stake if he defied Lieutenant Cruz.

It might just be his life.

The others would support whatever he decided, if it got them safely back to quarters, but the lie had to be plausible. More to the point, Rodriguez would need something in the way of evidence. He couldn't simply say the wagon had plunged into a ravine and was destroyed. Cruz would demand to see the wreckage, and he still might want the guns.

If they were ambushed by the rebels, if they suffered casualties . . .

No good. They couldn't very well draw lots to see who'd take a bullet for the squad. The losers might regret it afterward and carry tales.

So, something else—but what?

Rodriguez saw the clump of trees ahead, a rare oasis in

the middle of the wasteland. They could use a bit of shade, a chance to rest, perhaps refill canteens and sketch the outline of a story that would get them off the hook. It might require another day or two of searching, for the sake of credibility, but still—

The first scream could've been a hawk swooping for prey, but when it came a second time Rodriguez recognized a woman's voice. He also understood that it had emanated from the trees. Spurring his horse, he led the squad at full gallop across the dry, flat land, anxious for something—anything—to leaven the monotony of their pursuit.

Rodriguez saw the horse first, tethered to a tree and cropping meager grass around the twisted roots. A moment later, he could see two wrestlers grappling, man on top, slapping the woman, tearing at her clothes. Closer, he caught a flash of bare breasts as the woman fought to free herself.

The rapist was so focused on his mission that he didn't seem to hear the riders coming up behind him. Only when Rodriguez shouted at him, brandishing his pistol, did the man step back and face them with a vague, bewildered look upon his face. An instant later, he was smiling, as if they were long-lost friends.

"Welcome!" he said, beaming. "I hoped we'd find you soon."

Pepe Esparza woke to the insistent pain of something tugging at his flesh, and struck out blindly through a gauzy veil of delirium. His hand struck something dry yet pliable, reminding him of dead leaves in the autumn, but these leaves had ungodly squawking voices that berated him in some language he couldn't translate. Stranger still, if such things could be quantified, the raucous voices came from different sides, as if he was surrounded.

It cost him greatly to sit upright, but he managed. Barely. One eye opened on command; the other had been plastered shut by drainage from a scalp wound suffered when he fell. One eye was plenty, though, to see the vultures waddling in a circle just beyond his reach, hissing insults and imprecations at their uncooperative meal.

Lie down, they seemed to say. *Relax. Give up.*

They got no argument from Fabian or Tomas, stretched out where they'd fallen when the bastard Alcazar had opened fire without warning. As hazy as his mind was, still Esparza knew there was a body missing. Vultures were not large or strong enough to carry it away.

Where is Dolores?

Gone.

With Alcazar?

Esparza couldn't answer that one, but he knew what he must do. He had to tell Cesar.

But first, he had to stand.

It sounded easy, but it wasn't. When he struggled to all fours, the pain nearly defeated him right there. He held that pose for what seemed hours, trembling on hands and knees, while vultures watched and mocked his puny effort. Twenty feet away, more hungry birds were squabbling over tasty bits of Fabian, torn from his chest and face.

Esparza fought the pull of gravity and watched blood dribbling from his wounded side, into the dust. All things considered, he'd been lucky. Alcazar had fired in haste, still killing twice out of three shots, and there'd been no time wasted making sure of number three. The fall had knocked Pepe unconscious, thus contributing to the illusion while allowing Alcazar to take Dolores unopposed.

Esparza knew he would die here, and soon, unless he managed to get up and walk. There was no mystery about it, no magic required—simply an effort that would torture him like nothing in his life before.

Be quick about it then.

Calling upon reserves of strength he hadn't been aware that he possessed, Esparza pushed off from the dusty, blood-splotched ground, raised one knee to support himself, and rode the wave of agony until it buoyed him upright. Perhaps he screamed, or maybe it was just the surge of motion that dispersed his croaking audience. He staggered, nearly fell, but with his arms spread like a tightrope walker, he was able to maintain his balance.

Now, if he could just remember how to walk and choose the right direction, he'd be on his way.

There'd be no riding, damn it. Pepe didn't know if Alcazar had made off with their horses, or if they had simply fled the sounds of gunfire, but it made no difference. He would be walking back to camp, however far that was, if he could find the way.

The sheer absurdity of his position made Esparza laugh, a rasping sound the vultures might have taken as a greeting, for a couple of them answered him. That struck him as funny too, despite the fact that laughing drove a jagged lance of pain between his ribs. At least he wasn't gargling blood, like men he'd seen with punctured lungs, and he was capable of forward motion, even if his feet seemed to be made of lead.

Esparza risked losing his balance for a glimpse of the relentless sun, and found it had moved well past noon. That gave him compass points, and after he retrieved his crumpled hat—an exercise of startling difficulty in his present circumstances—he started shuffling westward, toward the mountains.

Trying not to think about how many miles they'd covered, riding out from camp.

Two hours, two years later, shuffling toward the skyline that retreated at a pace matching his own, Esparza heard a sound that struck him as familiar. A kind of huffing sound behind him, much like an exasperated sigh. Had the damned vultures followed him, dissatisfied with feasting on his friends?

Drawing his pistol from its holster, Pepe turned—and saw his piebald gelding trailing fifty feet behind him.

It was only then that he began to weep.

A somber day was ending in Zapata's camp, and Price took it to be his last amongst the rebels. He had given ample thought to the inducements that Zapata offered him, but he saw no advantage for himself in risking life and limb to win a future that he couldn't share.

Whatever lay in store for Mexico, however long he tarried there, it was not and would never be his home.

For once, he didn't play the old familiar mind game with himself, dissecting and translating "home" as if it was the key word in some ancient magic scroll, seeking its latitude and longitude. He was a foreigner in Mexico and always would be. For the moment, that was all Price had to know.

He would be leaving in the morning, but he hadn't told Zapata yet. There wouldn't be much argument about it, he supposed. Zapata had already made his case, and Price rejected it. He supposed the others would be relieved to see him go. It was a feeling he'd experienced in towns on both sides of the Rio Grande, a silent send-off that did not so much offend as sadden him.

He was the man who brightened any room by leaving it. Plain folk stepped wide around him, as if fearing contact with his shadow. It was different here—or had been, to a point—but he'd worn out his welcome and the road was waiting for him, leading who knows where.

He didn't think about Dolores more than once in every other minute, all day long.

Too late.

Burnt bridges were his specialty.

One of the widows from Sangre de Maria came around at dusk with food she had prepared for Price. The gesture took him by surprise and made him wonder what produced such people. Stripped of damn near everything they owned, robbed even of their family and loved ones, they still seemed to think of others first.

Price knew about the losing part, though it was different in his case. He'd run from home and family, instead of losing it to raiders or some natural disaster. Ever since that day, the friends he'd made were transitory and to some degree expendable. His chosen life demanded that he travel light, in terms of both possessions and entanglements. A friend was here today and dead tomorrow. Lovers looked too close and saw the death mask he was wearing underneath.

He'd nearly cleaned his plate, and it was almost dark, when some excitement on the far side of the camp drew his attention. From the tone and general direction of raised voices, Price knew that some unexpected visitor had passed inspection by the sentries and was on his way to join them. Reckoning that it would be no one he knew, nothing to do with him, Price kept his seat and finished with his meal.

Five minutes later, bulling through the crowd, Cesar

Zapata called his name. Price didn't go to meet him, knew he'd already been seen, but Cesar's agitation brought him to his feet.

"What's happening?" he asked.

"Pepe Esparza just came back," Zapata said.

"Don't know the man."

"I sent him with Dolores, to El Salto."

"And he's back already?"

"Wounded," said Zapata. "Close to death maybe. It's Alcazar. He shot the others, Matt, and took Dolores."

13

The day was going rapidly from bad to worse. That morning, exile from her brother's camp had been the worst torture Dolores could envision. Hours later, that had paled beside the murder of her friends and her abduction by Mateo Alcazar. His plan to rape her had been interrupted, but she wasn't saved. Indeed, Dolores thought she might be worse off with the *federales* than with Alcazar alone.

If it had only been Mateo, she imagined that she could've fended off his crude assault somehow. Or failing that, she might've lulled him into thinking that she liked it, waited for him to relax his guard, and killed him while he slept. The *federales,* though, were less concerned about her body—pleased to look, but under orders not to touch— than her potential value in their war against her brother.

Now I've hurt him twice, she thought. *Will this time cost his life?*

Dolores hadn't studied military strategy, but she was

only useful to the governor as bait. Somehow, her captors would contrive to lure Cesar out of hiding, either with a threat to her well-being or some plan to rescue her from custody. And when he came, the *federales* would be out in force to crush Cesar and anyone who joined him on the hopeless mission.

Was it hopeless?

Cesar had been caged, condemned to hang, but he'd been liberated by—

Matthew.

Where was he now? Had he remained in camp after she left that morning? Would he care that she was captured by the enemy? How would he even know?

The last question answered itself. Their enemies would tell Cesar his sister had been caught. How else could he attempt to free her? They would likely offer him a map and floor plan to her prison, if it didn't seem too obvious. The only bit of missing information would be numbers: how many soldiers and rifles were waiting to cut Cesar down the moment he revealed himself.

She thought about Mateo Alcazar, disarmed and riding with his hands tied some distance behind her, bound for the same undisclosed destination. The sergeant in charge had listened to Alcazar's story of treason, dissuaded from shooting him on the spot as a rapist, and decided his lieutenant should decide what happened to the pair of them. As to where or when that would happen, Dolores had no clue.

Back to Mateo then. If he had betrayed them—and who could deny it?—why hadn't he led *federales* to besiege the camp itself? Was he afraid, or did the enemy suspect that Cesar couldn't be defeated on his own home ground? Dolores wished they'd try it now, with the Gatling gun guarding the narrow approach to the camp, but Alcazar would doubtless warn them of that danger.

Unless she could stop him.

There'd been no opportunity to reach him since the *federales* had arrived upon the scene of her humiliation, but she wasn't giving up. Given half a chance, some kind of makeshift weapon, she would gladly silence Alcazar forever and repay the shame he had inflicted on her in the process.

Failing that, what could she do to help Cesar?

The obvious thing was to stop him from coming to help her, but how? She couldn't get word to the camp, and she knew that he'd ignore her pleas in any case. Cesar would not abandon her while there was any hope to rescue her alive.

And therein lay the answer.

Dolores wasn't a soldier. She hadn't been trained to maim or kill others, but she had a certain strength within her. Fueled by hatred, Dolores knew that she could kill Mateo Alcazar. And out of love for Cesar, she could end her own life for the good of all concerned.

It was a mortal sin, of course—a guaranteed ticket to Hell with no chance to repent—but what was one soul in the balance compared to dozens or hundreds of lives? She was prepared to face eternity in flames for Cesar's sake, and for the others she had grown to love during the years of struggle.

Anyway, if she wound up in Hell, she might find time and opportunity to punish Alcazar for his betrayal of the cause.

At dusk they camped, after a long day riding eastward. She was shackled, fed, and left alone. Still no one named their destination, and Dolores didn't ask. No matter where they took her, she would find a way to beat them at their own game, cheat them of their prize.

She simply had to watch and wait for Death to make himself available.

"You didn't find the wagon or the guns?"

"No, sir," the sergeant said.

Lieutenant Cruz narrowed his eyes, doing his best impression of a rattlesnake about to strike. "And yet, I see you here before me, in defiance of my orders. You have one minute to explain yourself."

Sergeant Rodriguez didn't need that long. "I've something better, sir," he answered.

Cruz had stalked into the meeting angry, warned by one of his assistants that the squad had come back empty-handed, save for two bedraggled prisoners—and one of them a woman. He was ready to destroy Rodriguez—strip the sergeant of his rank immediately, pending trial for dereliction of duty—but it couldn't hurt to let the doomed man speak his piece.

"Better, you say?"

"Yes, sir."

"I'm listening, but make it quick!"

"Cesar Zapata's sister, sir. It's her we have outside. Also some peasant named Alcazar who pretends to know you, sir. We caught him trying to . . . um, you know . . . with the woman, sir."

Cruz stood as if electrified. He instantly forgot about Rodriguez and his failure to retrieve the Gatling guns. He saw the opportunity to mend fences with his superiors and make himself a hero in the process. He saw glory, medals, a promotion, all laid out before him like a banquet.

"Bring the woman here at once, Sergeant," he said. "I'll question her myself."

"Yes, sir. About the other . . ."

"Hold him separately from the other prisoners. No one's to see him or to know we have him without my approval. Understood?"

"Yes, sir!"

Cruz stood before the mirror, studying his visage, while he waited for Rodriguez to return. Five minutes had passed, and he was getting edgy, when the sharp knock sounded on his door.

"Enter!" Rodriguez brought the woman in and was about to introduce her, when Cruz cut him off. "Wait in the hall, Sergeant."

"But, sir—"

"Dismissed!"

"Yes, sir."

Alone with her at last, Cruz said, "You are the sister of Cesar Zapata?"

"No, I'm not."

Cruz saw the flicker in her eyes. She was a novice liar, this one, as transparent as glass. "Your traveling companion tells a different story," he replied.

"That pig?" She snorted in derision. "He abducted me and tried to violate me. Ask your men."

Cruz studied her—the tousled hair, bruised cheek, her torn blouse barely held together over full, round breasts. He couldn't fault Alcazar's taste in women at least.

"Kidnapping and rape are capital charges, Señorita."

"Good. I look forward to his hanging."

"First things first. If you were kidnapped, as you say, your family should be informed that you are safe. It's part of my responsibility. I'm sure you understand."

"I have no family," she answered quickly. Learning, even now.

"You have my sympathy," Cruz said. "But I'm compelled to ask, in that case, how you make your living."

"Living?"

The lieutenant shrugged. "It may affect the charges," he replied. "Frankly, some magistrates do not believe a *puta*, for example, is entitled to the same protection as a decent woman."

"I am not a whore!" she raged at him, but she was wise enough to stand her ground without attacking.

"No, of course not, Señorita. What exactly are you?"

"I . . ." She hesitated, at a sudden loss for words.

"Allow me to assist you." Suddenly solicitous, Cruz stepped closer to the woman. She was too proud to retreat, a challenge molded in flesh.

"I think you *are* Zapata's sister," he continued. "We shall soon find out for certain, after I consult your friend. And if he can't convince me, there are various techniques to loosen stubborn tongues. You'll tell me everything I need to know, I promise you. And then, we'll plan a nice reception for your brother."

"Like the one in Sangre de Maria?" she asked defiantly.

Cruz smiled. "There is a price for treason, Señorita. Those who play the game must be prepared to pay up when they lose. As for your brother, he's already cheated justice once. His debt is overdue."

"I have no brother." She was turning sullen now.

"Too bad. In that case, you have nothing to trade."

"For what?"

"For your life."

"What have I done, Lieutenant?"

"Everyone's guilty of something, my dear. It's simply a

matter of framing the charges precisely. Now, if you were willing to bargain, there might be some hope."

"For this mythical brother?" she sneered.

"Or the gringo that helped him last time. I might settle for that, and forget what you owe to the state."

"Do your worst, pig."

Cruz moved closer yet, grabbing a handful of her hair and twisting it until she sobbed. "My worst is beyond your conception, *puta*. But you may see it yet, when your brother falls into my hands. You'll beg for favors then."

"I'd rather die," she hissed between clenched teeth.

Cruz wore a beatific smile. "That's easily arranged," he said.

Mateo Alcazar was furious and frightened, all at once. He merited a hero's welcome, but instead he occupied a stinking prison cell, ignored by his jailers and isolated from the other prisoners.

That part could be a blessing, Alcazar decided, since without a weapon he had doubts that he could fend off any larger, stronger inmates. But if there'd been someone in the cell next door at least, he could've tried to find out what in hell was happening.

He understood the stupid sergeant hadn't been expecting him, and didn't know about his mission for Lieutenant Cruz. The ride back with his hands tied was embarrassing, but Alcazar had suffered worse things in his time. What *really* galled him was the cage in which he sat, after the fools who'd captured him had told Cruz exactly what they'd found. He'd made a point of pleading with the sergeant to repeat his name, thus far to no avail.

Maybe he should've spelled it for the idiot.

Trying to calm himself, ignoring the fecal stench of his cell, Alcazar ran through the short list of problems that logically might've delayed his release. Lieutenant Cruz could've been called away on business, or perhaps he had a social engagement this evening. A colonel's daughter to squire, or a nice sassy whore. To the best of Alcazar's knowledge, no one else was aware of his dealings with Cruz, though he couldn't be sure who else the lieutenant had told of their collaboration.

That was the best he could hope for, implying a delay in his release from custody. Overnight perhaps, or at worst for the weekend, until Cruz returned to his post. When the lieutenant saw what Alcazar had brought him, albeit in slightly bruised condition, he would certainly be rewarded.

But what if Cruz didn't return?

Alcazar's mood veered from mounting annoyance to panic at the thought of being completely abandoned, cut off from his lifeline to the *federale* command chain. If Cruz had been killed or sacked, even if he'd simply been transferred to a new command, what would become of Alcazar? If no one else knew he'd collaborated in the past and had produced Cesar Zapata's sister as a token of his service to El Presidente, what would happen next?

At once, his cursed imagination conjured up an image of a dusty, pockmarked wall. He stood before it with his hands tied, while a firing squad marched into view and took position facing him. In Alcazar's vision he had refused a blindfold, but the muzzles of the leveled carbines frightened him and made him close his eyes. He heard the weapons being cocked, and then a voice called out—

"Wake up!"

His eyes snapped open to behold Lieutenant Cruz, fresh-faced and stylish in his best dress uniform. The *click-clack* sound of carbines cocking, he supposed, had been the guard unlocking his cell door.

Remembering his role, Alcazar rose from his corner—least filthy of the four available—and doffed his wilted hat. *"Jéfé,"* he said, "I was afraid you wouldn't come."

"Not come? Why would you think that, after all we've been through?"

Alcazar could only shrug, embarrassed by his doubt. Relief flowed through him like the warm rush of tequila.

"No," said Cruz, "I felt obliged to visit you and tell you where things stand. I didn't want the charges filed to come as a complete surprise."

"Charges? What charges, *Jéfé*?"

"Murder was proposed, but I've prevailed upon the prosecutor to remember that the men you killed were rebels and doubtless guilty of treason. Kidnapping also was mentioned, of course. The woman is quite outspoken on that subject, but a case can probably be made for citizen's arrest."

"That's what it was, most certainly! A citizen's arrest."

"Treason, of course, carries a penalty of death."

"Treason!" Alcazar felt his poor *cojones* shrivel at the very thought. "But *Jéfé*, I've been working for you!"

"In fact," Cruz said, "my notes reflect your arrest for attempted murder. The *puta* you slashed with a razor, remember? She shouldn't have laughed at your shortcomings, I admit, but your reaction was . . . extreme. Only in custody did you admit your service with Zapata's gang of traitors and agree to help destroy them, in return for charges being dropped."

"Well, yes, *Jéfé*, if you—"

"Which brings us to the present charge. Attempted rape. Even without the girl, I have a dozen witnesses who caught

you in the act. All *federales,* I might add, whose word will
certainly be trusted over that of a known deviate and traitor."

"Please, *Jéfé,* what is it you want from me?"

"Nothing, Mateo. You've provided everything I need.
This visit is a simple courtesy, and as a token of your service, I've waived the capital provision of the charge. You
won't be shot, Mateo."

"That's most generous."

"Of course, I understand that rapists don't do well in
prison. Something about felons and their families. And any
rebels in the prison you're assigned to may have questions
about your betrayal of Zapata."

"How would they—? You bastard!"

Cruz kept one hand on his sword as he retreated from the
tiny, reeking cell. The door clanged shut behind him, sepa-
rating them before Alcazar worked up nerve enough to
charge.

Smiling through the bars before he left, Cruz said,
"Something you might consider is attempting to escape. I
promise you, the guards are first-rate shots. They'll make a
decent job of it. Good luck, Mateo!"

Laughter echoed in the corridor as Cruz retreated toward
freedom. At last, an iron door slammed, cut off the mocking sound, and left Mateo Alcazar alone.

The new blouse didn't fit. It was too tight across the bust, a
trifle too low-cut, but at least it wasn't torn and dirty. With
her shawl, Dolores thought she could preserve some vestige
of her modesty.

What was the purpose of the gift?

After her quarrel with the lieutenant, she'd expected

something very different. Interrogators who would strip and torture her for information on her brother's whereabouts perhaps. A woman caged by brutal men never had any dearth of things to fear.

But when the guards returned, after she'd dressed and washed her face with water they provided, the lieutenant wasn't there. Instead, a captain took his place and intoduced himself as Elaminio Ruiz Valdez. Dolores didn't recognize the name from any conversations overheard in camp, but *federale* officers were all the same.

All enemies.

"Where are you taking me?" she asked the captain when he stepped aside, inviting her to leave her cell.

His answer startled her. "To meet the governor."

And off they went, winding through dungeon corridors and out into a crisp, cool dusk. More guards were waiting to surround them, carbines ready, as they crossed a courtyard and moved along a narrow alley to the side door of a larger building. There, they passed inside and followed more hallways where footsteps echoed on tiled floors. At last they reached an office where the captain entered by himself, then came back moments later to retrieve her.

"You wait here," he told the guards. Clutching her arm, he steered Dolores through the doorway. She considered jerking free, but guessed the *federales* would enjoy beating her down.

Escorted by Captain Ruiz, Dolores crossed an outer office to another door, hand-carved, and waited while a common soldier opened it before them.

The governor's office was lavishly furnished, as she had expected. Most Mexican villages could've survived for a year on the money expended for paintings and knickknacks alone, she supposed. The flag of Mexico against one wall reminded her of how rich men had robbed her country and betrayed its people in pursuit of profit.

Governor Neron stood in the middle of the room, before a massive desk. Dolores knew his face from posters that appeared from time to time in towns throughout the state. He studied her with an expression mingling curiosity, contempt, and something else she didn't recognize. Perhaps it was a hunter's satisfaction at the moment of the kill.

"Captain Ruiz, how good of you to come and bring a guest."

"Your Excellency, I present the sister of Cesar Zapata." Finally, Ruiz released her arm and stepped away, standing at ease, hands clasped behind his back.

"I'm not," she told the governor, deliberately omitting any title of respect. "There's been a serious mistake. I have no family."

"What's this?" Neron was frowning, eyebrows drawn together like two caterpillars urgently conversing.

"She lies, Your Excellency," said Ruiz. "We have confirmed through an informer that she is Zapata's sister. There is no doubt whatsoever, though she stubbornly denies it."

"Ah. Misguided loyalty. Of course, I understand." Neron stepped closer, dark eyes roving from her face down to her breasts and back again. "My dear, there's nothing to be gained from lies. You're in a perilous position as it is. Don't make things any harder on yourself."

"I won't betray him," she replied. "I won't betray the struggle. You will lose. Your days are numbered."

"That's the spirit!" said Neron, smiling. "And for the record, child, I don't expect you to betray your brother or his ragtag band of friends."

"Why am I here then?" she demanded.

Sudden pain lanced through her scalp as Ruiz clutched a

handful of her hair and twisted it. "You will address His Excellency as—"

. "Please, Captain," said Neron, "there's no need to defend me from this poor, misguided girl. Release her."

Ruiz did as he was told, leaving Dolores with a dull headache. "You haven't answered me," she said.

"I wanted to observe you at first-hand," the governor replied. "As for your function, you've fulfilled it. All that I require of you is that you be yourself. No doubt, your brother loves you and will spare no effort to retrieve you from my custody. I plan to make it easy for him . . . to a point."

Dolores saw red then, and flung herself at Neron's smiling face with fingers curved like talons. Ruiz struck swiftly, hammering a fist below her ribs that dropped her gasping to the floor.

"What spirit!" said Neron from somewhere high above her. "I'd say she's worth dying for, and no mistake."

Captain Ruiz believed a pair of corporals could've returned Zapata's sister to her cell, but he was in no mood to argue when Neron instructed him to take her back and then return without delay. One didn't contradict the governor, especially when one had just escaped demotion or dismissal by a fluke of fortune that would never be repeated in a million years.

As he retreated from the cell block for the second time that night, Ruiz considered just how lucky he had been to have Zapata's sister fall into his hands. Lieutenant Cruz had explained the curious chain of events, more or less, and while Ruiz assumed that his subordinate had tinkered with the facts a bit to make himself seem smarter, more industrious than nature painted him, Ruiz tried not to question success.

What was the gringo saying for an unexpected stroke of luck? *Don't look a gift horse in the mouth.*

He knew a hundred different mishaps might have spoiled the moment, could've left him empty-handed and compelled to grovel before his supervisor, but the new turn of events should vindicate him. Governor Neron should realize that Ruiz knew what he was doing, that he could be trusted to pursue Zapata's rebels to the bitter end.

The latter part was true at least. And he intended that the end would be more bitter for his enemies than for himself.

As for his colleagues . . .

Cruz had done well to recruit the rebel turncoat, better still to drop him after he delivered their prize hostage. Ruiz gave the lieutenant credit for his crafty strategy, and knew he'd have to watch his back in future. Cruz might slip the knife in when he least expected it.

Or maybe he would be another fallen warrior in El Presidente's struggle to maintain order in Mexico. Whether or not the rebels tried to liberate Zapata's sister, Ruiz knew the days ahead were fraught with peril. He would be first to recommend Lieutenant Cruz for a resplendent hero's funeral if for any reason Cruz didn't survive the next campaign.

Ruiz surprised the governor's attendant with his smile. Most *federales* summoned to a meeting with Neron wore grim expressions, ready for the kind of bitter medicine that stunts or kills careers. The jubilant expression on Ruiz's face had not been matched within those walls in living memory.

Ruiz lost it on the threshold to Neron's inner sanctum as he saw Captain Montoya standing rigidly beside the gover-

nor's desk. Montoya's face was bland, unreadable. If Ruiz
had surprised Montoya or discomfited him with the capture
of Zapata's sister, Montoya managed to conceal it well.
There was no tremor in the hand that held his brandy glass,
no trace of perspiration on his high forehead.

Neron beamed at him from across the spacious room.
"Captain Ruiz, welcome!"

Not *welcome back,* he noticed. Was the governor pre-
tending that he hadn't been inside this very office only moments earlier? What was the point of such a game, unless
he meant to deceive Montoya?

Wait and see.

"Brandy?" Neron inquired. "By all means, help yourself. I've just been explaining your triumph to Captain
Montoya. He shares our feeling that we must exploit good
fortune while it lasts. Strike while the iron is hot!"

"Indeed, Your Excellency." Ruiz sipped his brandy, sa-
voring its heat. "In fact, I have a plan to do exactly that—
with your consent, of course."

It was Cruz's plan, in fact, but why burden the governor
with needless details? As he took another sip of liquid fire,
Ruiz was pleased to see a first small flicker in Montoya's
eyes.

"By all means," said Neron, "please share this plan."

Frowning to make himself seem serious, Ruiz replied,
"My plan relies on what we know about the enemy, Your
Excellency. With a bit of prodding, they undo themselves.
The first step is. . . ."

Lupé Cortez had ridden hard through dusk and darkness,
slowing only when his horse could run no further without
suffering some grievous injury. He walked the animal to

rest it, fifteen minutes every hour, while he doled out sips of water poured from his canteen into his hat. Despite his urgent errand, Cortez didn't want to lose the stallion. He was fond of it, and he would need it for the long ride back.

Durango's taverns showed no signs of closing for the night as Cortez made his way along the main street of the city's vice district. From the east end of the avenue, he counted off a dozen places where a man could lose his money, memory, and anything resembling dignity within a few short hours. There was no shortage of sinful opportunity, but Cortez had no need to choose between the offerings of various establishments.

He'd known where he was going all along, and nothing short of death would keep him from his destination.

The cantina was known as Los Diablos, though the name appeared nowhere on any sign Cortez could see. Its reputation was sufficient to entice patrons or frighten them away, but Cortez wasn't scared.

Not much.

It was a well-known fact that *federales* were among the nightly clientele of Los Diablos. Not the officers, who gravitated toward a slightly higher-class depravity, but sergeants, corporals, and privates, thirsty after hours of beating down the people they were pledged to serve and protect. When they were lubricated with tequila, some forgot themselves and let slip information they should not have shared with mere civilians. It was said among Durango's freedom fighters that Mateo Alcazar—God curse his filthy name!—had gathered much strategic information in the smoky cave of Los Diablos.

Now, the mission fell upon Lupé Cortez.

The place was dark and claustrophobic, with a fog bank of tobacco smoke that stung Cortez's eyes. He made a beeline for the bar, wincing at the discordant music from a trio of guitars. No one else in the bar seemed to notice, their tone-deaf reaction a testament to the numbing powers of alcohol.

At the bar, Cortez found a place beside two *federales* who ignored him. He ordered cold *cerveza,* and received warm cat's piss in a dirty glass. He managed not to grimace as he sipped it, while his pesos disappeared into the fat bartender's hand.

Cortez leaned closer to the *federales* on his right, gaining a vantage point where he could smell their sweat and eavesdrop on their conversation. He'd expected to spend hours drifting here and there around the tavern, trying to remain unnoticed as he scavenged tidbits from the noxious air, but now he heard the name *Zapata* almost instantly.

". . . supposed to be his sister," one of them was saying. "They're afraid Zapata will come fetch her with an army."

"Where's she going then?" the other asked.

"To Hell most likely," said the nearer of the two. "*El Jéfé* has already sentenced her to hang."

"So soon?"

"Why not? Remember, she's Zapata's sister. Everything he's done, she's been a part of it. There's treason in the blood. Only one way to wipe it out."

"Where will they do it? Here?"

The sweaty sergeant shook his head. "They're taking her to El Palmito in the morning, for a necktie party Saturday."

"Why El Palmito?" asked the corporal.

"Christ, you don't know anything! It's where they came from, the Zapatas, once upon a time. *El Jéfé* wants to rub it in their faces."

Cortez took a swallow of his so-called beer and left his glass half-empty on the bar. Despite a sudden urge to run, he took his time leaving the tavern, breathing freely only when he reached the street outside. Likewise when he was mounted, cantering along the street as if he had nowhere to go and all night still to get there. Haste would only draw unwelcome notice, and the last thing Cortez needed at the moment was a problem with the roving *federales* on patrol.

There would be time enough for racing when he hit the open desert and the city fell away behind him. Cortez hoped the stallion was rested enough for the ride back to camp. He knew now what Zapata had sent him to learn, and the news was all bad.

It would be close to dawn by the time he arrived, and Cortez could already imagine the bloody sunrise. He didn't want to think about the slaughter that would follow, so he concentrated on the road and prayed for speed.

14

Around midnight, when it sank in that simple fretting didn't help, most of the camp had gone to sleep. Price tried it for a while, wrapped in his blanket near a dying fire, but after thirty wasted minutes he got up and made his way into the woods.

The trail was plainly visible, tramped down by two thirds of Zapata's following on Tuesday night, and Price had no trouble retracing his steps to the clearing. It wasn't a secret place anymore. The magic was gone, if it had ever been there in the first place. Maybe it had always been Dolores, though.

Price knew he wasn't qualified to judge such things.

He spent some time alone there, studying the place where he and Dolores had almost made love, where he'd killed Rufio Duarte. Price regretted neither act, but both had had consequences that kept going long after the deed was done—or interrupted, in the case of his abortive, one-time-only tryst with Dolores. Price wondered if he'd ever see the end of what was done that night, or of the things he'd done in bygone years, stretching right back to childhood on the farm.

And even as the question took shape in his mind, he knew the answer. There would be an end to all of it, the day he died.

Or would there?

The closest Price had come to church in recent years had been the day he stole the padre's robe in San Filipe, and he didn't waste a lot of time thinking about the afterlife. If it existed, Price supposed the best thing he could hope for was a second chance, an opportunity to choose a different path. If there was nothing on the other side but punishment for things that he'd already done and couldn't alter if he tried, there seemed to be no point in worrying.

And then again, maybe there was no "other side" at all.

The moon was past its full. Scanning the clearing, Price thought he could see the place where he had tumbled with Dolores, and the spot where Duarte fell. Most of the ferns had managed to survive that night, and Price took care as he passed through them, moving toward the boulder at the center of the clearing. There, he sat and tried to think of something he could do to help Dolores.

And he came up empty, all around.

Zapata had already run through a short list of options while Price listened, acting as his sounding board. The rebels could retaliate for Dolores's kidnapping, but the *federales* would expect that if they were behind it, and any target chosen by Zapata would be a potential trap. This time, unlike the skirmish on the road, the rebels couldn't count on luck and nerve to see them through the exercise alive.

The other side of aggression was submission. Assuming that Dolores had been taken as a lure or bargaining chip,

Zapata could end the game simply by surrendering. It would mean certain death for him, with no assurance of Dolores's release once he was clapped in irons, and while Zapata didn't seem to fear the noose per se, he'd finally decided that surrender wouldn't serve the cause.

One angle that Zapata didn't want to think about, which Price couldn't avoid, was an alternative reason for the abduction. Price had asked what they would do if it turned out Mateo Alcazar had snatched Dolores for himself, instead of as a present to their adversaries, but Zapata wouldn't hear it. He'd dismissed the notion as impossible, saying the weasel wasn't man enough to risk it on his own behalf.

Maybe.

But earlier that day, Price guessed Zapata would've said the same about Alcazar shooting three men on the trail and kidnapping Dolores. Still, he'd done those things, and if Zapata had misread his man, Price guessed he might be wrong on other points as well.

In truth, Price hoped Dolores *had* been kidnapped for the *federales*. If that was the case, he guessed that Alcazar would be more likely to deliver her unharmed. It wouldn't mean that she was safe by any means, but if the kidnapping had been a one-man deal, inspired by Alcazar's own passion, then Dolores faced a lethal risk by spurning him. She would be smart enough to know that, but Price guessed she wouldn't just roll over for a man to save herself.

If it was Alcazar alone, Price reckoned she might already be dead—or worse, if there was such a thing. Caged by the *federales,* she would likely have a day or two, at least, before they got around to hanging her.

Pale dawn was breaking when he started back to camp. Price heard excited voices as he cleared the tree line, saw Zapata speaking urgently with one of the riders he'd sent out last evening. Price didn't know his name, but the young man was talking rapidly, explaining something that held Zapata's rapt attention. As Price moved closer, Zapata noticed him and raised a hand to beckon him.

"Matt, hurry!" he called out. "We've found Dolores!"

"You're going on a journey," said Lieutenant Cruz.

The woman didn't answer, simply watched him through the gray bars of her cage. Haughty. Contemptuous. Cruz would've loved to break her, see her grovel for him—preferably naked—but the best that he could do for now was taunt her with a preview of her fate.

"You're going home, in fact," he told her. "El Palmito. You remember it, I trust."

"Why there?" she asked, surprising him.

"It's not your place to question why," he sneered, "but I suppose His Excellency means to let your people see what you've become. They need a lesson. This is what becomes of whores and traitors."

She ignored the insult, disappointing Cruz, and asked, "When do we leave?"

"Within the hour," he replied. "I trust that gives you time to pack."

She drifted closer to the bars. "You're very brave with people under lock and key. Is it the same in battle? I believe you soil yourself and run away."

Cruz felt the rage-heat in his face and answered through clenched teeth. "We'll see how brave your sainted brother is. Do you suppose he'll try to save you from the gallows, or will he remember how your lot left him to die?"

"Maybe you'll find out, if you tell him where I am."

Cruz laughed at that. "It's all been taken care of, *puta*.

Word went out last night, to every piss-hole in Durango. If your brother's famous spy network is worth its salt, he'll have the word by now."

"Maybe you'll meet him then, and have a chance to prove yourself a man." She glanced down at his fist, clutching the saber's hilt, and smiled. "You'd like to run me through with that—or is there maybe something else you want to use? Stay with the sword, *cabron*. It's all you have."

Cruz would've gladly rushed into the cell and slaughtered her for the insult, but that would mean his own head in a noose. Instead, he spit between the bars, full in her face, and turned away. Her mocking laughter followed him outside, into the morning's light.

Two captains supervised the preparations for departure, speaking to each other only when logistics made it mandatory. Cruz supposed that the arrival of Captain Montoya meant Ruiz was in disfavor with the governor, and yet they seemed to share command. On second thought, perhaps the mission had been deemed too great for one captain alone to take responsibility.

And where did that leave Cruz?

He still might distinguish himself, if the rebels turned out to rescue their hostage. In that case, he knew, the commanding officers were little more than window dressing. Sergeants kept the men together during combat, but their orders had to come from somewhere, and in this case it would be Lieutenant Cruz. If something evil should befall their troop in battle—if the two captains were killed or wounded, for example—then command in fact would fall to Cruz.

Something to think about. Perchance to dream.

He had selected fifty men this time, all seasoned veterans this time. The woman would be riding in a prison wagon, with a driver and a shotgun guard. The other forty-eight armed men, together with himself and the two captains, would provide security. When they reached El Palmito, they would occupy the town and lay their trap. Tomorrow morning, if Zapata came, he would be cut to ribbons with his men.

And if he didn't, well, the bitch would hang and they could all go home.

From Cruz's point of view, it was a winning situation either way.

"All ready then, Lieutenant?" asked Captain Ruiz.

"It's almost time," Captain Montoya said.

Cruz knew the trek to El Palmito would be a long ride. "We're ready, sirs," he said. And to his Sergeant Rodriguez he commanded, "Fetch the prisoner."

Cruz hoped she liked the prison wagon's rough bench seats, no cushions for a dainty passenger. He hoped that El Palmito had a tiny, stinking jail—or maybe none at all, in which case they could lock her in a shed, with rats and spiders. In the morning, Cruz would check the noose himself, to make sure that she didn't cheat the crowd by dying quickly.

He looked forward to the *puta*'s final dance.

Price helped retrieve the second Gatling gun. It had been hidden, with its wagon, in a narrow weed-choked canyon situated half a mile due south of the protected entrance to the rebel camp. Zapata obviously knew his stuff where squirreling gear and weapons was concerned. Price could've ridden past the spot a dozen times without detecting wagon tracks or any other sign of human activity around the place.

They had to draw the wagon out by hand, a five-man job made ticklish by the rattlesnakes inhabiting Zapata's chosen hideout. The reptiles were perfect for security, their whirring sounds enough to stop most animals or men from penetrating the first wall of tumbleweeds, yet Zapata moved among them as if he was charmed, or they were, nudging snakes this way and that with dusty boots, removing them from harm's way as the wagon was revealed and then extracted from its nest.

The big gun, broken down and wrapped in canvas, was in perfect form as far as Price could tell. He didn't want to risk a test-fire, which would mean setting up the gun and then dismantling it again, but it had worked without a flaw just three days earlier. There was no reason why it shouldn't kill again upon command.

No ammunition had been hidden with the gun. Zapata's men brought magazines and cartridges from camp, a satchel full of death for anyone who stood between the rebel leader and his sister. By the time the wagon team was harnessed, thirty riders sat astride their mounts and waited for the order to proceed. Twenty more were being left behind, to hold the fort or, failing that, evacuate the noncombatants to some safer place.

Wherever that might be.

"You see my army, Matt," Zapata said. "Is this a force to make El Presidente tremble in his palace?"

Price surveyed the horsemen from his saddle. "Hard to say. One man can do the job sometimes."

Zapata smiled. "You think we ought to fight a duel? Perhaps I'll challenge him, if we survive the weekend."

On Zapata's signal, they began the journey eastward.

There was no disguising who they were, no feigning any lawful purpose for their congregation. If they met patrols along the way, they would be forced to fight or flee, and Price knew that Zapata wasn't in a fleeing mood.

Around mile three, Zapata briefed him on their target. El Palmito was home, of a sort. Zapata and Dolores had been born there, watched their parents scratch the ground to raise a yearly crop of corn and beans, helped when they could in childish ways around the little spread. Taxes were steep, and punishment for failure to remit the pesos was severe. Zapata's parents went to hear a speech in town, some would-be politician who was working on reform one village at a time, but *federales* had shown up and fired into the crowd. Before he knew it, Zapata was man of the house, and then the house itself was gone, sold out from under them for taxes that his father hadn't paid.

The rest was history, five years of struggle at an age when most young men were students or apprentices or starting families of their own. Zapata chose another path, and he'd been striking back at those who'd killed his parents ever since.

"Today I pay the price," he said at last. "Dolores suffers for my pride and arrogance."

"She made a choice, the same as you," Price replied. "She could've married off and let you go your own way, if she wanted to."

"I know. But this is no life for a woman, even if she picks it for herself."

Price thought about his own as he answered, "I wouldn't recommend this life to anyone, you want to know the truth."

Zapata studied him. "You know my story now," he said at last. "What's yours?"

"The same old thing you've heard a hundred times. I don't like rules and taking orders. When my old man dished out more than I could take, I ran from home and just kept going. Here I am."

"I don't believe you learned gunfighting from your father."

"No, I picked that up along the way. At first, it was a necessary skill. Turns out I had a talent for it. Most folks don't. Now, it's just me."

"You don't enjoy it, though. Some do."

"Doing and liking are two different things."

"I think it's why you said no to Dolores, eh?"

"Part of it anyway. My deal, it's hard to see beyond tomorrow. Next week's just a fantasy. Also, she's spent enough time in harm's way."

"And that's my fault," Zapata said.

"Free will," Price told him. "You didn't chain her to a tree."

"With family, sometimes it's the same thing."

Price could only shrug at that. "I wouldn't know."

Dolores was surprised to find she had no feelings about going back to El Palmito. She knew people there, but few of them would recognize her. Fewer still would dare admit it, with the *federales* watching, listening. She wondered which among her former friends and neighbors would turn out to watch her die.

It didn't matter in the end, as long as Cesar stayed away. She hoped her captors were mistaken, that Cesar had no spies in Durango who would tell him where she'd gone, but she supposed they were correct. It was their job to know such things and plan ahead, to foil the freedom struggle any way they could.

Bastards.

They had prevented her, so far, from acting out her plan to cheat them of their prize. There had been nothing in her cell that could've served her as a weapon, not even a hook from which to hang herself if she had torn her skirt to make a noose.

Maybe in El Palmito they'd get careless, but Dolores feared that it was already too late. If it was true, what she'd been told, and Cesar knew where they were taking her, nothing short of a natural disaster would prevent him being there.

Dolores thought of praying for an earthquake or a hurricane, but she had given up on God. If the Almighty granted power to a creature like Neron, much less Diaz, He was unworthy of respect.

Dolores hoped that Matthew Price, at least, had left the camp before word came of her abduction and impending execution. Even though he hadn't chosen to make a life with her, she knew that Price would feel obliged to save her from the *federales*. He had done as much for Cesar when the two of them were total strangers.

But she didn't want his help, didn't want anyone to die on her behalf. If she could send her thoughts across the miles to reach Cesar, she would've asked him to protect himself and bide his time, strike only when he was assured of victory, inflicting maximum destruction on the enemies of Mexico.

He wouldn't listen anyway, she thought, and nearly smiled.

Caged in the prison wagon, she had no view of the town as they approached it, from the south. Her first glimpse of the people and their homes came as the *federales* entered El Palmito, riders staying close beside the wagon as if they were frightened she might squeeze between the bars and flee on foot.

Or were they frightened that Cesar was there ahead of them?

It was impossible, she knew. He had a full day's ride from camp to reach their former home, if he was coming, and the news couldn't have reached him much before sunrise. Some of the people watching as she passed might sympathize with Cesar's fight, but none of them were armed for battle. They would not be keen to risk their lives, their families and homes, to save a girl barely remembered, who had left them years ago.

Why should they, after all?

Dolores heard the sound of carpentry in progress, saws and hammers wielded by determined hands. Halfway through town they passed the object of attention, and she recognized it as a gallows. Now, at least, it was confirmed that she would not be placed against a wall and shot.

Was strangulation worse, or did it even matter in the end?

The wagon reached its destination, creaking to a halt. Some of the *federales* instantly dismounted, drawing carbines from their saddle scabbards, while the rest remained alert, prepared to charge at any instant, one way or another, up or down the street.

Lieutenant Cruz unlocked the wagon's hatch and crawled inside, using a second key to unfasten her shackles. Dolores couldn't stand upright until she was clear of the wagon, Cruz pressing close behind her. In the street, she was surrounded and marched toward a building that she didn't recognize from five years earlier.

The jail was new. What progress her hometown had made in five short years under El Presidente's rule.

Before she passed inside, Dolores took one last look at the people on the street and wondered whether they were proud of what their village had become, or if they were ashamed.

She wondered too how many of them would survive the coming day.

Zapata spun a word-picture of El Palmito as they rode eastward, the sun climbing before them, pausing briefly overhead, then lowering again behind their backs. In five years he had not revisited the town he once called home, but he had contacts there and news of El Palmito reached his ears from time to time.

"The main street runs from north to south," he said, watching as Price absorbed the information bit by bit. "There are four side streets now, two more than when I left. A few small shops along the main street, with a new jail near the center and a stable to the north. The other buildings, mostly homes. In El Palmito, people grow most of the food they eat. They have what you would call a dry-goods store, a blacksmith's shop, but nothing like Durango."

"There'll be *federales* waiting," Price remarked. "Where would they sleep?"

"I haven't seen the jail," Zapata said, "but there'd be room for some inside. Perhaps the stable, or they may intrude on private homes."

"You need to think about a bill of rights down here," Price said, half smiling.

"*Sí.* It's on my list, amigo. Come the day of victory, there will be many changes for the better made in Mexico."

"I guess there's no idea on when that day might be?" asked Price.

Zapata felt his shoulders slump, and made a point of squaring them again. "My people, I'll admit it, have a flaw. They're easygoing to a fault, not like Americans who grab a gun whenever someone sets foot on their property."

"It isn't all like that up north," Price said. "Some places pride themselves on being *civilized*. Won't even let you wear a gun in public, if you can believe it. Other places, though, you want that weapon handy when a stranger comes to call."

"Sometimes," Zapata said, "I wish my people could be more like yours. You are adventurous, aggressive—sometimes foolish too, I have to say it—but it almost seems you never rest. In Mexico, it's all siesta and mañana for too many of my folk. They've never tasted freedom, so they don't know what they're missing."

"How'd *you* taste it?" Price asked him.

"As a child, I saw the *federales* stop men on the street in El Palmito, question them, sometimes abuse them while their wives and children watched. The *federales* always laughed. I've hated them since then, as many of my people do, but when they killed my parents, it was just . . ."

"Enough?" Price suggested.

"That's it. I'd had enough. Nothing will ever change unless someone stands up and says, 'Enough!' We know El Presidente and the *federales* will not listen to our voices, so we speak to them with guns."

"Not many of you, though."

"Not yet perhaps, but we are gaining strength. Each month, each year, we win more converts to the cause. More men find the *cojones* they'd forgotten that they had and join us in the struggle."

"Are you winning?" Price inquired.

"We are surviving," said Zapata. "For the moment, that's a victory of sorts. In time, we will succeed. I'm confident of that. I may not live to see the victory in person, but perhaps my son will be there."

"You have children, Cesar?"

"No, but I will have a son someday. I'm confident of that as well."

"I guess that means you think we'll pull it off all right in El Palmito."

"I intend to free Dolores, by whatever means are necessary. We will send a mighty message to the governor, and to Diaz."

"I guess you know what preachers say about the road to Hell?" Price asked.

"Tell me."

"It's paved with good intentions."

"Ah, but we have strategy."

"You want to let me in on that?" asked Price.

"They will outnumber us, agreed? More men, more guns, more everything."

"Don't sugarcoat it now."

"But even though they are expecting us, we may effect surprise."

"I'm listening."

"There is a farm, five miles from El Palmito, on the road we follow. It is owned by friends of mine. Friends of the struggle. They will give us corn enough to fill the wagon and conceal the big gun, so the *federales* will not see it."

"Let's suppose they search the wagon," Price suggested.

"Maybe they won't find it," said Zapata. "Maybe we can bribe them. Maybe I shall simply have to kill them."

"There goes your surprise."

"You'll be surprised, Matt. After all, the *federales* are my people too. We simply have to play upon their weaknesses."

"All right. I figure two men on the wagon, tops. No gringos and no famous rebel faces. What about the rest of us?"

Zapata smiled. "Fear not," he said. "I have a plan."

Price listened to the rest of it, Zapata telling how he'd divide their force after the wagon left them, still at least two miles from El Palmito so they didn't have to worry about the *federales* that were bound to be in place when they arrived. Zapata's plan was simple, but Price saw no reason why it shouldn't work in theory. As for working in the real world, he would have to wait and see.

With two men on the wagon, they'd have twenty-eight remaining, split up into flying squads of fourteen each. One team would circle east of town, the other west. When they were still a mile or so from El Palmito, they'd dismount and leave one man on either side to hold the horses. The remainder—lucky thirteen, once again—would close on foot and finish on their bellies, crawl the last five hundred yards or so and try to infiltrate the sleeping town. At daybreak, if they hadn't tipped their hand ahead of time and ruined everything, they'd be in place and ready for the fireworks show.

The only part to which Price raised objection was Zapata's plan for *him* to lead the second team. "My Spanish may be passable," he said, "but they don't know me. There's no reason they should trust me in a pinch. In case you haven't noticed, I'm a gringo."

Zapata shook his head and chided, "Matt, don't tell me that you're prejudiced against *yourself*. Some of these men were with us when we took the Gatling guns. The rest all know the story, how you killed more *federales* in one hour than the rest have done since Christmas."

"I got lucky," Price replied. "I saw an opening and made a move, with no one's scalp at risk but mine. It's not the same as leading troops, and you know that."

"I need a man of courage, who won't wet himself and turn tail when the shooting starts," Zapata said. "My men need someone who isn't afraid to risk his life and lead them by example. Normally, that man would have been Rufio. Today . . ."

"If that's a play on guilt," Price said, "I promise you've misjudged me."

"No guilt. This is war. I trust you with my men. It's time for you to trust yourself."

They stopped to fill the wagon at a run-down farm with half a dozen children and some thirty chickens milling in the yard. A wiry, ageless man came out to shake hands with Zapata, led them to the barn, and pitched in as they filled the wagon bed with corncobs in the husk. Before they left, Zapata sketched a diagram of El Palmito in the dust and pointed out the vantage points for riflemen. In forty minutes they were on the road again, the little farm a fading memory.

An hour later, when it was fully dark, they stopped and watched the wagon rattle on without them. Price still couldn't see the town, which reassured him that the enemy holed up there wasn't watching him. There might be sentries posted in the desert, but Zapata didn't think so, and Price had resolved to trust his knowledge of their opposition—to a point at least.

When they reached El Palmito and the killing started, he

would trust himself as Cesar urged, and no one else. It was the way he'd stayed alive this long, against all odds.

And maybe it would get him through the night.

They waited on the wagon, let it gain a decent lead, then split off as agreed to east and west. Price took the west side, with a guide who knew the way spotting landmarks. They were in place by half past ten o'clock, dismounting and retrieving any battle gear they needed from their saddlebags.

Price didn't have a speech for them, but he risked a final warning as they waited for the order to proceed. "The only thing we've got on our side is surprise," he said. "Lose that, we lose it all. From here on in, that means no talking, no unnecessary noise of any kind. Watch out for those canteens, side arms, loose cartridges—whatever else you're carrying that might give you away. You all know where to go in town when we get there. When Cesar starts the ball, kill anything in uniform and do your best to stay alive. Questions?"

The silent men stared back at Price. He guessed they were as ready as they'd ever be.

"All right," he said at last. "Let's go."

Leading the way, he turned and started walking through the desert darkness toward a town he couldn't see.

15

Despite a sleepless night, Lieutenant Cruz felt vigorous and fit for anything when he arose at dawn on Saturday. The loss of sleep was no reflection on his quarters, though the room assigned to him was small and poorly ventilated. Cruz was simply too excited to relax, invigorated by the prospect of a hanging and a massacre of peasant rebels, all rolled up together in a single bloody package.

Governor Neron would be delighted, and he would remember those who laid that gift before him. Cruz didn't expect to profit from the victory on par with his superiors, but he was bound to gain something. Mere elevation to a captain's rank would satisfy him very well.

For now.

If he was honest with himself, though, he was looking forward to the woman's hanging most of all. She had insulted him, a *federale* officer, and that demanded punishment. The peasant women who observed her death or learned of it at second hand would be reminded of their place in Mexican society, and next time they would think twice before mocking Jose Cruz.

Magnificent in his dress uniform, Cruz checked his weapons again—pistol on the right hip, saber on the left—then made his way outside. It was impossible to walk the village streets without a layer of dust collecting on his spit-shined boots, but Cruz refused to let it spoil his mood. The other officers were still at breakfast, but he wasn't hungry.

What he *really* wanted was to see the prisoner once more, alone, before he led her to the gallows and her fate. Perhaps a night passed in the shadow of the noose had changed her mood. Contrition wouldn't save her now, but it would make the morning that much more enjoyable for Cruz.

The jail was two doors down from where he'd spent the night, behind the dry-goods store. Its owner hadn't argued when Captain Montoya told him *federales* would be sleeping on the premises to make his stock secure. Cruz had debated cleaning out the till, but finally decided not to bother. The thought of petty theft didn't amuse him on the eve of battle, when he would be tested as an officer and as a man.

The prisoner was guarded, but the sentries didn't challenge Cruz. He found the woman waiting for him, standing in the middle of her cage, apparently well rested.

"Is it time?" she asked.

"Not quite, but soon."

"Than what do you want?" That arrogance again.

"I thought you might be willing to . . . cooperate."

"With you?" Her tone was scornful. "I prefer the rope."

"Your wish is my command," Cruz said, hoping she couldn't see the angry color in his face. "It's not as easy as they say, you know. Hanging. It doesn't always break the neck like that." He snapped his fingers. "Sometimes, when mistakes are made, it takes a long, long time to die."

"Whatever pleases you," she answered. "Do your drooling somewhere else."

Recoiling from the bars, Cruz spit at her. "I hope your brother likes the show we've planned for him today. Save him a seat in Hell. He won't be far behind you."

People were all the same, Price thought. No matter where he went, they always turned out for an execution. Friend or foe, rich or poor, the gallows seemed to draw them with a magnetism Price had never really understood.

He would've guessed that most of El Palmito's residents admired Cesar Zapata at some level and despised the *federales,* yet they showed up for the hanging as if Governor Neron was doling out free food and liquor. To their credit, they were solemn and without the festive air he'd seen at many hangings in the States, but in his mind it would've shown more honor for the victim if they'd stayed away.

Or done something to stop the show.

But that was *his* job, crouched beside the wagon they'd unloaded late last night, ready to cover when his two amigos rose at the last minute to erect the Gatling gun. They had it locked and loaded, ready to be mounted on the tripod, all of sixty seconds' work for strong men who knew what to do.

From that point on, Price knew it could be anybody's game.

The *federales* were prepared for trouble, but their natural assumption of superiority still made them careless. One of them had wandered past the stable while Zapata's men were unloading the corn last night, but he'd asked nothing of the rebels, taking it on faith that his *compadres* had already checked the load and found it innocent. In fact, Price knew, there'd been no search at all and little in the way of an interrogation when the wagon entered El Palmito. Rebels were expected, but the *federales* obviously thought Zapata would come charging in like Custer with the Seventh Cavalry, instead of creeping in behind them, hiding snipers in the shadows here and there.

It was a lapse that would put some of them in early graves.

Price didn't know how many people lived in El Palmito, but he reckoned most of them were in the street three quarters of an hour past sunrise. Ideally, he'd have sent them home and cleared the line of fire, but there was nothing he could do to help them. When their town became a shooting gallery, they'd have to look out for themselves.

And maybe next time, when a public execution was announced, today's survivors would stay safe at home.

There should've been a drum roll, Price imagined, but a murmur from the crowd was all Dolores got as she emerged from jail surrounded by four *federales*. They'd already bound her hands behind her, but she didn't seem intimidated as she walked the fifty feet or so to mount the hastily constructed platform. As she passed the spectators, scanning their faces, many eyes were suddenly averted and a few brimmed full of tears.

The guards were something else. They had Zapata's men outnumbered almost two to one, by Price's count, but they were clearly visible, eschewing stealth. Price marked the officers, one escorting Dolores with a pleased expression on his face, two others standing stiffly near the scaffold, as if each was trying to ignore the other's presence.

"Do it!" he told the men behind him, and they hastened

to obey. Price heard the big gun settle on its mount, his two companions straining as they brought it forward.

Any minute now.

Price sighted down the barrel of his Winchester and waited for Zapata's signal to begin the free-for-all.

Halfway up the wooden stairs, Dolores realized that she was frightened of the gallows after all. Instead of crumbling, though, she bit her lip and concentrated on her posture. Shoulders squared, back straight, eyes focused on the dangling noose.

The scaffold placed her well above most of the *federales* and the spectators who'd come to watch her die. She had already scanned those faces, seeking any show of friendship, but instead she mostly saw embarrassment. They'd come to see her final moments, watch her jerk and strangle as the rope went taut, but even those she knew by sight and memory were strangers to her now. No faces from the camp among them either, which had been her last real hope.

And yet, surprisingly, that brought relief.

Perhaps the others had prevailed upon Cesar to stay away and seek his vengeance at some other place and time, when all the odds were not against him. Maybe—

The lieutenant stood before her, smiling. Rough hands on her arms positioned her above the trapdoor that would open in a few short moments, plummeting Dolores into darkness everlasting.

"Normally, we bind the ankles," the lieutenant whispered, "but I think they'd rather see you kick a bit."

Dolores somehow found the strength to smile at him and said, "I pity your poor mother, cursed with such a son."

She wondered whether he'd be able to control the fury

written on his twisted face, but there was no time for her captor to reply. Below them, on the street, the captain who'd escorted her to meet the governor was speaking to the crowd.

"Today," he said, "we execute a traitor who was born among you and dishonored your community by waging war against the government of Mexico. She is the sister of Cesar Zapata, who today is hiding like the coward that he is. Thus we punish all who stand against El Presidente and the constitution."

Stony silence from the crowd. When none replied, the captain turned and shouted up to his subordinate, "Proceed!"

"With pleasure," the lieutenant hissed. He reached up for the noose, then seemed to stumble, lurching forward. Even as Dolores heard the rifle shot, his deadweight bore her backward, sprawling on the scaffold with his warm blood on her face.

Price didn't hesitate after Zapata's shot dropped the lieutenant and Dolores in a heap atop the scaffold. There were still two living *federales* on the platform with her, and he tagged the nearer of them with a rifle shot that drilled his target's chest from left to right and sent him reeling backward, off the brink and out of sight.

By that time, half the *federales* in the village square were firing, even if they couldn't find real targets, and Zapata's men were shooting back from rooftops, alleys, nooks, and crannies where they'd hidden overnight. A storm of lead swept through the plaza, worsened when the Gatling gun let go in rapid fire, while scores of unarmed villagers ran screaming through the midst of it.

The last surviving *federale* on the scaffold knelt beside Dolores and the dead lieutenant, carbine clutched in one hand while the other groped his late commander, seeking signs of life. Beneath the corpse, Dolores wriggled, trying to escape, then started screaming as the *federale* reached for the lieutenant's sword, drew it, and raised it for a stroke that would behead her.

Price's bullet struck the *federale* just above one eye and slammed him over backward, while his flat-brimmed hat went sailing off the scaffold. Price pumped the rifle's lever-action, swung to face the point where he had seen two captains standing seconds earlier—and found them gone. There was no dearth of targets, chaos reigning in the plaza, and he saw four villagers cut down by Gatling fire, pummeled by bullets even as they fell.

Price rounded on the gunner, shouting, "Watch your goddamned fire!" He was too late, though, as a lucky shot or stray bullet from somewhere found the rebel on the Gatling's crank and cut a frothy blowhole in his throat. The stricken shooter lurched backward, clutching his wound, while blood spouted between his fingers. By the time Price reached the big gun, he was down and thrashing on the stable's plain dirt floor.

Price stood behind the Gatling gun and scanned the battleground for targets. There were *federales* on the far side of the street, but reaching them meant firing past and through civilians running for their homes or any other shelter they could find. That shelter was in short supply right now, as snipers craned from windows, doorways, anyplace at all where they could claim a bit of cover for themselves.

Windows.

Price saw two *federales* firing carbines from a second-floor window above the village dry-goods store. One fired, then ducked back to reload his carbine while the other took his place. Price crouched and raised the Gatling gun's six muzzles, framed the window in his sights, and waited for the switch.

A shooter leaned into his line of fire, Price spun the Gatling's crank, and ten or fifteen heavy bullets tore the window frame apart. His target flailed with rag-doll arms and toppled out of sight. Another burst along the wall beside the window gobbled up the last rounds from the Gatling's upright magazine and tore handfuls of dry adobe from the wall.

"Reload!" Price told the rebel crouched beside him. "You're the gunner now. And make damn sure of who you're blasting with this thing!"

"*Sí, Jéfé*. Only *federales*!"

"That's the ticket," Price replied, and then he broke from cover, out into the open killing ground.

"For God's sake, do something!" Captain Montoya shouted.

Hunched beside him in the scaffold's shade, Captain Ruiz sneered back at him, "What would you have me do?"

"Command your troops! Locate the enemy and kill him!"

"They're your troops as much as mine," Ruiz answered. "You lead the way."

His hand ached from its death grip on his pistol, but he hadn't fired the weapon yet. Montoya, pompous fool, had worn no pistol, but he held his saber ready, just in case one of the rebels called him out to fight a duel. Ruiz was busy looking for a target, but the pandemonium around him left his senses reeling. Puffs of gun smoke wafted here, there, everywhere, but Ruiz couldn't tell which weapons were the enemy's and which were friendly.

Not that it would matter, if a bullet found him cowering beneath the gallows. Loyal lead would snuff his life as quickly as a rebel's slug, and he would never know the difference.

As if in answer to that silent thought, a bullet struck the ground six inches to his right, spraying Ruiz with dirt. His uniform, already filthy, was no longer a concern, but the indignity of cringing from an unseen sniper made him furious.

Beside him, on his knees, Montoya raged, "I *order* you to do something!"

Scowling, Ruiz answered, "I will," and shot Montoya squarely in the chest. At point-blank range, the .44-caliber slug knocked him sprawling, dead before he settled in the dust.

Ruiz glanced this and that way, searching all around himself for witnesses. It seemed that no one had observed him, meaning that he simply needed distance from Montoya's corpse to wash his hands of all responsibility. Zapata's rebels would be blamed, and who would really miss Montoya, after all?

The trick was finding somewhere safe to hide, reaching the spot he chose, then rallying his men to slaughter every traitor they could find in El Palmito.

For Montoya had been right about one thing. If Ruiz didn't *do something,* and quickly, it might be too late to save himself. If his men were beaten, Ruiz could expect no mercy from the victors. They would shoot him on the spot, or hoist him with the rope he had intended for Zapata's sister.

Wait!

Where *was* the woman? Cruz had been cut down before he got the noose around her neck, and yet—

A droplet of warm, tacky liquid struck Ruiz's neck and trickled down inside his collar. Swiping at it with his left hand, he saw blood smeared on his fingertips. A quick glance upward showed Ruiz that it was dripping through a crack between the scaffold's planks.

Zapata's sister might be there, and if she was—

Ruiz was on his feet and moving as his mind completed the plan. He cleared the shade, then hesitated for a moment before racing up the gallows steps. Atop the platform, he was just in time to find Zapata's sister wriggling out from under the remains of Jose Cruz.

Crouching beside her, Ruiz seized a handful of her hair and pressed his weapon's muzzle to her cheek. She gasped, stared up at him, as he declared, "I see I'm just in time."

Cesar Zapata recognized the bastard crouched beside his sister on the scaffold. Elaminio Ruiz Valdez commanded federales in the sector of Durango where Zapata's camp was located and where he carried out most of his raids. Every atrocity committed in the district for the past three years had either been directed by Ruiz or sanctioned by him retroactively.

The only targets more important to Zapata would've been El Presidente or his lackey in Durango, Governor Neron. But he would happily accept what Fate had given him.

Zapata found Ruiz with his rifle sights, caressed the weapon's trigger with his index finger—and froze, as Ruiz lurched to his feet, drawing Dolores after him. One instant, the captain was crouching beside her in plain view; the next, Dolores stood before him on tiptoes, shielding Ruiz as he moved backward, toward the gallows steps.

Zapata mouthed a curse, shifted positions in the flat roof of a single-story building thirty yards southwest of where the scaffold stood, but Ruiz knew his business. Moving constantly, the *federale* turned Dolores this way and that as he backpedaled toward the stairs, making sure that no snipers would have a clear shot.

The stairs helped him, Ruiz descending first, pulling Dolores after him, always one step above him, so the captain was invisible from where Zapata lay. Once he had reached ground level, Ruiz could duck into any building on the west side of the street, and he'd no longer need Dolores as a shield. If he decided she was useless then, there'd be no reason not to kill her.

Frustrated and furious, Zapata grimaced as a stream of bullets from the Gatling gun bit chunks of pale wood from the scaffold, chopping at its upright beams and mauling the two corpses on the platform.

"Stop, you idiots!" he bellowed, but his voice was lost in screams and gunfire from below. He saw Ruiz move down the steps, Dolores almost toppling over backward as the *federale* pulled her after him.

Zapata scrabbled to the north side of the roof, rolled over it, and dangled by one hand to drop the last eight feet into a narrow alley. Near its mouth, one of his soldiers lay entangled with a *federale,* both men bloody, slack, and still in death.

Zapata stepped around them, saw Ruiz retreating with his sister toward the nearest doorway opposite, and raced into the bright, corpse-littered street.

•   •   •

Dolores felt as if her hair was being pulled out by the roots. She stumbled as her captor started backing down the stairs, then felt his pistol gouge into her back and kept her fragile balance with an effort. The captain must've feared a fall as much as she did, for he slowed his pace, supporting her without releasing his tight grip upon her tresses.

Awkwardly, she staggered backward down the wooden steps, groping with first one foot and then the other. All around her, gunfire echoed through the plaza, punctuated by the angry shouts of men, the panicked screams of women, and children sobbing for their mothers. When the Gatling gun cut loose, it sounded like a huge saw ripping into giant trees, and then Dolores realized that it was spraying bullets over and around the gallows, splintering the scaffold's frame and sending tremors through the steps on which she wobbled so precariously.

"Hurry up!" the captain hissed at her, and started dragging her again.

Dolores lost her footing then, surrendering to gravity. She felt the muzzle of her enemy's revolver jab between her shoulder blades and wondered whether it would pierce her flesh, or if the sudden shift in weight would trigger an explosive shot into her back.

It was too late to save her brother by the simple act of dying, even though that option now seemed readily available. Why was she clinging even now to life, when Cesar had been sucked into a trap where he would almost surely die?

They fell together, tumbling to the bottom of the stairs, where she immediately tried to free herself by twisting from the captain's grasp. Though he was shaken, maybe even stunned, Ruiz clung fast and threw one leg across her flailing thighs, a posture almost simulating sex that managed—the pistol gouging at her flesh—to quell her struggle.

"On your feet!" he rasped at her. "One more smart trick like that one and I shoot, no matter what. *Comprende?*"

As she rose, the captain dragged her backward, toward a doorway that appeared to serve a private residence. With no free hand, her captor didn't knock or even try the knob. Instead, he threw his weight against the door, then swung Dolores to her right and jammed her face against the panel.

"Open it!"

"My hands are tied!"

Cursing, the *federale* grudgingly released her hair and reached around her, fumbling for the knob. His pistol ground into the base of her skull as he found the knob and gave it a twist. The door swung inward, hinges squealing, and a moment later it slammed shut behind her. Suddenly, the sounds of gunfire from the street were muffled—and she thought the firing had become more scattered, as if there were fewer weapons in the battle now.

Was Cesar dead already? Were the *federales* wiping out her friends?

Was Matthew Price among them?

Standing in the main room of a small but tidy house, Captain Ruiz told her, "You have a choice to make. Come willingly with me, or die now where you stand."

"Come where?" she asked him. "To another gallows?"

"If you help me get away from here," he answered, "I can have the charge reduced."

"What charge?" she challenged him. "Being related to my brother?"

"Yes or no?" he hissed, and leveled his revolver at her face.

•   •   •

Halfway across the street, Price saw Zapata coming on a near-collision course. He'd tracked Dolores and the captain this far, and her brother must've done the same. They reached the closed door almost simultaneously, one man flattening himself to either side.

"Don't you have troops to lead?" Price asked Zapata.

Breathing heavily, the rebel answered, "They know how to deal with *federales* on their own."

Price glanced around the street, littered with bodies. Some of them were wearing bloodied uniforms. Nearly as many were civilians, cut down on the run by shots from one side or the other. On the far side of the street, he saw one of Zapata's men sprawled slack in death, a rifle propped across his chest.

"All right," Price said. "I'm first, you follow." He expected a dispute but got none. With a nod, Zapata braced himself, clutching his rifle close and ready to rush in on Price's heels.

If they could clear the door, that is.

Price took a chance, leaned in to reach the knob, and when it turned he knew there wasn't any time to waste. He pushed through, diving to the floor and off to one side as a gunshot echoed from his right. Price didn't see the muzzle-flash, but heard the bullet strike above him, crumbling adobe on impact.

A second shot kept Price moving, scrambling for cover in a sparsely furnished room. He saw movement in his peripheral vision and heard Zapata charging in behind him, holding fire in case the enemy still planned to use Dolores as a shield.

Instead, when Price turned toward the sounds of shots and scuffling feet, he saw Dolores stretched out on the floor, almost within arm's reach. Her eyes were closed and there was blood on her forehead, but whatever had struck her skull didn't appear to be a bullet.

Price fired at the fleeing captain, missed, and heard Zapata's first shot echo through the house. Price jacked another round into the rifle's chamber, rising to pursue his adversary, while Zapata moved to kneel beside his sister.

Price knew he could let the captain go and help Zapata haul Dolores out of there, but that kind of unfinished business had a way of coming back to haunt him. Pushing on, he tracked the sound of footsteps moving through the house, moving parallel on the other side of an adobe wall, and then he realized the target had reversed directions.

He was doubling back.

Price cursed and turned to follow, knowing he was too late when two weapons fired almost together. As he reached the spot, Price saw Zapata toppling over backward, falling with one arm still wrapped around Dolores while the other clutched his rifle. It was difficult—perhaps impossible—to cock one-handed, and Price saw the *federale* captain lining up another pistol shot.

Instinctively, he triggered a round from the hip that caught the captain just above his belt. It might've been a killing wound, but Price wasn't inclined to gamble at the moment. As his target dropped to one knee, turning slowly with the pistol still outstretched, Price found his mark and put another slug between the *federale*'s eyes.

"It looks worse than it feels," Zapata said when Price stood over him a moment later, watching blood soak through one shoulder of his shirt.

"I'll take your word for that," Price said. "We need to stop the bleeding, though."

"Please, help Dolores first."

Zapata felt beneath her jawline for a pulse and found it strong, steady. "She took a beating," he informed Zapata, "but I think she'll be all right, once she gets past the headache. Now, about that shoulder . . ."

Price was suddenly aware of silence from the street outside and matched it with his own. On second thought, he realized the town wasn't completely quiet. He could still hear women sobbing, somewhere in the middle distance, but the gunfire had entirely ceased.

He wouldn't know if that was good or bad until he looked outside.

"Stay here," he urged Zapata, but the wounded revolutionary was already lurching to his feet. As one, they saw Dolores stir, and so Zapata knelt again to stroke her face, speaking softly and helping her with gentle hands to rise.

Leaning on Zapata, she seemed dizzy and disoriented from the blow that recently had rendered her unconscious. Blinking at her brother, then at Price, she seemed to sense the outer silence for herself.

"What is it?" she asked dreamily. "What's happening?"

"That's what we're going to find out," Price said.

He reached the door first, taking time to work the rifle's lever-action and be sure he had a live round in the firing chamber. There'd be little time to aim as he was opening the door, but if they found a hostile army on the other side, at least the targets would be close.

As ready as he'd ever be, Price flung the door back, dropping to a crouch and sighting down the barrel of his Winchester.

"Don't shoot, amigo!" One of Cesar's men stood with his hands raised in a mock surrender, others ranged behind him, still more moving in the street, checking the dead.

"It's over?"

"*Sí,*" the rebel answered. "I think we surprised them this time."

By the time Zapata's wound was bound, the horses had arrived and Price had stowed his rifle, freshly loaded, in his horse's saddle boot. He found Dolores with her brother, steady on her feet now, managing to cover any pain from superficial injuries.

"I think it's best if we go back to camp, instead of staying here tonight," Zapata said. "Neron may send more men when the patrol does not return."

"You go ahead," Price answered. "I'll be heading north."

"You won't stay, even for a little while?" Dolores asked.

"It's best I don't. You wouldn't thank me in the end."

She came to Price and kissed him softly on the lips, whispered, "Good-bye," and turned away to leave the men alone. Price focused on Zapata's face and let her go.

"You're sure about this, Matt?"

"I may regret it," Price replied. "But yeah, I'm sure."

"Texas?"

"Something a little further west maybe. I've seen enough Lone Star to last a while."

"You're always welcome in my camp, amigo, if you change your mind."

"I might just take you up on that," Price lied.

Zapata's grip was firm when they shook hands. Whatever blood loss he had suffered hadn't cost him any strength. "*Vaya con Díos,* Matt," he offered. "Go with God."

"I travel better on my own," Price said, and turned back toward his roan.